CW00866861

ESCAPING River Creek

ESCAPING
River Creek

JASON BLAYNE

Copyright © 2020 Jason Blayne.

All rights reserved. No part of this book may be used or reproduced by any means, graphic, electronic, or mechanical, including photocopying, recording, taping or by any information storage retrieval system without the written permission of the author except in the case of brief quotations embodied in critical articles and reviews.

This is a work of fiction. All of the characters, names, incidents, organizations, and dialogue in this novel are either the products of the author's imagination or are used fictitiously.

Archway Publishing books may be ordered through booksellers or by contacting:

Archway Publishing
1663 Liberty Drive
Bloomington, IN 47403
www.archwaypublishing.com
844-669-3957

Because of the dynamic nature of the Internet, any web addresses or links contained in this book may have changed since publication and may no longer be valid. The views expressed in this work are solely those of the author and do not necessarily reflect the views of the publisher, and the publisher hereby disclaims any responsibility for them.

Any people depicted in stock imagery provided by Getty Images are models, and such images are being used for illustrative purposes only. Certain stock imagery © Getty Images.

ISBN: 978-1-4808-9902-5 (sc)
ISBN: 978-1-4808-9903-2 (e)

Library of Congress Control Number: 2020921650

Print information available on the last page.

Archway Publishing rev. date: 11/18/2020

Doris Jean Holbrook 1955-2020.
A loving mother who supported her children
into the arts and entertainment.

CONTENTS

CHAPTER 1

Welcome to RiverCreek

Life. That's a funny term in some parts of the world. They say to live life to the fullest, or live like you're dying.

In a suburban community about an hour away from Minneapolis, life just isn't easy when you know everyone there. Most of the residents who don't leave remain to work in their families' businesses scattered around town. Those who graduate from college make the drive from RiverCreek. It's their way of staying out of the city, thinking it's a safer place for their children with its low crime rate.

Every year it's the same old thing repeated, and to most around town, it doesn't seem to age. The Catholics hold an extra midnight Mass. The Baptists put on a play in front of their church. The Methodists gather together and sing Christmas carols on the corner.

The few atheists go around and fling objects at anyone participating, trying to cause a ruckus. The sheriff usually lets them off with a warning and community service in lieu of paying a fine.

The only other thing that matters in this town is the high school varsity hockey team. It makes a deep run into the state playoffs almost every year. The team hasn't won a state title since the late 1980's, when most of the current roster was born. That's where this story begins, with Cory Dubois, the team's second-best scorer and leader in goal assists. He is an above-average student dreaming of one day becoming a general surgeon. He dreams of the day he can finally escape RiverCreek.

Cory is of French-Canadian descent. He is six feet tall with medium brown hair and hazel eyes. He has the typical athletic lean build from all his years of playing on the ice.

His best friend growing up, who always has his back, is an African American kid, Rick McGuiness. Rick, who wears his hair in cornrows, is also in great shape. He runs the one-hundred-meter dash for the track team. The two are nearly inseparable. They always make sure the rich kids don't get too rowdy when the races go down every Friday night near the point where the Minnesota and Mississippi rivers meet.

It's a usual snowy December night, and the kids are at their hangout spot. By the time Cory and Rick arrive, the festivities have already started with a hockey game out on the edge of the banks, where the ice is the thickest.

"C'mon Rick, I'm late!" Cory calls out, popping the hatch to his '93 Toyota Celica.

"Go on, bruh. I'm coming. Gotta finish up business with my girl first," Rick says, holding his hand over his cell phone.

Cory shrugs it off, snickering to himself, and hurries down to the ice.

"So, baby, we still hooking up when I come over after I watch my boy mop the floor with Frankie and his boys, right?"

"Oh, you know it! I've been waiting all week for my parents to go caroling so I can get alone time with my boo."

The only thing Rick can do is smile his cheesy grin. "All right, cool. I got the love gloves, so get ready to rock the boat, baby."

They share a laugh; then Rick closes his flip phone and gets out of his all-wheel-drive navy-blue Chrysler Minivan to cheer his best friend to victory.

With no refs to monitor the action, the game gets violent, with lots of hard hits as the boys get rough and rowdy. They use it as an excuse to fight since it's always the hometown kids versus the rich snobs.

"You're going down this time, Cold Core," Frankie threatens, skating behind him and using his stick to cross-check him between the shoulders. Cory hits the ice hard enough that his helmet slips off. Stopping over him, Frank and his cronies laugh.

"Serves ya right. Just remember: you're still second-best to me, garage boy!"

Frank has always been jealous of Cory. Cory's a better player even though Frank's the captain. Frank is also jealous that he's only second-best to Cory when it comes to grades and his physical build. He can't seem to get the lean-cut tone to his muscles. He appears a little skinnier than Cory. Frankie is a natural redhead with fair skin, jade-colored eyes, and freckles all over.

Having enough of Frank's mouth, Rick shouts out from the snowbank, "Hey spaz ass, why don't you try hitting him from the front and see how hard he plants your rich sorry white ass!"

Frank looks over to Rick. "Yeah, strong words from a scared skid mark."

Stunned at first, Rick stands there motioning for him to come over. "Come say that shit to my face, ya little bitch, and see how bad I beat you down right here, right now. C'mon, let's see what you all got!" Rick waves them on after unzipping his heavy coat.

Frank shakes his head and skates away, so Rick tries to entice the fight further. "Yeah, skate away, bitch. I'll beat your ass just like my boy's Celica whooped that junky Scooby last week!"

Frank's best friend, Joseph, stops, turns back, challenges either Cory or Rick to a race. "Hey, smartass, wanna line 'em up then? Guarantee he doesn't beat my Eclipse since it's all-wheel drive and turbocharged just like his."

Not wasting time, Cory slides over off the ice. He wants to cool Rick down before it escalates any further. "Hey, man, ease up. I don't wanna race right now."

"It's cool, dawg. You got this. I got faith in my boy and that car of yours. Tell ya what, though. I'll handle this fool on my own." Lowering his head, Cory clutches his hand over his eyes, frustrated.

"Line it up, then! I'll get my van, and we'll race. Hell, anyone can beat your Mitsi-Bushy!" The insult causes everyone to roar, excited to see the race.

"Go get it. I wanna shut that fat lip of yours, bitch," a pissed-off Joseph says. Joseph follows his friends a little farther down the embankment. He slips out of his skates and back into his shoes, and he puts on his Beavers pullover jacket. Before he begins to walk toward his car, Frankie grabs him by the arm.

"Wreck that piece of shit van. He may call it the 'Man-Van,' but put it out of commission."

Nodding, Joseph slides into his car. The competitors line them up at the end of the parking lot, ready to race from end to end.

"First one down and back wins," Frank announces, pointing to the designated area and back to where they're waiting to start.

Both young men acknowledge the instructions and begin revving their engines hard. Sighing, Cory places his stuff in the hatch of his car and watches, hoping he can stay out of the action. "Go," he hears Frank yell, and the squealing of tires heating up the ice-covered pavement follows.

Both vehicles hurl down to the turnaround spot, but Joseph backs off, giving the advantage to Rick. "Yeah, I knew he was scared of a little ice!" Rick screams, pounding on his steering wheel.

Rick's about to steer to pull out of the turn and come back when Joseph locks up his brakes, slinging his car the opposite way. He slams the very edge of his car into the rear quarter panel of the van, causing Rick to swerve out of control.

Everyone panics for a moment, but once he regains control, he stops. Rick gets out to check the damage. His opponent finishes the race and keeps going, along with all his friends as they want to avoid a physical backlash.

"Spineless bastards!" one of the kids yells, rushing over to make sure Rick hasn't been injured.

"Oh man, my ride, the Man-Van; it's ruined," Rick screams, holding his hands on top of his head. "Damn it, I can't afford to get this fixed. I sank everything I had into the back, making it a party van. Ugh. Now what's the point of putting CO_2 lines in for that old fountain machine and all the stuff to make microwave food? I'm gonna shoot those guys!" Rick continues to blow off steam as the crowd begins to break up once they see the sheriff charge in with lights flashing, but without the siren.

Pulled up between the Man-Van and the Celica, she crawls gets out. Holding onto the door, the sheriff looks over at her son.

"Hi, boys. Everything fine? Got a call there was a hit and run during a race." Rick's head is dipped down, and Cory knows he can't lie to his mother.

"Yes, ma'am. We were racing, but a patch of ice caused us to skid. I'm sorry, Mrs. Dubois. Just boys being stupid."

She walks over to Rick and looks at the damage to his vehicle. "Well, I think Mr. Dubois can take care of that at the shop. You're like our second son, so take it to him."

Rick smiles. Just knowing he's not in serious trouble is enough to make him feel empowered. He gets into his van and pulls away, leaving his best friend there to talk to his mother.

"Get in the cruiser, son. Now." Cory does as his mother says. Stuck in the passenger seat, he waits for the usual lecture.

"What are you doing out here? I can tell you've been out on the ice again. How badly did you get hit this time?"

Hanging his head in shame, Cory opens up to his mother. "Just once in the back. But it doesn't hurt that bad. I promise, Mom. I'm just trying to kill time until I can get out of this boring town."

"What's wrong with this town? It's been a peaceful place for the longest time."

Looking over at his mother, he answers, "Exactly. Nothing ever happens here, outside of the holidays being a bust for you. I want excitement. I want stuff to happen. I want to see how I handle anything that can happen at any time. Mom, it sucks here, and I want out."

She huffs over her son's boredom, Sherriff Dubois places her hand on the back of his head. "Oh, my sweet boy, you have only one more year of school left, so your wait is almost over."

Cory gives his mother a look of disdain before a call comes over the radio.

"Sherriff, you're needed out at the Hunter residence immediately."

Picking up the mic, she replies, "I'm on my way, Patty. Sherriff Dubois out. So how about nothing happening in town now, kid. Hate to do this, but Mom's gotta go. See you at home."

Cory hops out of the mid-90s brown Crown Victoria cruiser and heads back to his car after his mother speeds away with the lights still flashing.

"She's probably needing groceries again or her cat got out. Like I said, nothing exciting in this entire place." Pulling out his car keys, Cory heads home to relax. The season-opening game is a couple of days away. It's the one thing he looks forward to every year during Thanksgiving break.

Once he's home, showered, and settled into his shorts with a gray muscle shirt, Cory takes a seat at his computer to hop online to chat with anyone in the AOL locally created chatroom.

Feeling bored reading everyone chatting about the time down by the meeting point of the two rivers, he sits back after exiting the chatroom and visits the college he hopes to attend on scholarship.

Still in his own world after placing headphones over his ears, Cory isn't aware that his dad's home. He stands there in his son's bedroom doorway staring at the screen wondering what he's looking at with such intensity.

Mr. Dubois stands a little over six feet and is extremely skinny due to suffering with severe diabetes. His hair is beginning to turn gray; it's thinning a little in the back, but his brown hair and baby brown eyes still capture Cory's mother's attention each day she stares into them with the same passion she's had since they were kids growing up.

When he shoves off the frame, he strolls up, placing his hand on Cory's shoulder.

Startled by someone touching him, Cory jumps up, swinging his chair around. He's relieved to see his father standing there in his garage uniform. With a sigh of relief, he stands up to greet his father.

"Hey, kid, just looked at Quick Rick's so-called 'Man-Van.' Who hit it like that? I know it wasn't done on ice. So spill it. I won't tell your mom." Removing his headphones from his shoulders, Cory spills the beans.

"Don't tell Mom. Frankie's friend Joe mouthed off and got him to race. Well, he did it to try to wreck his van, and when Mom drove up, everyone scattered." His hand on his hips, Mr. Dubois shakes his head.

"You boys need to end this poor against rich stuff. In the end, you're all the same. You bleed red, and you all want out of this place, but I got him fixed up, and he'll have it next week."

Cory just smiles. "Thanks, Dad. I'm sure he appreciates it."

Mr. Dubois takes his cue to leave when an instant message pops up on the screen. Curious to see who's messaging him, Cory takes a moment to read the message before realizing it's his ex-girlfriend, who is away at college.

"Hey, sweet stuff, miss me still?"

Tapping his fingers on the keyboard, he sits there thinking it over. *"Yeah, I guess. Been busy with hockey practice and stuff. You know I got to get ready for SATs and whatnot."*

"Well, I miss you, and it's lonely here, especially since I'm not coming home for Christmas break. Maybe you could come visit me and stay in my dorm for a couple days?"

Corey cringes a bit. *"I'll see what I can do, but you're a long way away."*

"So! I gotta see you and soon. I really do miss you."

He sits there for a minute in hopes to make his ex-girlfriend sweat. *"I'll see what I can do."*

As they carry on their conversation, Rick sneaks into Cory's room and silently sits on the bed watching him chat with Vanessa.

Shaking his head, he can't stand the lying little two-faced bleached-blond twit. Rick knows for a fact that she's cheated on his boy more than once.

"Yo, homie, leave that bitch the fuck alone." Rick startles him enough that he closes the instant message, putting up an away status.

"Oh, damn, man, how long have you been there?" Twisting around to face Rick, Cory notices the look of disappointment staring back at him.

"Long enough, but I'll tell you what. Since you're my boy and all, I feel for ya like my brother. I'll take you there after ya game on Saturday. I'm telling you, Big C, she's playing you like a fool."

His own expression of dissatisfaction, Cory downplays the situation. "Nah, man, she ain't gonna do that anymore. I think she loves me."

"Whatever you say, man, but we'll see." Closing his eyes, shaking his head side to side, Rick's gut instinct screams that something isn't right with Vanessa.

From the kitchen, the boys hear Mrs. Dubois yell. "Hey boys, pizza's here. Come get something to eat."

That ends their debate for the moment.

Cory can't wait to prove he's right in the coming days, but as usual, he has no plans to tell his parents as the duo already has their plan to fool Cory's parents.

"Hey, Mom, Dad, do you care if I crash over at Rick's Saturday after the game?"

His parents look over at each other. A couple of head nods give him an answer as he tries to read their eyes.

"Yeah, but no racing or going out late—and definitely no partying like we caught you two doing last time."

Both the boys nod their heads, agreeing to the terms as it's set in motion to sneak away.

The rest of the evening is spent hanging out in Cory's room. They become rowdy, playing games online or sitting around on the PlayStation, killing time.

CHAPTER 2

Who's Right?

Cory says nothing to Vanessa about traveling to Northern City Central College. He spends his free time chatting back and forth, trying to rekindle their old flame, buying into everything she tells him.

"She can't be fooling around. She's always on here." Cory's convinced himself until he tries to webchat with Vanessa and she continuously clicks "Deny Request." Beyond mad, he can't understand why she's refusing to let him see her.

Why won't you click connect? He waits a couple minutes for the most significant thing that makes him begin to doubt her so-called commitment.

"They charge us for using webcams. It's a private school, so they charge for every little thing, baby. I'm sorry."

She sends a frowny face right after that, but all that does is infuriate Cory.

"Yeah, sure. Whatever. Gotta go. Love ya. Later." He logs off and begins packing his bag.

Marching out of the house, Cory is met by his patiently waiting mother, wearing her game gear.

"Ready to play?" she asks, getting out of her chair walking to the door with her son.

"Yeah, I'm ready to win!"

Able to conceal his fuming anticipation, Cory marches out to his car, tossing in his bag, and follows his mom to the rink where he begins getting ready to face the Plymouth Penguins.

Cory laces up his skates, sitting beside Frankie, who's refusing to talk to him.

"Hey, Frank, listen. What we do outside of here is one thing, but let's work together like we used to in middle school. You know together we can't be stopped."

Twisting to face Cory, Frank quickly thinks it over. "You're right. Here we're teammates, but don't get me wrong. I don't like you, and I'm not doing this for you. College scouts are going to be watching you this season, and I want a chance too. After all, I am team captain, and you're still beneath me."

Cory uses his hands in a cool-down motion.

"I get that, okay? Just chillax, man. I just wanna win. I wanna get the state title this year. Last year we made it to the semis. Well, this year, I wanna get it all."

Nodding in agreement, Frank extends his hand, taking Cory's offer on a pact to start their old double team maneuvers.

Out on the ice, Cory and Frank dominate with time of possession as they speed around the ice. They keep a defensive position out in front as the other speeds to catch up with a fake or quick pass. It provides them with a pair of goals for a two-to-nothing lead through the first two periods.

At intermission, the coach goes over things he's observed and praises the duo for their effort with the goals against a strong defensive team.

"All right, here's what needs to happen. Cory, they know you're going for the assist with Frankie. So now let's add in an enforcer."

The coach begins drawing a diagram on the dry-erase board.

"Wayne, when you're playing protector for either one of them. Just stop. Cory and Frankie, take turns passing it. Then, Wayne, skate up and slap that damn puck in for a goal. It won't work too many times; let's just expose that huge hole to the left of the net. That's your best chance, boys." The team gets fired up as they march back out to the ice.

The coach's plan is placed into action quickly, and the boys make it a three-to-nothing game. The Penguins players quickly decide to take out one of the three players controlling the tempo of the game.

The next faceoff, it's Frankie coming up to try to snatch the puck. The instant he sees it touch the ice, he goes for it, unaware of the stick mashing him in the face, followed by the player punching him as they tumble to the ice. Stunned by what's happening, Cory quickly throws down his stick, trying to pull the Penguin player off Frank.

"Get off him, ya piece of shit!" Cory yells. The refs grab him, pulling Cory away from the fight.

Cory watches as the crowd goes silent on both sides as the refs and medical personnel help Frankie back to his feet.

Frank's covered in blood, with a swollen eye that's nearly shut. He's barely conscience when he's escorted from the ice to the locker room. In need of a microphone, the referee makes an announcement.

"Ladies and gentlemen, due to unsportsmanlike conduct, Plymouth has been disqualified. Thank you for attending today's game. Players, you are dismissed. See you next week as RiverCreek faces their archrival, the Twin Cities Dragons."

Cory rushes to the back to see Frankie being ushered into the back of an ambulance. "Yo, Frankie, feel better!" Cory yells before the coach comes up behind him, placing a hand on his shoulder pad.

"C'mon, Core. Let's hit the showers so you can get home. I'll go check on Frankie."

After lowering his head, Cory returns to the locker room, gets cleaned up, and meets Rick out in the corridor.

"Ready to roll, homie?"

As he shakes his head yes, Rick walks beside his best friend until they reach their vehicles and pull away for to Rick's house. That's where they'll take one vehicle to make a surprise visit to Vanessa's place on campus.

Once they're on the way for the north end of St. Paul, the boys take advantage of the clear roads since it's not supposed to snow for a few hours.

By the time they arrive on campus and use a directory map,

the duo has found the location of her dorm, and Cory calls her room from Rick's cellphone.

"Hey, what are doing? You sound winded."

"Oh, hey. Just uh exercising some. Trying to stay in shape."

Cory gives her a compliment. "That isn't hard for you, but listen: we'll be there in about five minutes, so surprise!"

Rick rolls his eyes as he listens.

"Well, that is a surprise, but it's not good right now."

Cory is stunned. "Why?"

With nothing but silence in the air, the line goes dead when she can't come up with an answer. Pissed, Cory goes to get out of the Man-Van, but Rick quickly pulls him by the shirt collar.

"Wait right here. Let's see if she comes to greet you."

That quickly gets an answer as Vanessa comes running out with a guy, his arm wrapped around her shoulders.

"Son of bitch!" Cory yells, seeing red with tunnel vision, right at Vanessa.

"I'm not going to say it, homie, but now you see it firsthand. I'm sorry, man, but don't say anything. Let's just go home."

Fighting back the pain within, Cory shakes his head yes, staring out the window.

Vanessa hears the van come to life and looks over to see them pulling away. All she does is wave and give a devilish smile, knowing she's hurt Cory. She's gotten her revenge for him breaking up with her when she left for college.

"Let it go, Core. You deserve better, bruh. Just think: by this time next year, we'll be going into our last year of high school, and then it's off to Grambling and Western Michigan for us."

That's when Rick goes into a preachy, taunting tone. "Almost there, my brother. Just gotta paddle through the shit to get to the promised land."

"Amen, my brother. Let's go home. I just wanna get fucked up." Slamming his fist into the side of the door, Cory can't control his emotions at all.

"Nah, homie. We're going home but we're going to relax and not get wasted. Not this time. Sorry to disappoint."

Finally arriving back home, the boys rush inside just as the whiteout begins. Rick's mother stares, hearing them walk into the living room from the mudroom.

"Hey, Ma. Yeah, we're back, and wow, is it coming down!"

"Oh, good you boys are home. I was worried you'd be stuck out in this."

"Hi, Mrs. McGuiness. It's good to see you," Cory says, feeling a sense of calm come over him.

"Hey, sweetness, you look awful. You feel okay?"

Rick speaks up for him to cover for his best friend's anguish. "Nah, Ma. He's feeling the game and stuff. Plus, you know, guy stuff going on.

She takes the hint as Rick gives her his worried stare. "Oh well, tell you what: give me a few minutes, and I'll bring you boys some hot chocolate with mini marshmallows."

"Yeah, buddy." Rick nudges Cory's arm as he can tell he's putting on a fake smile.

"That'd be great. Thank you," Cory says, following Rick as they head upstairs.

He takes a seat at the computer desk. Cory jumps online to see if there is anything from Vanessa explaining her actions.

The AOL welcome greets Cory as he instantly goes for the mailbox. "Welcome … You've got mail …"

"Core-man, c'mon, let it go. She's not worth a flying—"

Rick is cut off as his dad walks into his room.

"Not worth a flying what, son?" he asks, standing tall over his son, looking down with concern.

"Crap, sir. I wasn't gonna swear, Dad. I promise."

Easing his gaze, Mr. McGuiness takes his son's word. "Good. You know it looks bad when the preacher's son uses a sinful mouth; it's just like giving into those sinful temptations. You need to outlast that, son, and that goes double for you, Cory."

"Yes, sir, Mr. McGuiness. I'll do my best."

Bowing his head, he hopes the boys will heed his advice. He smiles and walks away when he hears Mrs. McGuiness coming up the carpeted steps.

"Here we are, boys: two hot chocolates. Enjoy, and, oh, Cory, your mother called while you were out and said to call her when you got back here." Looking over at her, Cory nods his head, waiting for his drink.

"Here, brother, use my cordless." Rick tosses his phone into Cory's lap. The phone in his free hand, Cory calls home to find out what his mom needs.

Cory rolls his eyes after about four rings.

"Hello," his mom finally answers.

"Hey, you wanted me to call."

"Yeah, hey, listen, Ms. Hunter passed away, and her daughter is coming up to handle things. Since it's going to take some time to handle the funeral, plus going through her mother's stuff, she's bringing her daughter. So, when she arrives on Monday, make her feel welcomed here."

With an annoyed sigh, Cory agrees, "Yes, ma'am. I'll be polite and be her guide."

"Thank you, and, oh, did you tell Vanessa hi for me?"

Cory tries to deny it. "We didn't—"

He's cut off before he can lie.

"I know you went. Pete seen you both leaving town."

"Oh … It's over. She was with someone else."

His mom hears the anguish in her son's voice. "I'm sorry, son, but let her go."

"Yeah, but I'm going to get off here and chillax. See you tomorrow." Cory ends the call, placing the cordless on the computer desk.

He's about to sign off when a message pops up from Vanessa.

"GET A GOOD VIEW OF A REAL MAN?"

Before he can type a reply, Rick scoots the chair away to finally handle the situation.

"Bitch listen, here. My boy can do better thank yer skank ass, so get to stepping, ya white piece of trailer trash."

Once Rick says his peace, he copies and pastes her screen name to Cory's block list.

"There. It's done, and that slut is gone for good!"

After taking a sip of his steaming hot chocolate, Cory mutters, "Thanks."

After logging Cory off, Rick turns on the TV, then changes the subject.

"So what'd ya moms need?"

Cory takes a seat on the floor, leaning back against the bed. "Eh, there's a new girl coming on Monday to school, and since I have first block free, she's using me as an escort."

"Oh snap, son. I bet she's a hound too, ya know? All geeky and stuff, and you got to be seen with her."

Rick continues to taunt his best friend until they find a college football game close to halftime that catches their attention. Cory crashes there the rest of the weekend since the snow is falling relentlessly over more than half a day straight.

Before he realizes it, Monday morning arrives, and Cory's forgotten all about his appointment. He's sitting in the office about to go spend part of his free time in the weight room when the principal catches him just as he's about to walk out the door.

"Excuse me, Mr. Dubois. Has it slipped your mind about accompanying our newest addition through our fine educational establishment?"

Dropping his head, Cory turns around. "I'm sorry, Miss Woodard. I completely forgot."

Cory lifts his head and he's lost for words when he sets his eyes on her. Up from her seat in the principal's office, the new girl, Tara, smiles nervously as she approaches Cory. He's taken by the sight of her tanned, glowing skin and almond hair, which complements her deep sea-blue eyes. She's an obvious athlete given her slender figure, which is evident from her form-fitting outfit.

She waves anxiously to Cory, and he even takes a moment to notice her nails with the bright pink tips, motioning for his attention.

"Hi, I'm um … Cory, and welcome to RiverCreek. Did I say that I am Cory?"

With both of her hands clutching the straps on her backpack, Tara timidly speaks in a Midwestern accent, mingled with a hint of Southern.

"Hi, I'm Tara Marie Rose, and I'll try not to bug you too much. I learn fast, so you can show me around, and I'll be on my way."

Cory chuckles, waving her to follow him as he tries to hide the glow in his cheeks, feeling an instantaneous attraction.

While they sway down the corridor together, Cory tries to break the ice. "So where ya coming here from?"

After a shrug of her shoulders, Tara keeps her voice low.

"Little Rock, Arkansas. My mother was raised here and left with my dad when he became a truck driver."

Cory huffs before he replies. "Lucky lady! This place is Dullsville. I have one more year, then it's off to, hopefully, Western Michigan on a hockey scholarship."

That's the instant Tara shoves her foot in her mouth for the first time around him.

"I bet you're just as hot playing hockey as you are."

She slaps her hand over her mouth as she blushes a light shade of pink.

"Thank you. You're, uh, very pretty too," Cory says, causing himself to blush so she doesn't feel too far out of place.

"Thank you," she's able to mumble through her hand, not turning her head to look at Cory.

Together, they waltz around the hallways, chitchatting back and forth. They're able to break through the barriers and slowly shift away from talking to flirting.

"Well, here's the Arts Center. Uh, what class do you have?" Cory asks, trying to peek over to see her schedule.

"Home Economics. I want to get into culinary school and work on cruise ships before I have a family one day. What about you? Become a pro hockey player, I take it."

Laughing, Cory corrects her assumption. "No, actually, I want to get into medical school and become a surgeon. Ah, here we are. The only Home Ec. classroom in the entire school."

Tara takes her time to get another moment with her guide. She slowly begins playing with her long hair.

"Well, I guess this is where you go away." She's hinting, hoping to get asked for her number.

"Guess so, have fun!" Cory smiles and waves, acting as if he's about to walk away.

Tara huffs and drops her hand from her hair down to her side.

"I'm kidding, okay? Would you like to go out sometime? Like after you get settled in, or maybe next weekend? Gimme a second to get my pen, and I'll give you my number."

"Or I could give you my cell number."

Cory's blown away. "That'll work too. Didn't know you had one."

"You didn't ask, ya rude ass," Tara says mockingly, taking out a pen from the side of her backpack.

She writes down her number neatly on the back of Cory's hand. "Call me … soon." Tara grins as she returns to playing with her hair before entering the classroom and leaving Cory to walk away, staring at his hand, forgetting all about Vanessa.

CHAPTER 3

Tara's Arrival

Ever since the minute he leaves Tara at her class; Cory can't get that first image of her out of his mind as he sits through his next class.

Damn, she's really pretty, and she was flirty. Hey, wait, what if she's like that with other guys too? Ugh, great, now I'm back to another Vanessa situation. Lowering his head, he sees a note sitting on his desk.

Rotating his eyes over, he sees Rick motioning slightly to open the note he tossed. "Open it," he mouths, wanting Cory to hurry up while the teacher writes notes on the board.

Hey, so how bad is that girl you had to show around school? I've heard both sides—that she is smoking hot and that she's ugly as hell. So which is it? Also, you ain't stopped smiling since you got in here, so what's up?

After he flattens out the note to hide it from the teacher, Cory quickly jots down why he seems so chipper. *She's beautiful, man. Long brown hair and tan. Funny. She seems smart, and just wow! I have her number on my hand, so when we get out of here, I plan on asking her out.* He folds the note back up and heaves it through the air as Rick snatches it seconds before the teacher turns around.

Rick barely gets his hand down before the teacher sees him. Both boys sigh a bit of relief as they keep their eyes forward to avoid having their note read out loud for the entire class to hear, as the teacher imitates their voices mockingly for entertainment purposes.

When the chance to finally unfold the note to see his boy's response about the new girl. Rick is taken by surprise when he looks over to Cory, nodding his head just before they both close their books and binders, waiting for the bell to ring.

Once the sound of freedom dings, the fellas head to the lunchroom.

"So I have an idea, my brother of another mother. Let's find this girl, or hell use the school's payphone to call her and leave a message, giving her your number. Then ask her out on a double date with me and my girl."

Cory is about to take up Rick's idea when they enter the game room, where they see Tara getting hit on by a tall but kind of chubby male, brushing his ear-length long black hair back out of his eyes.

"Yo, Lloyd, back off. That's Cory's woman!" Rick yells to their friend. They both begin to laugh when Rick and Cory come strutting over.

"Hi, I'm Tara, and who might you be?" she asks, extending her hand out to Rick.

"I just might happen to be Rick, the eyes and ears of all that is RiverCreek. Wow, what an accent. But your beauty makes that Southern sweetness complete. My boy was right. You are a sight to behold."

Blushing and hunkering her head down, all Tara can manage to squeak out is "Thank you," enjoying the attention.

"Excuse me!" Rick hears coming up from behind him.

"Sorry, honey. I was just trying to be nice. You know how I am, and Cory's into her."

"He best be, or else you ain't walking out of here with your balls intact," a female voice calls out.

Rick goes wide-eyed, covering his genitals, turning around to face his girl. She's standing there with her hands on her wide hips and head cocked slightly sideways. She might be short, but everyone knows her attitude is nothing compared to her temper when it blows.

"It's true, Kayla. He's into her. In fact, it was my idea to see if you wanted to double date with them this weekend, if she's interested," Rick babbles to save his ass.

Cory immediately blushes a right shade of red when Tara looks over at him, hiding her playfulness.

"Really … I'm the new girl in town, and you think you can get with me just like that?"

Cory picks up the hint that he's about to get shot down when Lloyd takes up for him.

"Hey, give 'em a break. He's a good guy. I say do it, let him show you around and maybe go watch him play on the ice," Lloyd says, then adds, boosting the bass in his voice, "He should be captain, but the preps around here control all that with Mommy and Daddy's donations to the school."

Everyone agrees to that statement, but the subject quickly swings back to Cory and Tara.

"So what ya say, Tara? Give him a chance." She places her hand under her chin, pretending that she's thinking it over.

"Well, you've talked him up since I mentioned him in class. I guess I could do Mr. Shy Bones here a favor and say yes."

Cory makes a huffing noise, standing there in the middle of everyone.

"Well, then, I guess it's a date," Rick teases, slapping Cory on the back, then walks away with Kayla stepping in line for lunch.

"C'mon, you two love birds, let's get something to choke on," Lloyd comments, tugging on Cory's shirt.

Cory follows closely behind Tara to the end of the line and watches her ass wiggle along the way.

"Like it?" She mentions, letting him know she was doing it intentionally.

"Yup. So how were your first two classes?"

"Really! I'm here flirting and hitting on you, and all you can do is ask about my classes. Well, I guess it's better than most other guys. They was fine, I guess. I have American History next with a Mr. Desmond."

Cory's luck kicks in when he speaks up. "As do I. So I guess you can sit next to me, since I am one of the smartest kids in school."

That causes the entire group to laugh as they look back at them.

"You're sweet, Core, but c'mon. Don't be the geek you usually are. I mean, she is pretty and so much nicer than that bitch Vanessa," Kayla mentions, looking over her shoulder.

Caught off guard, it grabs Tara's attention when she asks, "Who's that?"

Kayla motions for her to come to her as they engage in girl talk while the line continues to move slowly.

"Yo, man, looks like you got the hookup and, you're welcome, by the way," Rick tells him, smiling, glad to see his boy out of the funk he was in over the Thanksgiving Break.

Lloyd takes his turn helping to assist Cory to get out of his shyness, which is a first for them to witness.

"Yeah, bro man. All she's done is talk about you since Home Ec. She's into you and loves the fact you're not a typical football or basketball jock."

Tara covers her mouth when Kayla brings her up to speed about how Vanessa has treated Cory and all the times she's cheated on him. "What a slut!" she barks out. Unfortunately, a teacher passing by overhears the insult.

"Excuse me, young lady. There is no need for such foul language around here. Give me your name. I'll have an incident report sent to your principal this afternoon.

"Tara Rose, ma'am, and I am sorry."

The teacher notices her thick accent.

"You're not from around here, are you?"

"No, ma'am. It's my first day."

Feeling pity for the new girl, the teacher let's her off with a warning. "Well, I'll let it slide, but just this time. Next time it's an incident report, but welcome to RiverCreek High."

A grateful Tara dips her head. "Thank you, ma'am." The teacher begins to walk away as Tara looks horrified at being overheard so easily.

"Wow, you really are a spitfire. I like her! Cory, you're keeping this one. I like making new friends."

Cory responds in a sarcastic tone, causing the guys to laugh at his mockery, "You got it, girlfriend!"

"Say that one more time and you won't go home as a mister." Cory backs away, holding his hands up, still chuckling.

"C'mon, girl. You're with me for now. You can deal with his goofy butt in class." The girls turn around, ignoring the boys as they take their food from their grip and walk out of the game room.

The guys search for a table near the back of the room, where the sun is reflecting off the snow covering the ground.

"She seems really nice, bro-man. Like, f'real. And she is hot," Lloyd says after tearing into his soggy school pizza.

"Yeah, homie. Do what me and Kay are doing and go slow. I mean, we tease and whatnot, but ya know we don't wanna screw this up."

The boys laugh as they wait for Cory to say something.

In a single deep breath, Cory reveals something. "Yeah, the instant I looked her in the eyes, I forgot about Vanessa, and she is just … wow. I'm thinking Friday night should work since I have a game on Saturday at one."

"Cool. Tell ya what. Let's make an evening of it. Dinner, movie, and hey, if you wanna impress her, then show up with something sweet," Rick says, thrilled to see the way his best friend glows in delight.

Cory looks over to Lloyd and asks him if he's coming with his own date. "So you think you and 'George' are gonna be brave enough to come out and join us?"

Lloyd sighs, rolling his eyes. "He's still afraid to come out and admit he's gay. I mean, we've all known this about me since, what, sixth grade or so? But he doesn't want to hurt his parents' feelings. I doubt he'll come along, but, yeah, I'll be there as a wingman for sure. I got your back, Cold Core."

Before anything else can be suggested the bell chimes for the next group of students to come to lunch. Kayla escorts Tara back to the edge of the game room where they wait for the boys to walk together. They break away when they head toward their next class.

The last two to walk to class are Tara and Cory, still feeling out of place, not knowing what to say.

Cory takes any chance he can to get a glance at Tara. She sees him and smiles each time she notices him looking over at her. When she brushes her hair back behind her ear, she slowly takes her hand and plays with Cory's hand, teasing him to take hers.

"So does this mean we're a thing for sure?" Cory asks, taking her hand and interlocking their fingers.

"Guess so, cutie." They stop and smile at each other for a moment.

The moment continues to build, and they're feeling the connection of wanting to kiss. Cory keeps in mind what Rick has suggested and turns his head, pointing with his free hand to their classroom a few doors away.

"There's our class. C'mon, let's find a seat close together." Tara feels a little shunned, huffing as Cory leads her to the classroom.

Walking into the room, they're greeted by stares from Frankie and his friend Kevin.

"She's cute," Kevin whispers when he notices the couple letting go of each other's hand, taking a seat near the door.

Kevin gets up, walking in front of Tara. She looks up to see an extremely skinny, short-haired boy looking down at her with intensely with his olive-green eyes.

"Can I help you?" she snarls, leaning back in her seat.

"Yeah, you and me, tonight, my place, alone," Kevin suggests, placing his hands on the corners of her desk, leaning in with a kiss gesture on his lips.

"Ugh, as if, bean pole. Get lost!" she replies, shoving her hand into his face, sending a quick wave of anger through his body.

Cory gets up, standing off to the side of Kevin. "You heard her. Get lost, Kev, or else," Cory warns him, standing there, ready to strike.

"Or what, ya worthless little townie?" Kevin goes to turn to Cory when the teacher walks into the room.

"Okay, boys, take your seats before I send you both to detention. As for everyone else, please take out your books to page three hundred and ninety-four, 'The Industrial Revolution,'" Mr. Desmond demands, taking his spot in the front of the class.

As the lecture begins, Cory begins jotting down the notes he needs but also has a spare piece of paper to write a note to Tara. After quickly scribbling down what he wants to say, he folds it in half, passing over to Tara, and waits as she quickly reads over it and replies to him.

Checking to make sure it's clear to open the note, Cory places it under the notes for class and reads it.

Thank you for taking up for me before class. It was sweet. And yes, I would love to see a movie and go to dinner. I love eating pizza, and I love Applebee's too, by the way.

Plastered with a smile, he looks over to shake his head and mouths "okay" to Tara. Before he can look back to the teacher, he sees Frankie staring at them with a glare of anger. With his mouth he silently says "what" over to him, Frankie quickly flips him off, turning around so Cory doesn't stare at the damage done to his face from the game.

Ignoring his teammate, Cory returns his attention to Mr. Desmond. He's now anxious for Friday night to come. That's all that's on his mind the rest of class as he exchanges smiles and winks with Tara. She giggles quietly and smiles when their eyes meet.

When the bell rings for them to head off for the final class of the day, Cory escorts her to class before he takes off to the gym on the other side of the school, trying to beat the tardy bell.

Through the door, just seconds before the bell rings, he gets the coach's attention. Then he heads to the locker room to get changed. He quickly finds himself cornered.

"So you think you can already claim that new townie?" Frankie calls out as he walks up behind Cory.

Sliding his gym shirt on, Cory turns around, preparing to assault Frankie if he needs to.

"Yeah, I'm making the first move. I'm not having you do what you did with Vanessa. You used her to get back at me. And, hey, you want her? Go get her, man. She's nothing but a tramp."

Frank can't help but rub his face in the past. "Yeah, I know, she sucked my dick several times when you two dated all because she said you couldn't get it up. So what you hiding? You a rear-packer like Lloyd, just trying to hide it still, or what?"

Cory takes offense to Lloyd being taunted and shoves Frank into a locker. "Listen here, you rich bastard. I tried to treat her with respect, and if she was fucking around, why risk getting something? Judging by that shit on your face, I'd say she's got something bad. Oh, wait, that's right—she's the one who had the dick between you two, am I right?"

Curling up his fist, Frank slugs Cory in the jaw. Before Cory can come back at him, Kevin steps in, stopping the punch.

"Your boy ain't here now, so you wanna make this two on one, or do you wanna get out of here alive?" Kevin threatens, clinching Cory's fist, ready to interject himself into the fight.

Realizing it's not worth it, Cory steps back, allowing Kevin to release his grip.

"Thought so, ya little punk ass."

They both walk away, laughing at how they kicked Cory's ass. Pissed off at the incident, Cory rubs his jaw as he leaves the locker room last and goes about playing basketball for the duration of class.

Still angry about the team up in the locker room, Cory hurries up to the front of the school. He is waiting to see if he can get a glimpse of Tara before he heads to practice.

"Hey, Cory," he hears. He notices Tara walking up from the west side of the sidewalk.

"Hey, you, wanted to say I'll call you when I get home from practice."

"Sounds good. I'll have my phone on me, but I see my mom waiting on me. Call me for sure, and think about me," she says, blowing him a kiss, going over to the silver Honda Accord sedan waiting for her.

"Will do, beautiful," he says, waving as he walks backward to his car to head to practice.

CHAPTER 4

Forming Their Bond

In a rush, Tara pitches her bag into the backseat, watching as Cory walks away. Tara opens the passenger door, getting into her mother's car.

"Hi, Momma," she says, keeping her eyes locked on her new boy toy.

"Well, look at you. Here for a day and already finding boys. So who is he, and what's his story?" her mother wants to know, pulling out of the pick up are.

Sucking in a long breath, she begins with what little she knows about him.

"Well, his name is Cory, he plays hockey, and he wants to go to Western Michigan to play. He wants to be a surgeon. He's like, oh so cute, Momma, and really shy and nice, and he asked me out Friday. So, like, Mom, please can I go?"

Her mother snickers at it all, pretending she's going to deny her daughter the chance to go out. "Well, I don't know, young lady. I mean, he sounds nice and shy and, like, oh so cute, but Friday, your father is coming off the road for the weekend."

She taps her fingers off her chin, teasing her daughter.

"Mom! C'mon, please. It'll give you and Daddy time alone, and it's just a movie and dinner."

Happy and able to play off her daughter's excitement, she shakes her head yes. "You can go, but I want to meet him first."

Tara squeals, shaking her hands fast, wanting to hug her mother's neck. "Thanks, Momma. Thank you, thank you, thank you!"

Reaching into the center console, Tara takes her phone and holds onto it as they continue down the road.

The feel-good sensation doesn't last long.

"I have something to tell you, and you're probably not going to like it." Not thinking twice about her mother's tone, Tara turns to listen to what is about to happen.

"Well, you know I got laid off a few months back, and well, they're going to stop my unemployment, so I talked to your dad this morning, and we're selling the house back home."

Tara can hear the disappointment in her mother's voice. "The factory is shipping every job down to Mexico, and Mom left me the store."

"So we're not going home like you said we would?"

Her mother attempts to hold back the tears. Tara's mother confirms it with a shake of her head.

"Well, that's cool, Momma. I guess it's not too bad up here. I mean, I've made new friends, and I could always go visit Aunt Suzy over the summer to see my friends back home."

Tara's mood goes from happy-go-lucky to feeling a little bummed out—not over being stuck in RiverCreek but because she felt betrayed by her parents not wanting to bring her into their decision.

"That's my girl. I'm so sorry to spring this on you like this, but it's better than being homeless, you know, and it's not like we can't remodel Mom's house and make it our own."

Tara's voice shows her frustration, as she wants to drop the subject. "Mom, really, it's fine. I mean, I kind of have a boyfriend now, and all I'm gonna miss are my friends. Plus, no tornados up here, and look, we can have a white Christmas for once. It's cool, Mom, so drop it, okay?"

It doesn't take them long to reach the grocery store in the heart of town.

"Here we are, Hunter's Groceries. Soon it'll change affiliation. I'm going to turn it into a Foodland International, and try to bring in a little more culture to this place. I'll say this though, it has increased in size since I left. So maybe it won't be so bad."

"Yeah, sure. Care if I go check it out before I have to do my homework?"

"Sure thing, baby girl."

Tara gets out and walks inside, bumping into Kayla when she comes from the office with her apron on.

"Hey, Tara, what are you doing here?"

"Oh, hey, girl, just checking it out. My mom's taking it over, and I guess I'm a little curious, but you work here?"

Tying her apron, she answers with frustration. "Yeah, my dad's the store manager, but you didn't say your mom was taking over the store. That's a relief, though. Almost everyone does their shopping here—either here, or they head over to that run-down-looking Dollar General for basic things."

"Yeah, I just found out, but hey, do you know where Cory practices at? I wanna get out of here, to be honest."

Kayla scopes out who's nearby. She motions for Tara to follow her into the office. "I'll have Rick pick you up on his way to see his dad at church."

"Oh, thanks. You're a lifesaver." She stands there and listens as Kayla convinces Rick to pick Tara up and head over to the arena.

"Thank you, love bug. We owe you, but I gotta get to my register. I love you, and I'll see you when I get off. Bye." The girls scramble out of the office as Tara waves, walking away. Kayla takes her place at the register, waiting on customers to enter her line.

It takes Rick nearly ten minutes to arrive. He sees Tara waiting by the soda machines and strolls inside, leaving his Man-Van running while he gets her attention to come on. Seeing him waving, Tara darts out the side door of the building, getting into the van without her mother knowing that she's leaving.

"Can't get enough of my boy already," Rick teases, cranking up the heat in the van.

"Nah, my mother pissed me off, and I want to get away for a bit."

Rick gives her a thumbs-up for the rebellious defiance as they make their way over to the arena where Cory is busy with practice.

"Well, here we are. Just go through those double doors there, use the steps to the right, and sit in the bleachers. I have to take my dad a few things for his service on Wednesday, and then I'll be back to catch up with you two afterward. Ugh, coach hates spectators, so stay quiet, and you'll be cool."

"Got it. Thanks, Ricky. You're a cool dude," Tara says, making him laugh as she slips her way over the icy sidewalk into the building and disappears when she finds the steps he mentioned.

She takes a seat at the top of the bleachers, Tara turns down the volume on her phone. Luckily for her, it's a smart idea, since it's her mother calling, and she is furious about her leaving without permission.

"Yes, Mother Dearest." She pulls the speaker away from her ear when her mother yells back.

"Don't give me that lippy mouth, young lady. You took off without permission. Where are you so I can come get you?"

"I'm at the ice rink. Hey, turnabout is fair play! You didn't mention moving up here for good, Mom. That's wrong to do when we promised we would talk more about not keeping secrets since you and Daddy worked things out."

Silence falls over the phone when Tara realizes she can still use that trump card against her mother.

"You're right, and I am sorry. It was wrong. You deserve to have been part of our decision. Just don't do this again, please. You scared the living hell out of me."

"Yes, Momma. I won't, I promise. I'll see you when I get home." Tara hangs up her phone and turns her attention to the ice, where she sees the players being coached. He's in uniform, participating firsthand with the team.

A bit of boredom sets in, and Tara takes out her book. She begins to go over her assignments when she hears the coach yell again.

"Dubois, come over here and show these guys how to shave around a defender like you do."

She looks down as they begin to skate back and forth. Cory shines as the best player on the ice.

"Go, Cory," she whispers, placing her things down, giving him all her attention without him realizing it.

"Now, that's how you get the edge, gentlemen. Remember, it's not enough to skate fast. You also must get into their head and make them feel like they have you. Then make your move. That's how Frank and Cold to the Core do it, and you saw how it worked last week. So remember that, and let's do a little three-on-three action, going both ways, and we'll call it a day after that."

The players match up road jerseys versus home jerseys. The coach refs the team as they skate back and forth, working on position skills.

"Go, Cory, you got this. C'mon, cutie pie, score," Tara continues to whisper to herself, gawking down at the ice as Cory gets a one-on-one break.

Stealing the puck, he gains distance as the goalie watches him speed toward the net. Closely watching his actions, the goalie comes out just a couple of feet, preparing to stop Cory's attempt to score. "Come on, Core. Let's see what you got!" the goalie screams through his mask, slowly skating backward.

"Here you go!" Cory replies, seeing an opening as the goalie slides back to the pipes. Cory takes the shot, knocking the puck into the net off the goalie's inner shin pad, giving his team the goal and the win.

The whistle blows as the coach skates back to center ice. "That's it, boys. Hit the showers and see ya tomorrow. Oh, and Cory, since Frankie has opted to sit out until further notice due to his injuries, you are taking over as captain for now." Everyone stops at the announcement.

"Yes, sir, Coach. I got this!" Cory says as his teammates' applause his rise from assistant team captain.

Tara's beyond enthusiastic for him, as she's the first of his friends to hear him get the opportunity to lead the team.

Inside the locker room, most of his teammates pat Cory on the back as they shower and change back into street clothes.

"Go, Cold Core. You're the man now, the way it should be!" one of the guys shouts as Frank and his friends listen to them.

"Fuck off, you pieces of shit. I'll be back soon enough. Cory ain't got half my skills."

"Yeah, he has way more, ya rich punk!" another teammate comments, slipping on his boots.

"Hey, fuck you too, assclown!" Frankie replies before leaving the locker room in a pissed-off mood.

He bumps into Tara, who's found her way down to the locker room area, where she's waiting with Rick.

"Hey, tell your boy to watch his back. I'm still leading this team," Frankie reminds Rick, walking past and shoulder checking him.

"About time someone put you in your place." Rick mentions, daring Frank to come back by extending his arms open, ready for a fight.

Out from the locker room, Cory is surprised to see Tara and Rick standing there waiting. "Did I miss something?" Cory asks, placing his bag on his shoulder.

"No, ya girl here wanted to come see how good you are," Rick tells him as he scoots Tara closer to his best friend.

She begins to feel embarrassed until she's caught off guard by Cory planting a kiss on her cheek. "Hi there, gorgeous. Glad you came," he whispers, putting his hands on her hips.

All she can do is giggle as she tries to control her urge to press her lips against his. She bites on her lower lip, staring into his eyes as Rick stands there observing the whole scene.

"This is a Kodak moment," Rick says, breaking their attention to each other as Cory pulls away from Tara.

"Hey, anyone hungry?" he probes, hoping to get an impromptu dinner date.

"I would say I am, but I'm gonna go see Kay on her break here in a few, but you two should hit Gina's Diner. It's suppertime, which means fresh cherry pie." The couple laughs at Rick rubbing his stomach and licking his lips.

Taking her by the hand, Cory leads the way out as Rick walks the other way parked in the visitor's section of the arena.

"C'mon, I'll take ya there. You'll love it. It's Lloyd's mother's diner. It's where we usually hang out after games."

Not thinking twice about it, Tara allows Cory to take her hand, leading the way as his shyness slowly fades away. After they walk out the rear exit, they're greeted by the last few teammates leaving for the diner as they see Cory with the new girl. They whistle, giving him props.

"Well, I think they like you," he tells her, popping the hatch to his Celica and unlocks the doors, opening the passenger side for his date.

"Aw, aren't you just the sweetest thing," Tara says, rubbing the palm of her hand on the cheek that was punched earlier in the day.

"I try," he tells her as she settles into the seat, placing her bag between her legs.

Closing the door, he circles around the car, getting inside and starting it up. He releases the emergency brake as he slowly lets the clutch come out, pulling away. "You can drive a stick shift. Impressive, and this is such a pretty car!" he hears. Tara stares around while they make their way over to the diner.

Once they arrive, Cory parks and rushes around the car to open the door, once more helping Tara to her feet. "Thank you," she says, refusing to let go of his hand when he shuts the car door.

"Any time." Cory smiles, feeling her hand still gripping his own as they walk toward the entrance together.

The bell over the door rings and the waitress calls out to them. "Find your own booth, you two. I'll be with you shortly." She scurries about the floor, trying to keep up with everyone inside. As they sit in the waiting area, orders ring in from the kitchen.

Quickly they spot an open booth. The newly coined couple head over and begin to chitchat as they play footsy.

"Are you going to officially ask me out or what?" Tara begins, hoping to shake things up a bit.

"Well … um … uhh … how about now? Would you like to start going out?" Cory asks, caught off guard by her request.

"I'll have to think about it. So … um … how about … hmm … let me think see … gotta check my calendar … so … yes," she teases back as Cory sits there with his jaw slightly dipped open.

"I'll remember that miss thing," he warns her, flirting again until the waitress comes over to them.

"Well, hello, you two lovebirds. What can I get for ya?" she questions, pulling out her order pad and a pen.

"I'll have a sweet tea and the bacon burger with fries," Cory says, looking over at his date.

"Well, uh, a Diet Coke and the grilled chicken sandwich with a salad, pretty please."

The waitress chuckles. "Watching that figure, I see. Good for you, sweetie. I'll get those in and bring your drinks. Oh, and Cory, she's pretty. I'm sure your mom will like this one."

"Thanks, Marge. She's new to town, and, well, someone's gotta show her around, you know," he comments, keeping his eyes locked on Tara's.

"You're cute together. And, honey, may I say, I love that accent. I'm gonna guess Mississippi?"

"Arkansas, actually, but thank you. It seems to be the first thing people have noticed about me so far."

"Well, it'll fade in time, but welcome to RiverCreek. This one here is a good egg. I've known him since he was little," she states as Cory blushes, hunkering down in the seat.

The waitress walks away, giving them time to sit there and stare at each other, making them wonder what the other is thinking at that moment. The music from the jukebox carries throughout the diner when a slow song begins to play.

Hardly anything else is said even after they eat. They sit there exchanging goofy expressions and smiles, feeling their connection blossom. Nearly an hour passes by, and the sun slowly begins to settle behind the town.

"Well, guess I should get you home before it starts icing over out there," Cory tells Tara, leaving money for the tab on the table.

"I reckon so, huh," Tara says, scooting out of her seat, following Cory to the door, which he holds open for her.

When they park in front of her house, he places the shifter in neutral. They sit there with the heat on, keeping the windows from fogging up.

"Well, I had a great first day here. Thank you, Cory. You are so very sweet," Tara says, taking her hand and resting it on his cheek.

"My pleasure. I'm glad it was me that got to show you around school. So I'll see you tomorrow?" he asks, struggling against the urge to keep from kissing her.

"Yes, you will. Bye, honey bunny." She pulls her hand away from his cheek and thrusts it behind his head, pulling his lips to hers as she braces for their first kiss.

From the warmth of her lips, Cory opens up to it more as they continue to keep it locked tightly between them. Unable to pull away, he slides his hand from his shifter to the back of her neck, pulling her closer to him, wanting to feel her closer to his body.

The passion swells as the seconds pass. When Tara is finally able to pull away from the kiss, she can't say or do anything except smile. Her hand on her bag, Tara slowly crawls out of the car. Secretly touching her lips as she makes her way up the icy walkway, she can still feel the sensation that rocked her more than she ever expected.

Finally, she's able to get through the front door. She stands there watching as Cory pulls away, her hand still pressed to her lips. She fails to notice her mother, who witnessed the entire thing, standing there.

"Well can he kiss?" her mother asks, startling her.

"Oh, yes. That was the best kiss I've ever had," she tells her mother, walking upstairs to her new bedroom to finish her homework and get settled in for the night.

CHAPTER 5

Unsettled Nerves

As she settles down to finish her homework, Tara's cellphone rings. The number on her caller ID indicates it's her best friend from Little Rock.

"Hey, Janet, what's up?" Tara asks with excitement, but out of nowhere, her best friend begins to rip into her.

"Well, I don't know. You never called me today to let me know what it's like up there or if you found out how long it'll be before you're coming back home."

Rolling her eyes, Tara turns over onto her back to explain what's happened. "Bad news. I ain't coming home. Mom said the factory is shutting down, for, like, ever, and she's taking over my grandmother's sto—"

She's cut off in the middle of her statement.

"What? Doesn't that fucking blow cow chunks on a hog's ass! I need you here. Stan is getting out soon, and I need you to be my maid of honor."

Her eyes clinched shut, Tara shakes her head.

"Girl, he's always gonna be nothin' but a jailbird. You can do so much better than him."

Janet huffs into the phone before she speaks again. "Uh, whatever, girl. It ain't your life, ya know. Speaking of which, Bobby said he wants to surprise you by coming up there to get you when you're eighteen and bring you home. I think he got a trailer for you guys that way you can finish school back here."

That's when the bombshell drops out of nowhere. "Um ... I kind've found someone else already. Bobby just wants me to stay home and have babies while he's out working for his uncle with a state job and forget about my dream of culinary school."

"Excuse me, honey, but what's wrong with that? What, you too Yankee for us now?"

"No, I just wanna manage or run my own place. I don't wanna be a stay at home, Mom, especially this young."

That's the final straw for Janet to lose her cool. "Let me tell you something, princess. I am not going to sit here and listen to you go on about some guy you just met when you got a real man back here who wants to take care of you. But fine, whatever, be that way. When you come back to your senses, call or text me. Until then, peace out, homegirl."

Tara scoffs at her best friend, giving her hell for wanting something more in life. She tosses her phone on the floor and gets comfy in the middle of her bed, cracking open her book to complete her assignment.

About an hour and a half later, Tara's temperament settles back down. A hot, steaming shower along with her favorite CD helps most of the relaxing. She's coming back into her room when her phone begins to ring.

"Uh, hello," she answers, unable to recognize the number.

"Hey, it's Cory, I just wanted to call and see if you needed a ride in the morning."

"Oh, oh, hey cutie pie, I need to save your number. Nah, my mom will drop me off, but I hope I get there early enough to see you before class."

Cory gives her details for the morning. "I'll meet you by the office then. I wanna talk and get to know you more. I'm sure you hear this all the time, but you are the most beautiful girl I've seen."

Even though Cory can't see her, he hopes she has the biggest smile on her face, hoping it'll improve his chances that no one will swoop in to steal her away.

"Aw, thank you. I don't think I'm that pretty, but you are pretty damn cute and sweet."

"Thanks! I'll let you go. I just wanted to check. I will see you tomorrow. Bye, baby."

Using her sweet and innocent tone, Tara replies with "bye" as she closes her phone and places it on the charger on her nightstand.

After yawning and stretching, Tara makes sure her door is locked and drops her towel into her hamper as she returns to her dresser, getting a pair of mini-shorts with a pink tank top, slipping them over her soft, silky skin. She stops when she tugs her shirt down to glance at herself in the mirror.

"He thinks I'm that beautiful, huh? I hope he thinks that, because Bobby never told you that once, girl," she tells herself, frowning as she stares at her reflection.

She lowers her tone so her mother doesn't hear her as she continues to glare at herself in wonder. "Sure, he wanted me, but outside of wanting to sleep together, did he ever listen? Am I just good for that, or could I actually be pretty enough to find a good guy?"

A few minutes later, a soft knocking echoes from her door. Her mother is calling out to her. "Tara, honey, time for bed, sweetie. Good night. I love you."

"I love you too, Momma. Night," she calls back, walking away from the mirror to kill her lamp beside the bed, crawling under the covers and snuggling to get comfortable.

The next few days leading up to Friday night's double date, Tara and Kayla go off at lunch for their girl-talk sessions while the boys generally choose to shoot pool or stand around chatting while they eat.

Other than those few moments at school and after practice, Cory would spend his time chatting over the phone with Tara. They get closer as they discuss anything that they can to keep a conversation alive. The night before their date, Cory finds out what gets her going more than anything.

"There's something I have to know. What made you decide on culinary school?" he asks, hoping it can rekindle a sluggish evening between them.

"Well, I watched the cooking channel a lot since my mom always worked overtime, and my dad is an over-the-road trucker. I got tired of microwavable TV dinners, so I started getting into more of it. From there, I started making dinner for me and my mom every night."

"Oh, well, that's neat. Yeah, I'm not much of a food maker." They finally share a laugh together.

Cory is caught off guard when he's given an offer. "Tell you what: I'm sure tomorrow is going to be fun, but Saturday, why don't you come over here and let me show you a few things. I don't want to say I'm comparing you to my ex-boyfriend back home, but I want to see if you can show interest in something other than my looks."

Not taking a nanosecond to think it over, he answers immediately.

"Hell, yeah, baby girl, I'll be there after my game. Shoot, I'll come get you, and you can go to my game at one, and afterward, I'll chill at your place."

Her giggles travel through the receiver when Tara thinks it over. "You got it! I will see you almost all day then. I like that almost as much as I like you."

"Good, I'll see you tomorrow then. Goodnight and sweet dreams, my Tara."

In a soft, sweet, seductive tone, Tara tells him, "Rest easy, handsome. I can't wait to taste your lips."

They each end the call and settle in for the night. In the morning, they meet up and walk around the hallways until they reach Tara's Home Economics class.

"I guess I'll go see my counselor and register for classes out at the votec."

Tara has a baffled look on her face.

"Wait … why would you be going out there?"

Taking hold of her free hand, Cory begins to explain.

"Well, they have a surgical tech program that I can enroll in from next semester through graduation. It'll give me college credits and help me understand surgery a little better."

A gesture of disappointment creeps into his girlfriend's eyes. "Oh, well, have fun with that then, babe."

Able to sense her sadness, Cory suggests an idea to her.

"Hey, why not ask your teacher about going out there for the advanced classes? Buses run from there to here and such."

"Really, they do that here?"

Cory's mouth pops off before he realizes he's talking. "Well, yeah, doesn't your old school have programs like that?"

Shaking her head, she reveals a little more about where she came from in Little Rock. "Most girls by now are pregnant or have a baby. I want more, which is why I don't mind being here now."

He is amazed by that fact, but Cory doesn't show it. "Well, go ask your teacher and let me know, baby girl. I'll drive you there and back if I have to."

Cory releases one of her hands so she can rub the side of his cheek.

"See, you're sweet and so thoughtful. I got to get in there, though, cutie pie. See you around after class."

Cory leans in, giving her a kiss on the cheek, and walks away as she slips inside to her seat, along the stationary island in the middle of the classroom.

Knowing Cory could be around less in the coming semester messes with Tara's head. It goes unmentioned until lunch, when Kayla has her alone for their girl-talk session.

"Hey, girl, what's up with you?"

Sitting down along the edge of the bench just outside the game room, she broaches the issue in a hushed tone.

"Cory told me about going to the votec program. Well, I want him to stay here with us."

Kayla begins to giggle when she motions for her girl to come closer. "Honey, if you keep thinking he's gonna find someone else, then chill."

Shrugging her shoulders, Tara sips down the last of her milk before she mentions what Cory told her to do.

"Well, it's not just that. There's something about him that makes me wanna be around him all the time. I've never felt this way—not even with my last boyfriend."

A hand on her friend's shoulder, Kayla makes sure she has Tara's undivided attention. "He is a really good guy. So who can blame you for that? C'mon now, girl, relax. It'll be cool. I'll be here still. Rick's going out there too, for pre-engineering classes."

Tara's still unsettled about how she feels inside. She gets what Kayla is telling her, but the sudden rush of feelings for Cory makes her feel a little uneasy.

"Okay, but he mentioned going out there too, for Home Ec stuff."

"Then do it. If he wants you around and it feels right, then do it."

That's when she lets it slip out. "It feels too fast. I like him and all, but I mean, I just got here, and we're making plans."

Rubbing her shoulder to maintain her attention, Kayla eases those fears. "Okay, tonight, then, I will do this. I'll pull ol' boy over to the side and remind him to go slow."

Their eyes meet as she spills out the rest of the news. "Girl, he's crazy about you from what Rick's told me."

"I'm crazy 'bout him too. He makes me smile and feel good 'bout myself."

"Then just chill. I got your back, girl. That's what I do. C'mon, let's ditch the boys and do our own thing." The girls dump their trash and walk away with their arms locked together.

When the bell rings and Cory can't find Tara to walk with her to class, he gets a nervous sensation in the pit of his gut. It nearly causes him to be tardy for class. When he slides through the door, he sees her sitting there with a blank expression on her face.

"Hey, I was looking for you," he says, taking his seat.

While keeping his eyes locked on hers, she pretends to ignore him.

"I'm sorry, but we need to talk," Tara whispers when she finally turns her attention to him.

"Oh, okay, did I do something wrong?"

She returns to ignoring him for the duration of class as she takes notes and doesn't break her concentration from the teacher.

Butterflies fill his stomach for nearly ninety minutes. Cory begins to overthink what he might have done to make Tara this pissed off.

I don't get it. Everything was fine when we got here this morning. Wait … is she pissed that I'm going to votec next semester? Ugh, damn it. Hurry up, ya fucking bell. This is killing me.

Cory then begins to tap his index finger frantically on his desk until the bell gives him the chance to shoot out the door and wait for Tara. Over by the edge of the lockers, he's dying to know why she's acting strange.

"Listen, you've done nothing wrong, but let me explain before you say anything, please," she begins as she stares at the tiles on the floor.

Cory stands there motionless with his thumbs hooked together against the straps of his backpack when she begins to mumble.

"I like you, Cory—like, a lot—and it's really fast for me to feel this way. I feel like you're actually a really good guy. That scares the hell out of me because of how my last boyfriend treated me and what he wanted me to do for my life." She pauses for a moment. "And, and, and here you are, just openly ready to help me make my life better. You wanna be there to support my dreams. You scare me because you are so sweet, and when I kissed you … well …"

Cory is fearing the worst is about to slip from her lips.

"I never felt that kind of spark hit me before. It was so hard to let it go because I wanted it to last forever. I mean, we're only seventeen, and you know …"

Without realizing it, Cory has shifted his right hand under her chin. Slowly pulling her face so they can meet eye to eye, Cory ignores her request to stay silent.

"I like you a lot too, Tara. I would never stop you from living your life, and anyone who would is an idiot." That's when his maturity virtually slaps her in the face.

"If you need some space, then fine. I have a team meeting after school to prepare for tomorrow's game, and then we have our date. If you want to cancel, then cool. No biggie."

Playfully punching Cory in the midsection, Tara goes from timid and scared to a lip-curling, eyebrow hunkering scowl.

"I don't think so, mister!"

Cory playfully laughs, taking a step back. "Okay, chill, snow kitten. Reow." He continues to taunt her with hissing noises for a few seconds, causing her to laugh.

"There's my beautiful smile. So I'll see you tonight when I pick you up?"

"No, I will see you there. I'm riding with my bestie, Kayla."

Cory nods and walks away, leaving Tara feeling a little more relieved as she walks to her final class of the day.

Since clearing the air with Cory, things instantly begin to feel like they're going to be okay. While in her final class, Tara goes over everything and considers taking up his offer of checking out the classes at the votec on Monday.

Time seems to soar as the week comes to an end as Tara rushes for her mother's car.

Slamming the door shut after shucking her backpack into the floorboard, Tara hurries to fasten her seatbelt.

"What's the rush. Got a hot date tonight?" her mother jokes, forgetting about Tara's plans.

"Yes, actually, I do, and I wanna be ready when you meet Cory tonight."

Shocked, Tara's mother lets her jaw drop. "Oh, my goodness, I forgot, but good, I can finally meet this mystery boy that keeps you smilin' all the time." Tara blushes as they pull away for home.

"Now does that mean you like it here?"

Shaking her head yes, Tara goes on about what all she likes about RiverCreek. "It's not only Cory I like here. It's the snow on the ground. I have friends who want more than being housewives. Here people have dreams of wanting more."

Her mother listens as she continues to babble.

"I can be open and be me here. Like, for example, this morning, I found out they have like classes at the votec that could help me get into a good culinary school. And, oh, Momma, I wanna do it."

Chuckling at her excitement, Tara's mother develops a renewed sparkle in her eyes. "Yeah, I forgot this place can be a blessing with good people. I loved Little Rock, but yeah, people there are a little old fashioned."

The chitchatting continues as they drive home.

Swiftly, the afternoon evolves into the early evening. The sun sets by six twenty-five. Tara's just getting out of the shower with only a towel wrapped her torso. She's taken by surprise when she overhears laughter coming from downstairs.

Curiosity gets the best of her, so she struts down the steps and stops at the next-to-last step when her mother sees her there with soaking wet hair and her towel wrapped around, barely covering her lower half.

"Tara! Get back upstairs, young lady!"

Tara's frozen when she notices Cory is sitting there with his back to her, talking with her mother. It isn't until she's screamed at once more that she regains her senses.

"Tara, upstairs now, or you're not going!"

Hearing her rush back up the stairs, Cory sits there trying his best to keep from turning around. He wants to see what the commotion is all about but knows it will not go well if gives in to temptation. Seeing the relief in Mrs. Rose's eyes, Cory smiles, trying to appear as innocent as he is polite.

"Thank you for not trying to turn around to see her standing there like that in only her bath towel. You really are a good, kid, aren't ya, Cory."

Blushing, he sits there kicking himself on the inside now. Cory just sits there, smiling for a moment.

"My mother wouldn't have me any other way, Mrs. Rose. Besides, she is the sheriff, and if I don't treat ladies with respect, well, it's not a good thing with her."

Oliva sits there, laughing lightly at the rehearsed corny response. "If you say so, kiddo, and please call me Olivia."

"Sorry, Olivia."

"It's okay. And tell me this: I understand you play hockey, and you asked my daughter to come watch you play tomorrow. Now, why should I allow my innocent little girl to go see something so violent? Before you answer that, I heard about what went down during that first game."

Taking his time thinking it over, Cory comes up with what he hopes is the best answer.

"Well ... Olivia, why don't you bring her and see for yourself. You can come watch the game, and afterward, I can come here for dinner because Tara wants to show off her cooking skills."

"Is that a fact? Hmm. Well, then, I guess I'll consider that offer to come watch, and then I'll let Tara show you how good she is at what she does best. Thank you for the invitation."

As he smiles nervously Cory begins to fumble with his thumbs.

"Tell ya what, I can tell you're a little uncomfy with this, so just relax. I'll go help Tara get ready so you can get going. I mean this. You do seem like a polite kid. And you are good to her. The last feller she went out with took advantage of her."

That's when she turns on mommy mode.

"So just a little warning—hurt my daughter like he did, and I'll hunt you down and mount your ass on my wall."

Swallowing hard, Cory nods his head while giving his response. "Yes, ma'am. I'll remember that."

Pulling her body from her seat, Olivia trots up the steps into Tara's room, where she sees her daughter struggling with what to wear.

"Hey, gorgeous, need some help?" her mother offers as she sneaks through the door.

"Yes, please, Momma. I can't pick out which blouse to wear. Or should I go with a sweater since it's already getting dark and cold?"

With the door behind her, Olivia goes over to the bed to see the assortment of options spread across the blanket.

Olivia glances over at what she sees and leans over, picking up a low-cut gray tank top along with Tara's favorite black button-up blouse.

"Try this. You wanna make an impression and wow him tonight. Then either leave this open or leave a button or two undone and watch him drool," Olivia suggests, advising her daughter on the art of foreplay.

"Mom!" she lets out in a whispered tone.

"What? I was young once too, you know. And hey, nothing like drawing in a good man with a little teasing at first. It worked with your father, and hey, after sitting and chatting with Cory, well …" She shrugs her shoulders as she finishes her statement. "He's a bit of the shy type I think, so c'mon, bring that boy's wild side out and make him proud to be seen with you. Make a bold statement. You're my daughter, and this is a brand-new start for you." Holding up the options, she continues. "So hurry up. He's down there waiting alone. Go blow dry your hair quickly and let it curl up some, then slip this on and go have fun. Love you." Olivia turns to leave, knowing she's embarrassed her daughter by suggesting she use a little sex appeal.

"This ain't you, Momma. What changed you to be more open like this?" Tara asks before her mother opens the door.

"You said he supports you. Well, if he does, then why not get your hooks into him and keep 'em around. Trust Momma. She knows a thing or two about boys."

Able to shake off the embarrassment, Tara slips into what her mother suggests and stands in front of her mirror as she blow dries her hair, hoping it's good enough for the evening.

Once it feels dry in her hands, she rushes downstairs to meet Cory, who's still sitting there.

"Ready to go?" She's caught off guard when she sees what Cory is wearing.

"Um, nice jersey, and what's with the khakis?" she asks when he stands up and turns to greet her.

"Team tradition. All starters wear this the night before we play, and since I am now team captain, I have to set the example."

A puzzled look creeps over Tara's face

"Okay, well, we better get going if we wanna make dinner before the movie."

Cory twists back around to give his farewell to Mrs. Rose. "Well, it was nice talking to you, Mrs. Rose … I mean, Olivia."

"It was nice meeting you too, Cory. You two have fun. Remember, young lady, curfew is eleven thirty." Tara nods her head, slipping her jacket on and grabbing Cory as they rush out the door.

"Bye, Momma. Love you. Mean it. See you later."

She's literally dragging Cory to his car so they can get away from her mother before she has another opportunity to embarrass either of them again. Anxious to get their first official date underway, the couple pulls away to meet up with their friends.

Olivia stands in the doorway, staring at the snow flurries, and wraps her arms across her chest. Still unsure if moving back home is the right decision, she at least gets to see her daughter more often now with a boy that gives her a positive vibe and treats Tara like a lady.

CHAPTER 6

Double-Date Time

On the drive to Applebee's, Tara and Cory both barely speak for a few minutes. Neither one was still unsure of what to say about what occurred back at Tara's house, not until Cory finally just blurts out what he's thinking. "Well, your mom is something else, isn't she?"

"Uh, yeah, and thank you for not running off. She can pick up that you're shy. Take advantage of that."

Shifting gears, Cory takes a millisecond to reply, "Oh."

Tara shifts her body away from the window. She decides to try something her mother suggested.

"Did you get a good glance at me standing there or running in only a bath towel?"

Cory's eyes say it all when she witnesses them grow. It now dawns on him why her mother warned her to run back upstairs.

"Uh no, I missed it," he teases back, hoping to get Tara to keep playing along.

"Well, what if I give you a little preview of what you missed by unbuttoning my blouse and letting you get a decent look down my tank top?"

Cory can't resist dropping his jaw when he sees from of the corner of his eye that Tara is slowly pulling her jacket back and unbuttoning the top three buttons on her blouse. As she listens to him huff, she pulls back away to the door, lowering her head with a seductive smile glowing toward Cory.

"Wow, just yeah, holy hell," Cory mumbles, wanting to take his eyes off the road, but he knows he can't since black ice is horrible.

"Maybe some other time I'll let you get a much better view," Tara teases as she buttons up her blouse, zipping her jacket back up.

"Anytime you wanna. I won't complain." Tara chuckles and knows it has been effective when she stares over at Cory's khakis and notices that he's trying to hide the fact that it has had an obvious effect on his desires.

Now that the tension is finally broken, the couple drives into the heart of town, where they notice that Rick and Kayla are just pulling into the parking lot.

"Wow, I figured they would've been waiting on us," Cory admits, curious as to why they are just arriving a few cars ahead of Tara and himself.

Cory parks beside his friends.

"Ready to eat?" he asks his date, looking over at her with a soft, comforting look in his eyes.

Mesmerized by the glow of his eyes, Tara finds it difficult to speak. "Y-yes, I am ..." she's able to muster up as she waits for him to travel around the front of the Celica to open her door to take her hand, helping her out.

"Thank you. I love how you do that for me."

"You're a lady. You should expect that respect."

Once he closes the door gently behind her, Tara softly places her hand on his cheek to distract him for the first kiss of the evening.

"Woah! Get a room, you two," Kayla teases when Rick helps her out of the Man-Van.

Cory and Tara ignore the mockery and continue to kiss. He wraps his arms around her in hopes of making it feel more romantic.

"C'mon, let's get our table," Rick whispers, seeing his friends embraced in their moment.

Feeling her body wanting to give in to the temptation to forego the date, Tara finds a way to break away from the moment where her world is at a standstill.

"Oh, wow, that was better than the first time, but we better get inside. I think they went on in," Tara's able to mutter, touching her lips with her icy hand.

"Yeah, yeah, good idea. Let's go," Cory says, taking her hand.

Holding the door open for Tara as the couple walks inside, Cory is acknowledged with a "thank you" as they walk by him to get out of the cold.

"Hello, welcome to Applebee's. Just the two of you?" The host asks, getting menus out for them.

"No, actually, our friends came in a minute ago, and I don't see—"

Cory is cut off when he hears Rick hollering to get his attention. "Hey, Core, over here, homie!"

He points over to Rick. "That's them," Cory says. The host reaches to get a couple of menus and guides him and Tara over to the booth.

"Well, glad you two could finally break apart to join us," Rick teases, a smirk forming as they sit down across the table.

When an easy kick lands against her shin, Tara looks up from the menu to see Kayla motioning to follow her to the lady's room.

"Hey, boys, we will be right back."

Taking Tara by the wrist, Kayla quickly yanks her from the booth, giving Rick the time to explain why they were late.

"Hey, Core, you are not going to believe this, homie. She finally gave it up. Almost a year of waiting, and she finally gave in tonight. I got a surprising letter offering me a scholarship to Marshall City University. Well, since she's going to Central Michigan, that means we can stay closer than we thought."

Cory ignores the first half of what Rick has just said. "Wait, you're not going to Grambling?"

Stunned by what he's just heard, Rick acts like he's reaching over to slap Cory.

"Didn't you hear me? I finally got some action, brother."

That's when Cory gives two thumbs-up for approval.

While Rick shares his enthusiasm with Cory, the girls stand in front of the sinks, reapplying their lip gloss. "Was that the first kiss?" Kayla questions as Tara continues to glow.

"Oh no, but it was definitely one that made me weak in the knees."

Tara's eyes nearly roll back in her head.

"Girl, just wait. I finally let Rick get me, and—oh my God, I haven't ever felt anything like that. The heat, the feeling of him over top of me. The sensation of feeling him breathe in my ear and all the way inside of me and goosebumps all over my body."

Tara notices that Kayla begins to wiggle a little, remembering the sensations pulsing through her body.

"I kinda know that feeling, girl," Tara says, slapping her hand over her mouth.

"Oh, shut up! You're not a virgin?"

"Ain't most not one by our age?"

Dropping her mouth open even more, Kayla is beyond shocked by the revelation.

"Well, I guess not, but when I found out Rick's going to a Michigan college, I couldn't resist. I love that man."

"I thought I loved my ex too, which is why I slept with him. Then I found out he just wanted to try to get me pregnant so I wouldn't follow my dreams," Tara says, checking on her makeup.

That's all it takes for the shock effect to end and the protective best friend to take over.

"I'll kick his ass myself! Thank goodness Core isn't that way, and girl he'll bend over backward to do anything for you. We saw that with Vanessa, but she couldn't keep from fucking anyone except him."

Tara blushes as they begin to walk out of the bathroom so they can join the boys waiting for them.

"Now, I see Cory as a shy little brother, and you're exactly what he needs," Kayla finishes as they approach the table.

Taking her place beside Cory, she's taken aback by the fact that he guessed correctly that she would enjoy a sweet tea. "How did you know I like tea more than pop?"

The three of them give her a standoffish glare. "What's pop?" Rick asks, looking over at the others.

"You know, Coke, Pepsi, Dr. Pepper—soda pop."

When they realize what she means, Cory speaks up next.

"We call it soda here. You had us a little confused with 'pop.'"

Tara slightly draws into her seat, feeling out of place again compared to Little Rock. "Sorry, y'all. Guess it'll take a little to get used to things up this way," she says. Her twang is still heavily present with certain words.

Quickly erasing the moment of cultural confusion, the two couples return to joking around, enjoying their time out before the movie. They sit and watch as Tara inhales every bit of steaming goodness from her plate once their food arrives.

She begins to show off her love for food when she looks around at everyone's plate. She tries to inhale the smells from what they ordered without having to ask.

Looking at the time, they realize that they need to get going if they want to make the movie on time.

"Hey, you all we need to pay and get moving if we wanna make this flick," Rick says as he reaches for his wallet; he stops Cory from getting his when he notices he's doing the same.

"Oh, hell no, son. Leave that wallet in your pocket. This is our treat for you two and our way to say welcome to miss Tara."

"Aw, that is so sweet, Rick, but, really, you don't have to."

Rick waves her off. "I know I don't, but I want to. This might not be the South, but we're still good people up this way."

Tara is touched and speechless by their acts of kindness. "Thank you," she manages to say, feeling special enough to cry with their acceptance.

The moment they walk away from the table, Tara clutches onto Cory's arm tightly as they approach the door. That doesn't settle well with the host since she's friends with Vanessa.

"Oh, fuck that sight. My girl isn't gonna like this," she mutters.

No one thinks anything of it as the fun keeps rising the longer the double date goes on. As luck would have it, the movie theater isn't far from the restaurant. Cory and Rick find a place to park along the curb. The boys look over the titles playing as they walk around to help the girls out of the vehicles.

"I guess it's girls' choice?" Rick asks, rolling his eyes between Tara and Kayla.

"Yup, and you know it's a chick-flick kind of night, boys," Kayla says.

Both boys drop their heads as they're escorted to the window to pay for tickets.

Once inside, the boys gently remove their dates' jackets. "What ya want? We'll come find you inside," Cory says as they approach the concession stand.

"Popcorn with lots of butter and something to drink. I'm a simple girl, and I like simple things," Tara says, allowing Rick to tease her, twisting her words.

"Well, that explains why you're so into our boy here. He's simple and shy, for sure!"

Cory begins to blush when Tara fires back without thinking, "Kiss him, and you'll find out differently. I can promise you that ain't simple at all."

Looking over at Cory, Rick extends his arms, continuing to play along. "Well, come here and gimme some sugar, big daddy."

Cory can't help but laugh as he pushes Rick away. "Sorry, man, not with that garlic breath!" he shouts, making a face of disgust as everyone watching can't help but laugh at their goofiness.

Once they're finished, they walk up to the counter and tell the cashier what they want, but they're taken aback by what she tells them when they go to pay.

"Boys, that was the funniest thing I've seen in a while. This is on the house since you made my day go so much better. This is my way to say thank you. Enjoy, gentlemen."

Taking the items, Cory says, "Hey, anytime. Glad we could help, and thank you."

The boys walk into the theater and start gawking around. They can't seem to locate their dates. They're caught off guard when the girls come from behind them, scaring them when they reach out, tickling the side of Cory's and Rick's ribs.

"Oh shit, don't do that!" Rick cries out, trying to contain his laughter. Cory is unable to contain himself as he pulls to the side, laughing.

"Okay, okay, you win!" he squeals, trying to get away.

The two girls giggle, having fun as they follow the boys to their seats just as the lights go dim. Settling into the seat, Tara leans over, resting her head against Cory's shoulder. All he can do is smile and stare at the screen so he doesn't make her uncomfortable.

One advantage to his slight discomfort is the angle. Cory can see down along the edge of Tara's blouse since it's just loose enough to give him a better view than he had in his car.

Damn, she's hot! Ugh, gotta be good, gotta be good, but can't look away, he says to himself over and over, trying to keep from drawing attention to the fact that he's staring down her shirt.

Forcing his concentration back to the screen, he sits there along with Rick, feeling bored as the movie plays. A couple of yawns near the end of the movie become noticeable when Kayla can feel Rick's chest expand and contrast.

Cory's a little better at hiding it when he sucks in air and coughs as he exhales. Leaning up to whisper in his ear, Tara stops when she feels her phone vibrate in her purse.

When the credits begin to roll up the screen, Tara reaches for her phone. Seeing that she has a voicemail waiting for her, she steps aside to listen as the people walk by her.

"Hey, it's Momma. Listen, I'll extend your curfew because your father made a surprise visit home. So, yeah, take your time, and I'll let you get away with it just this once. Love ya, kid. Goodnight. Don't stay out too late."

Listening to the voicemail, Tara has a disgusted expression written all over her face.

"Ugh, like that's so gross!" Concerned over what she heard, Cory walks over to her.

"What's wrong?"

She leans in, cups her hand, and whispers into his ear, "My parents told me not to come straight home because they're having sex."

A puzzling stare creeps over Cory face as he's not sure how to reply to that just yet.

"Well … you could … I don't know … go with me down to the edge of the river, and we could chill with some music and talk."

Able to overhear what they're talking about, Rick speaks up, knowing that sitting in the Celica won't set the mood.

"Wait. Hold on. Oh, hell no. Here's what you two do. We take the cars, drop yours off around the corner from Kay's house. I sneak in so we can spend a little more time together and I let you take the Man-Van. Hell, my parents already know I'm crashing with you tonight, so we're good."

"I'm good with that, but don't think you're getting in my pants." Tara explains, shoving her phone back into her purse before she struts out of the movie theater.

She leaves Cory standing there as Rick and Kayla begin to walk behind her.

"I'm insulted. I'm better than that!" Cory says as he slowly begins to pick up the pace.

They wait for Cory to catch up before they all walk out into the blistering cold, windy night. The town appears to resemble a ghost town as they get into their vehicles, start them up, and idle, waiting for the heat to build up.

"Holy hell, it's cold!" Cory cries out, breathing into his hands, trying to keep them warm.

"Yeah, I'm not used to this at all," Tara reveals, chattering her teeth.

"Give it a minute. The turbo helps the car get warm quick."

Within a matter of minutes, the lights inside the theater go out, but luckily, there's just enough heat for Cory to start to pull out as he follows Rick over to Kayla's house and swap keys.

"Make it worth it, homie," Rick whispers, winking at his best friend.

Cory nods, just to keep Rick from making another comment. In the Man-Van, Cory drops it into gear and heads for the river's edge. By the time they arrive, Tara's comfy in the back, looking over the setup that Rick has slowly assembled in his ride.

"Wow, I've never seen hot plates, a microwave—and is that a fountain machine plus a mini sink?" she says, signaling for Cory to get back there with her.

"Yeah, it's pretty—"

He's cut off when she gets a grip on his shirt, pulling him down beside her.

"Am I really that pretty?" she asks him as they both use a folded arm to prop themselves up.

Cory reaches out, placing his hand on her side. He slowly begins to move his hand up and down along her blouse.

"Absolutely, my beautiful girl. Actually, you're beyond beautiful. You literally took my breath away when I first saw you."

Tara begins to blush and roll away, which causes Cory's hand to slide up underneath her blouse and undershirt. "Oh, I'm sorry I wasn't trying to—"

She places a finger on his lips. "Shush, it's okay. And if it wasn't, I would've removed your hand. You really are timid, but you're also awfully sweet—one of the reasons why I like you more every day."

"Likewise, with you. I can't stop thinking about you, and out of anyone, you picked me. I'm not sure why you did. I am not special. I just play hockey and dream about getting out of here."

"That's what makes you special—the fact that you're determined to do that and you believe in me."

Just as they both feel the urge to lean in for a kiss, they are interrupted by a set of headlights beaming directly into the Man-Van.

Leaning up, Cory's already beginning to sweat when he sees the cruiser switch on the lights.

"Oh, fuck me. It's my mom!" he groans, trying to help Tara scoot back up into the front seat.

Over the bullhorn, Sherriff Dubois isn't aware who is in the Man-Van, but he assumes its Rick and Kayla trying to find a spot for a quickie.

"All right, kids, get heading home. This isn't the time or place. Now, get going before I call your parents."

Cory hopes the floodlight will continue to conceal them. He

quickly slides into the driver's seat and pulls away, trying to avoid getting busted by his mother.

"Thank you, and see you at the house, young man," she announces when the Man-Van pulls away.

Mortified, Cory takes the quickest route to Tara's so he can drop her off and end their date.

"I am so sorry that happened, but at least we didn't get busted," Cory says, feeling humiliated.

"It's cool, sweet pea. One day after practice, come over and we'll continue this. Hell, since my dad is home, my parents may go out and you can come over then."

Cory shakes his head as he pulls up as close to the house as he can to drop off Tara cut off. He watches to make sure she gets inside before he pulls away to wait on Rick to get his car back before they take off for home.

CHAPTER 7

Intensity

Cory speeds back to Kayla's house. He pulls up behind the Celica, flashing the high beams a couple of times. He waits a moment while Rick stumbles out the bedroom window, trying to slip on his overcoat. Fumbling into the Man-Van, Rick appears pissed by the interruption.

"What the hell, homie? You know I was busy in there and her parents almost caught us!"

Cory's expression refuses to change. In fact, he glares over at Rick with a look of disdain.

"Hey, my mother nearly caught me and Tara. She thinks it was you and Kayla. Now we need to get our asses back so she doesn't go looking for us—or worse, call your parents."

Rick gulps hard as he learns about the turn of events. "Guess we should go then," he stutters as he begins to pull out the keys to the Celica.

Cory snatches his keys from Rick's hand.

"Yeah, let's roll on out of here, man," Cory says, opening the driver's side door, then running through the cold night air to his car.

Rick waits for Cory to pull away before he drops his Man-Van into drive to follow him home. By the time both vehicles pull up alongside the curb, they notice Mrs. Dubois sitting in her car, waiting on them. She kills the engine to the cruiser and gets out to wave the boys over before she cups her hands together to protect herself from the frigid cold air.

Once out of the night air, the three of them take a minute to warm up once the door is closed before anything is said.

"Well, boys, how was the date?" Mrs. Dubois asks, slowly removing her leather jacket.

"It was … g-g-good, Ma …" Cory manages to mumble.

"Well, that's a good thing. Now, young man, I'm disappointed in you, taking Miss Kayla down to the riverfront like that. She's a hard-working, classy gal. You better treat her like a lady and not some two-dollar hooker. Hooking up in the back of your van—I'm ashamed."

Caught in disbelief, Rick nods his head, responding, "Yes, ma'am," taking the rap for Cory and Tara.

She chuckles at his pathetic apology. Sherriff Dubois hangs up her jacket and lumbers to her bedroom.

"Thanks for covering for me, man," Cory whispers, placing his jacket up last before they stroll to the bedroom.

Once the door is closed, Rick replies, "Hey, it was my idea, so it's all good, but if you don't mind, I'm gonna jump online and talk to Kay for a minute."

He waves Rick over to his computer. "Nah, go ahead. I'm gonna sit on the bed and read."

The boys sit and dive into their own thing for about an hour before the feeling of exhaustion slowly creeps in as their eyes begin to feel heavy.

"Hey, man, let's get ready to crash. Got a big game tomorrow, ya know," Cory says during an extended yawn.

"Yeah, I was about to jump off anyways. Let's call it a night. I wanna see you kick ass tomorrow."

Lifting the mattress, the boys set the spare one on the floor. Cory motions for Rick to take the bed while he sleeps on the spare mattress on the floor.

"Nah, man, I'm good on this one," Rick argues back.

"You're the guest, so go ahead. My way of saying thank you for saving my ass with my mother."

Not wanting to argue over it anymore, Rick flops onto the bed and covers up.

"Night, brother."

"Night, man."

Cory turns out the light. Not long after, he is caught off guard by Rick's snoring.

It's nearly ten o'clock when the boys are woken up by Mr. Dubois.

"Wake up, boys. I'm making breakfast. Hey, Rick, I made my famous brown-sugar-coated morning ham." Mr. Dubois opens the door wider, holding the plate with Rick's favorite breakfast food, letting him get a whiff of it, then walks back out of the room.

Slowly, Rick sits up with sleepy eyes. "Oh, that smells so good, sir. I'll be there in a minute." Rick stretches and slams a pillow down onto Cory.

"Ugh, you dick. I'm up, man. I'm up," he groans, pulling his arms from under his head.

"C'mon, ya dads got us food made." Rick rolls out of bed, bending over, yanking the blanket from Cory.

"Ugh, I'm up. C'mon, ya big pig. Let's go eat," Cory barks, pushing up off the mattress.

Stumbling into the kitchen, the boys find a place at the table.

"Well, there they are. I was about to put out an APB for you two," Mrs. Dubois teases, holding onto her coffee mug.

"Morning, Ma," both boys groan out as they continue to wake up.

"Get some juice. Get some sugar in ya, boys," Mrs. Dubois suggests, placing the jug of orange juice in front of them.

Breakfast comes and goes as everyone eats saying little to nothing. Once she's finished, Mrs. Dubois makes sure her robe is tied tightly enough so she can get ready for Cory's game.

Mr. Dubois is already dressed in his work uniform. He begins reading over the paper once he's finished with his meal.

"Gotta work today, Dad?" Cory asks, hoping his dad will come to his game.

"Yeah, just something small—oil change and tire rotation. I

should be done by noon at the latest. I will make it—I promise, son. I wouldn't miss today's game for nothing. Plus, your mom said your girlfriend is going, and I wanna meet this new one."

Cory goes silent, but that doesn't stop him from scarfing down the last bit on his plate. Finished, he gets the plates around the table and rinses them off in the sink.

"Well, if you'll excuse me, you all, I am going to head home and get cleaned up for the game."

Cory and Mr. Dubois wave as Rick rushes to get his jacket and vanishes behind the door.

"Well, son, I guess I need to get going too. I will see you later. Behave or be brave! I know you'll play well today." Mr. Dubois pats his son on the back as he passes by and makes his way through the living room and out the door.

As his nerves continue to build up for his first game as team captain, Cory walks back to his room, getting his jersey and a clean pair of khakis. He sits online for a while after getting dressed until it's time for him to leave to pick up Tara to take her to the game. When he arrives, he notices a semi-truck parked at the end of the corner and figures that's her dad's rig.

Parked directly behind Mrs. Rose's car, Cory runs to the front door, where he finds a note taped to the door.

"Cory, parents wanted to come to the game too. We will see you there. Love, Tara," he reads out loud.

Not only is the pressure building to win, but now his parents and Tara's parents are going to meet, and if it goes as it did between Vanessa's parents, it'll be fireworks exploding in his face again.

Taking in a couple of deep breaths, he takes the note and dashes to his car. Still tapping his fingers on the steering wheel, he starts the car and rushes over to the rink, where the crowd for both teams have started to arrive.

Parked outback, Cory dashes inside and toward the locker room. The team is yelling back and forth to psych themselves up. Everyone pats Cory on the back when he finally arrives.

"Team captain in the room!" one of the teammates announces

as they begin to bang on their lockers, chanting his name, a tradition to get the team captain worked up.

"Let's kill 'em guys!" Cory yells, raising an instant uproar from the entire team.

Hearing all the energy from the team, the coach comes out from his office.

"There's our leader. Get dressed, Cory. We may still have some time before the game, but let's go get a feel for the ice and pay our respects that our former team leader isn't playing with us today."

Frank stands there clapping his hands with a look of resentment in his eyes.

"Kill, guys. Go kill those losers!" Frank screams as the team heads out to the ice without Cory.

Frank walks over to Cory and leans up against a locker.

"Hey, don't play nice out there. Play like you did in the last game, before I got hurt. Become an animal on the ice."

After he finishes fastening his pads, Cory faces away from Frank as he gets ready.

"I'm not a pansy, as much as you think I am, Frankie. I've played just as long as you have. I just don't get ape shit crazy trying to hurt people. I'm in it to win it all—something this team hasn't done since before we were born."

Frustrated, Frankie shoves off the locker.

"Just don't blow it, okay. If we win today, then we stand a chance to actually have a high spot in the playoffs when March comes."

The short exchange brings out a side of Cory he doesn't usually express—unless he's feeling ignored.

"I said I got this, Frankie. Jesus Christ!"

Joining the team out on the ice, Cory glides into the open spot as they bend over to gently touch the ice to pay respects to Frank not being medically cleared to play.

"All right, team listen up …" Cory calls out, gaining their attention. "This is our time. From the first drop of the puck, this is our house, and we will protect our home!"

The team and home crowd begin to cheer.

"We're going to skate faster, hit harder, and keep the offense fast paced. Let's send them out of here with the worse thing in any rivalry game—a goose egg on the scoreboard! I'm talking shutout. Let's keep them on ice!" he shouts, motioning to get going over to the bench.

The team works at keeping themselves psyched up while time passes by for the game to begin. Cory sits off to the side by himself, keeping his eyes closed, replaying every negative moment in his life to keep his anger flowing.

He sits there patiently until the coach stands screaming. "It's game time, boys, let's get another 'W' for this house, our house!"

The starters rush from the players' bench, ready for action.

Once the puck is dropped, Cory leads the charge as the team follows his instructions. They keep up a heavy offense and continue to pound away on their archrivals.

By the end of the second period, they're already up four to nothing. During the intermission, the team rests, trying to keep their spirits high, but their energy begins to fade.

At the start if the third period, things take a turn for the worse. The Twin Cities Dragons come out skating hard. In the first few minutes, they cut the score in half; it's now four to two in favor of RiverCreek.

The crowd begins to roar up as each side cheers harder for their respective team. Cory looks around to find Tara and everyone else cupping their hands around their mouths, cheering. He's downright angry out of fear of letting them down. He rushes back down the ice to get on defense.

Skating at full speed, Cory slams into the Dragon with the puck so hard that they both go sliding across the ice, until they hit such thunderous force that it makes the glass tremble from the impact. The referee blows the whistle as a member of each team helps them to their feet.

"Penalty, RiverCreek, number fourteen, two minutes for charging," the referee announces, taking Cory by the arm and guiding him over to the penalty box.

The entire team cheers as they see their captain escorted to the box.

"Yeah, go, Cold Core!" one of the kids screams from the stands as Cory turns and smiles, waving, feeling proud of finally gaining some recognition.

"Hey, hey, hey, c'mon, get out there for the faceoff. We have a game to win!" the coach yells, getting his players organized once more.

Thanks to the momentum generated by Cory, the team rallies to once again take over the tempo of the game, playing with ruthless aggression. That style continues once Cory is released from the penalty box. Once again, the team begins slicing through the Twin Cities Dragons, scoring two more goals before the final buzzer sounds.

The RiverCreek Beavers stays out on the ice as the Dragons skate away with their heads held low.

"Yeah, boys, we did it! We destroyed them this time!" Cory shouts as they all form a circle in the middle of the rink, pounding their sticks against the ice in victory.

One by one, after gathering in the middle of the rink, the players slowly take their turn skating off the ice to return to the locker room. The feeling of victory continues to echo throughout the locker room and down the hall as the boys get cleaned up, taking their time going home.

Cory is one of the last ones to head for the door, but he's taken by surprise when he notices Frank sitting there, waiting for him.

"Hey, great way to rally the team. You did good today, Core. I guess you could be a real team captain. Honestly, I'm tired of playing, so it's your team now. I have more important things to do. I'll return when I'm ready and not a minute beforehand.

Stunned by his revelation, Cory stands there with his bag over his shoulder.

"I don't get you Frankie. Once minute you're an ass, and then, when it's just us here, you're a decent human being. What the hell is the matter with you?"

As he puts his hand on the back of his neck, Frankie doesn't respond. He walks away and vanishes down the hallway. Cory stands there, trying to put the pieces of the puzzle together with no luck at all. Finally able to wave it off, he remembers he has a date waiting on him and darts out the door.

Cory dashes out to his car, speeding to Tara's. Parking alongside the curb, he begins to feel a little nervous about meeting her father. With a hard gulp, he pulls himself from the Celica and walks toward the door.

When he gets directly in front of it, he knocks at first and waits. Nearly a minute goes by, and he knocks again with no answer, pounding harder on the door. Cory waits as Olivia finally approaches.

"Hey, sweetie. Tara's busy in the kitchen. C'mon inside and relax. Her dad took off to the store for a few last-minute things."

She steps aside so Cory can come in, getting out of the blistering wind.

"Thank you, Mrs. Rose."

Sliding his coat off, he tosses it up onto the coat rack.

"You're welcome. You played a rough game out there today. I never knew you had a bad side, kid, but keep it out there on the field and away from my little girl."

There's a quick snicker before Cory corrects her terminology.

"I think you mean 'on the ice.' The field guy is Quick Rick; he runs track in the spring."

Rolling her eyes, Mrs. Rose replies, "Whatever." With a huff, she walks away.

Cory follows behind her, taking a seat in the living room, waiting for either Mr. Rose to arrive back at the house or Tara to finish cooking.

He continues to sit there in the living room with Mrs. Rose, who has it tuned to the Arkansas football game.

"C'mon 'Backs, get 'em, hit 'em, kill 'em!" she screams at the TV. Cory isn't sure how to respond other than with "Go, team."

"Now, that's not how you cheer for the Razorbacks, son," a deep male voice says from behind, startling him.

He turns to see an extremely tall, slender man, with grey eyes to match his salt-and-pepper hair, standing behind him, holding a bag of groceries.

Olivia gets a good glance at Cory's eyes, laughing in her seat when Mr. Rose surprises him.

"Oh, uh, yes, sir," Cory mumbles, getting to his feet to greet Mr. Rose with a handshake and to introduce himself.

"Hello, sir. I'm Cory, Cory Dubois, your d-d-daughter's … boyfriend, sir."

Mr. Rose waves at Cory to retake his seat. After exchanging a handshake, Mr. Rose eases Cory's nerves.

"Sit down, kid, and relax. You're good. I seen ya earlier. I gotta say, you're respectful. I like that, but if you'll excuse me, Tara needs these." Mr. Rose looks over to his wife and smiles, giving his initial impression that he likes Cory and the values he was raised with to show his elders.

Not to disturb Tara's concentration, Mr. Rose drops the bags on the kitchen table and stands there to observe her in her element. He inhales the smell of the food and can't believe how much his little girl has grown up—especially now that she's brought home a new boy whom he so far likes, at least more than her deadbeat ex-boyfriend from Little Rock. It's a relief that sends a calming wave over his soul.

CHAPTER 8

Removing Her Past

In the front room watching the game with Olivia, Cory slowly begins to learn more about the team.

"Are they playing a really good team, huh?" Cory asks, not knowing much about the landscape of college football.

"A nobody team from Idaho, but they're playing like hog shit. C'mon, carry the damn ball!" she screams, flipping off the players on the screen out of frustration. Cory's getting a kick out of it even when Mr. Rose enters the room and carries on with his wife.

"C'mon y'all. Can't beat 'Bama down the stretch if ya play with a trough full of slop!" he yells, turning Razorback red in the cheeks.

He remembers that Cory is still in the room; Mr. Rose finally introduces himself.

"For heaven's sake, I'm sorry, son. I'm Dewey, but everyone calls me Wane. It's a pleasure to make ya acquaintance, young man."

Cory looks and nods as he reintroduces himself as well. "Well, as you know, I'm Cory. Nothing special to call me, other than Core."

Wane chuckles and waves him toward the kitchen, sensing he would rather spend time with Tara.

Once he's out of the room, Wane looks over to Olivia with a smirk on his face. "You was, right, nice kid. I like him already. Maybe this Yankee town ain't gonna be that bad after all."

Olivia slaps him playfully on the knee. "Yeah, it'll work out for the best, I think."

They return their attention to the TV, yelling at the referees again for what they see as a missed penalty.

"Hey there, hot stuff, need a hand?" Cory asks at the edge of the counter.

"No, just take a seat at the table and talk to me," Tara orders as she keeps her eyes on the skillet sizzling with four oversized pork chops.

"Can do, honeydew!" Cory takes a seat and stares at her.

Tara is hustling around, checking on her rolls in the oven and stirring the variety of vegetables boiling on the stove.

"Smells amazing!" Cory says, taking in a whiff of it all.

"Thank you, sweetness. Hope ya actually enjoy it, since it's gonna be like nuttin' you had before."

She keeps up the hasty pace and is asked questions as she continues to add seasonings and spices.

"What's that you're adding to it?"

"Well, I've melted down some butter and sprinkled in some garlic powder, rosemary, seasoning salts, and ground pepper—with just a hint of lemon pepper seasoning. It makes the pork taste a lot better, if you ask me."

Cory pops off without realizing it. "I did ask, so yeah, it sounds as good as it smells."

She scoffs and snickers as the butter pops in the skillet.

It takes her roughly ten minutes finish cooking. She picks up two plates to plate each dish in a fancy matter.

"Would you care to take these to my parents and then come back to get each both a beer, please? You don't know how much I would appreciate it," Tara pleads, using a hand towel to wipe her brow.

"I think I could manage that."

Cory struts up, pecking her on the cheek as he clutches the plates in his hands, walking back into the living room. He announces out loud to get their attention, "Food is served, compliments of the house chef."

Wane and Olivia laugh as they take their plates from Cory's grasp.

"I will be right back with your drinks," he says as he scurries away.

Hurrying back into the kitchen, he sways over to the classic icebox refrigerator, taking out two cans of beer.

"Be right back, beautiful." He quickly makes his way to and from the living room so he can take his place at the kitchen table, waiting on Tara to finish.

Just as he settles onto the thin, rustically fashioned seat cushion, he notices that a plate appears under his nose.

"Oh wow, breaded. You didn't mention that," Cory says, scooting his chair closer to the edge of the table.

"Something special for you. My parents don't really care much for it since I make it thick with breading, but enjoy."

Tara wiggles away, getting Cory a tall glass of her own sweet tea, and takes over her plate.

Cory waits patiently for her to take her first bite, even though his stomach is roaring.

"Dig in. No need to wait on me," she advises him, sticking a fork into her food, slicing it with a knife.

"Yes, ma'am," he replies, following her actions, slicing into the juicy, tender piece of pork.

Shoving the first bite into his mouth, his senses are thrusts into overdrive. His eyes light up with delight, which Tara sees immediately.

"So ...?" she asks, picking up her glass of tea.

"Oh my gosh. This is the best thing ever!" he says, slicing a second portion. Tara grins and returns to eating as she sees Cory inhaling his food.

Once they're finished and Cory politely rinses off their plates, the kids head into the living room to find Tara's parents, now lounging in their seats with empty plates resting comfortably on their guts.

"I'll call you later. Let me get all this cleaned up, and we'll make plans for later or tomorrow," she says, ready to tackle her mess in the kitchen.

Cory acknowledges her request and follows closely behind her as they walk toward the door.

When they embrace in a farewell hug, he whispers into her ear, "I wanna kiss you, but not in front of your parents."

When Tara begins to pull away, she lip-locks him as her parents sit there teasing them.

"How cute, but let the boy breathe there, Tara," her father says with a sarcastic clap.

She pulls away and backs off, giving him room to walk out the door. Once it's shut, her parents sit there, staring at her with a stern look.

"Keep it at—kissing only, young lady," her mother warns, pointing at her.

"Yes, Momma."

Tara goes over and takes her parents' plates and returns to the kitchen. After she finishes washing and putting everything away, she takes off for her bedroom to relax.

Hoping to catch either Kayla or Cory online, Tara jumps on to kill some time. The instant she logs on, there's an immediate instant message.

I heard ya done got yaself a brand-new fella. Guess that means I'm just another free bird to go do as I please?

She reads, realizing it's her ex.

Do whatever ya want, Bobby. Ya do anyway. You cheated on me enough, and I ain't comin' back to Lil Rock!

She sits and waits to see what he has to say before she blocks him.

Bitch, now listen here. You be mine, and you are gone come back home 'cuz you still with me and not some Yankee snob. You will have my kids, and you will do what I say when I sa . Now pack ya shit. I will be up there by Christmas to get you.

She loses her cool and begins yelling at the screen, loud enough that her parents rush into her room.

FUCK YOU, BOBBY. GO FUCK GLORIA KILGORE OR MARILOU EDWARDS, LIKE YOU DID BEHIND MY BACK, YA SHORT DICKED BASTARD!

Not bothering to knock, her father barges in, nearly taking the door down when the handle sticks.

"Hey, what in tarnation is going on up here?"

Tara steps aside and shows him the message from her ex. Her father is instantly pissed off by what he reads.

"Oh, now that boy is gonna be in for a ass-whipping. I'm gonna go make me a call. You print that out and block his worthless ass!" he orders, his temper getting the best of him.

"What's the matter?" Olivia asks, following Wane stomping down the steps.

"Bobby and threatening our daughter. I'm gonna have his ass locked up this time talking to her like that. She's still a minor."

She stops on the next-to-last step, standing there while Wane talks to his old friends down at the police station back home.

Tara's nerves are shot now, and she's ready to rip Bobby's head off his shoulders. She does as her father insists and prints out the conversation, placing it on her desk, then flops on her bed.

He wouldn't dare show up! She tells herself in her mind, taking a pillow and resting it on her chest with her arms clutched tightly around it.

"Yeah, Ronny, you'd be doing that town a favor, locking him up. He's nothing but a damn fool, if ya ask me, thinking he's gonna run my little girl's life and threatening to come kidnap her. Handle him, or I will!" he warns and listens into the phone.

"Well, do whatever you gotta do, and thank you. Bye, old friend." Wane slams the cordless phone on the end table and takes a seat, waiting for a return call.

It takes almost two hours before Wane receives a response. When the phone rings, Tara tries to sneak up to her door and crack it open to listen for the details. By the time she's almost to the door, her cell phone goes off. Running and diving over the bed, she picks it up, hoping it's Cory.

"Hello?"

That's when the results of her father's phone call reach her. "You bitch. How could you get Bobby arrested? He's your damn soulmate, and you have him set up by the cops as a favor for your old man. That's messed up, and now he's off to jail for driving with an open container and charged with intent to deliver!"

Tara laughs with a hint of uncaringness to her tone.

"Good, he deserves it the way he talked to me. I told you I was done with his dumb broke ass."

Janet rips into her with veracity. "You've changed, and I don't like it! Up there being all Yankee uppity and shit, now thinking you're better than us. Well, newsflash, Tara—you ain't a damn thing, and ain't gonna amount to a damn thing either. Next thing you know, you'll be sleeping with colored guys."

Hearing Janet disrespect others sends Tara into a frenzy. "Hey, Cory's best friend is black, and yes, he has a white girlfriend who happens to be my bestie up here. Don't you dare insult them, either. At least being here, I'm not judged for what I want to do with my life. You wanna go make babies, then do it, but yes, I am better than that, and if you don't like it, then kiss my fucking ass, and don't call me again!" Tara shuts her phone, tossing it onto the floor.

The pain of what Janet has said slowly twists from anger to pain. As she lies there crying into her pillow, everything she has heard replays over and over in her mind. All of it causes her to cry for a while, thinking of how happy Kayla is with Rick and how sad it is that people like her old friend will never accept anything like that.

"It's not fair or right!" she screams into the pillow repeatedly. She cries herself to sleep, missing a few phone calls from Cory.

Curious about how silent it is in Tara's bedroom, Olivia sneaks up the steps to investigate. Creeping open the door, she notices her daughter is out cold. She listens as a buzzing sound vibrates on the other side of the bed. Olivia tiptoes over she picks up the cell phone and answers the call.

"Hello."

Cory sounds worried when someone finally picks up. "Tara, are you okay?"

Quickly taking the phone out of the room, Olivia gives Cory an update of what's happened. "Hey, Core, it's her mom. She's asleep right now. Robert, her ex, caused a ruckus earlier, and she must have passed out. I'll tell her you called, though."

Panic sets in, as Cory doesn't know what to do.

"Is she okay? Do I need to come over and help with anything?"

Olivia calmly eases his fear. "No, no, it's handled, and he's going to jail, but you don't know what it means to have you ready to come take charge of things. I'll get her number changed soon so it doesn't happen again. She'll be fine. Just be there for her, and treat her like a princess."

He takes her advice and assures her with "Yes, ma'am" as his only response.

"Now, go enjoy your Saturday, and see you soon. Bye, Core." Olivia closes the flip phone and takes it downstairs with her.

When Olivia puts the phone down on the end table, it begins to vibrate again. Wane picks it up, looking at the phone number flashing on the mini screen.

"It's a Little Rock number. Better not be who I think it is." He opens the phone to accept the call.

"You fucking little tramp! You dare get me arrested!" Bobby blurts out.

"She didn't call the law, boy. I did, ya little hoodlum. You ever talk to my daughter that way again, they ain't gonna ever find your body. Just remember, I drive a truck, so you coming up missing ain't gonna hurt nobody, and your ass would certainly make some fine gator bait."

Bobby sits there for a minute, stewing as he thinks of something to say.

"C'mon now, boy, you wanna threaten a little girl? Threaten me like that—I dare ya to! You may have bamboozled her for a while, but you ain't part of her life now, so get lost and stay lost. You even think about showing up here, and you're dead—understand that."

The line is filled with heavy breathing as Bobby doesn't say a word.

"I'll take that as a yes. As much as I love the South and loved Arkansas, what's best for Tara is to be here and away from the likes a' you. Now, goodbye forever, Bobby, and don't ever bother us again. Oh, and God bless whoever for putting you behind bars yet again." Dewey closes the phone and places it in his wife's hands.

"Tomorrow—I don't care what it costs—get her number changed, and make her a new AOL handle too."

"Yes, dear. I can handle that, and thank God we got her out of there before he knocked her up."

Wane agrees with a head shake. "I need a drink. We got any whiskey?" he asks, heading toward the kitchen, frustrated and pissed off.

"Pour me a double!" Olivia requests, flopping down in her recliner.

A few hours pass by before Tara finally comes back to the world. The sun has set, and her parents have drunk enough that they have passed out in their chairs. She makes her way downstairs and sees her phone sitting on the end table between them.

Shit, they have my phone. Guess I can use the cordless to call Cory and get out of here for a little while, she says in her mind, wanting to escape before something else goes wrong.

Taking her time to get the house phone, she sneaks back up the steps to her room. Before she dials his number, she plans ahead in case she convinces him to pick her up. She goes over to her dresser and selects a low-cut tank top with a built-in bra and a lacey white thong to hide under her yoga pants, with the idea of seducing him.

Tara slides into the more comfortable selection, then she dials the number to Cory's and waits for someone to pick up.

"Hello," she hears Cory answer.

"Hey, sweet stuff, it's me. Hey, listen, when your parents pass out, think you could sneak out and come over for a bit, or maybe we could go out and drive or something. I need to see you—like now!"

"Yeah, my parents pass out pretty early, and I could run over to your place if you want. My car would wake my folks up. You're not that far from me, so it'll be a hop, skip, and jump away, babe. How are you feeling? I talked to your mom earlier, and she said you was pretty upset."

Here's Tara's ticket to beginning her seduction.

"That's why I need you here or me there. I need to see you, feel you, kiss you, rub you, anything to feel better," she whispers seductively.

"Sounds good, but if you just need to talk or vent or cry, you can too. I'm not with you just to try to sleep with you."

That sends chills through Tara's body. "You're sweet, but we'll see. Just come get me, or I'm coming to you. There's the basement we can go to so my parents don't hear us making out or anything."

Cory's body is feeling the urge to want to take Tara's offer and go with it, but his conscience is fighting back.

"We'll see when the time arrives, but for now, let me get off here, and I will see you soon. Bye, Tara."

"Bye, Cory. See you soon." Tara places the phone on her bed and stands there, debating what to do.

She turns to look in the mirror and sees how her clothes don't make her figure pop enough. She slips out of the yoga pants and pulls off the tank top. Once again, she stands in front of the mirror, feeling her body, trying to set herself for the mood.

"He won't be able to say no later. If anyone gets me, it'll be him," she tells herself. Her pain is the driving force behind her desire.

Searching for easy-to-rip-off clothes that fit snugly over her figure, Tara dances in front of the mirror as she works to keep herself in the mood. Expecting to take no off the table, Tara waits until ten o'clock and then locks her bedroom door and gets a jacket from her closet. She sneaks out her window and climbs down using the latticework on the side of the porch.

Ignoring the shivering of her body, she makes a run for Cory's house. She rounds the corner when she realizes he's running in her direction. At full speed, she slides into his arms, wrapping her arms around his neck.

"There you are! Let's get back to your place and make the most of it," Tara whispers, fighting the urge to plant her lips on his.

"Let's go, then. You must be freezing!" Cory whispers into her ear, breaking the hug.

They turn toward the direction of his house and hurry along the snow-covered sidewalk, guiding her around to the back of house. They try to tread lightly as the snow crunches beneath their feet.

"Here we go. Just push it up and climb inside," Cory whispers, helping her climb through the window. Slowly pulling his way back into his room, Tara closes the window and removes her jacket, exposing a spaghetti-strap tank top with no bra.

"Get on the bed and shut up!" she demands in a low growling tone, taking him by the shirt.

"Yes, baby girl."

Cory steps backward until his legs give way to his bed.

"Good boy. Now shut up and scoot up more. You're going to enjoy this!" she teases, crawling over him as they crawl to the crown of his bed.

Tara gets her grip on Cory's shirt, pulling it off and tossing it onto the floor. Sitting straight up, she lifts her shirt, exposing her bare breasts, which are barely visible in the dimly lit bedroom, compliments of the streetlamp just reaching into the bedroom.

She can feel Cory's breathing intensify. To keep up with her desire, she rolls off him, stripping down to just her lacey thong. She reaches over, taking charge once again, positioning Cory on top of her body.

"Kiss me," she whispers softly in his ear.

Cory takes her request, gently caressing his lips with hers.

Taking her hand, she grabs Cory's to give him the signal to begin to feel her up. The subtle hint, he obliges as his hands caress her silky-smooth skin.

Unsure of how she will react, Cory breaks their long French kiss, positioning himself down to her left ear and neck. Softly dapping her with kisses between the destination, he listens to her moan softly and passionately.

"Oh, God, don't stop," she moans under her breath, beginning to grind against Cory's body pressing down on hers.

The urges pump through Cory nearly to the point of no return. His conscience smacks him back to reality when he remembers Rick's advice. Pulling away from Tara's neck, he scoots back to meet her in the eyes. She notices the glow in his eyes as she goes from hot and passionate to concerned.

"What's wrong?" she asks softly, placing her hand gently against Cory's cheek.

"Nothing. It's nearly perfect, but we can't yet." Confused, she speaks up again.

"You don't want to, or am I not attractive, almost naked?"

Cory can't hold back, keeping his eyes locked deeply on hers.

"Oh no, trust me, I want to—you can feel that—but Angel, it's too soon right now. And you're hurting, which is probably why you want to—to dull the hurt. You feel so good, and, ugh … it's taking all I have not to take advantage—"

She cuts him off.

"You're not taking advantage if I allow you to take control and make my man feel good, you know."

Cory shuts his eyes for a moment, resisting the vibe pulsating through their bodies.

"Yes, but I want this to be 'our' thing when we do something special, not like this. Trust me, I want to be touching your body. Goddamn, you're so fine and beautiful."

Tara smiles back at him. "That's what makes you so special to me already, so sweet and kind. You're fine as hell too, baby boy. God, those muscles—I can't resist."

Not taking his words to heart, Tara moves her hand from his cheek to the back of his head, pulling him down to her again. Unable to resist, Cory gives in to their mutual desires. His signal to her is when he places his hands on her breasts.

"Take me," she orders him, sliding her hands down his back, barely scratching her nails into his bare skin.

Doing as he's ordered, Cory kisses his way down along Tara's body. He pauses at her breasts to lightly kiss and play with them, causing her body to slightly arch from his tender touch. She gasps when he continues kissing down her body. When Cory reaches the middle of her flat and toned stomach, he shifts over to lightly kiss along the edge of her ribs, making her arch even more. Her body being touched tenderly sends her urges into overdrive.

"Oh, Cory, please keep going," she whispers between moans, smiling at her body, grinding harder.

He moves down, hooking her thong. Cory slowly slips it down her legs.

Sliding down off the bed, Cory unlatches his belt along with unbuttoning his jeans. To be safe, he bends over to take a condom from his wallet. Adjusting his pillows, Tara braces when Cory crawls back on the bed.

He places his body where he can feel the bare skin of Tara's under his own. She assists him by taking her hand to guide him to her opening. Cory slowly and easily slides inside Tara, causing her to deeply gasp when he's full inserted into her body.

"Are you okay?" Cory asks when he hears her exhale with force.

"Oh yes, just go slow, please."

Cory nods as he begins to moderately thrust in and out of Tara. She begins to breathe faster and harder as her body reacts to Cory's touch.

Overwhelmed with both desire and lust, Cory doesn't take long to reach his climax. Tara reaches hers seconds after he does but before his body collapses on top of hers. Still breathing hard from it all, Cory places his elbows to where he's positioned to meet Tara's eyes.

"That was wonderful," he mutters quietly.

"So worth it, Cory, don't leave me," Tara pleads after her minds clears.

"Never, Tara. I'll always be here for you."

To calm her new inner fear, Cory rolls off Tara's body and pulls her into his chest, where they nestle up for a little while without saying a single word.

Feeling his heartbeat, Tara does her best to place her worry at bay. She realizes that she is her own worst enemy, as she gets into her mind better than anyone else.

He's better than that, she says to herself. Letting go of her fear, she relaxes her body, which sends a clear message to Cory that all is well between them. He wraps his arms around her a bit tighter, and they enjoy most of the night, wrapped in each other's arms.

After such a short time, he can't believe this has happened. For Cory, this is the best moment of his life, as he holds Tara in his arms, not only to keep her warm but to allow his heart to fill with more love than he ever expected.

CHAPTER 9

The Aftermath

After getting dressed and escorting Tara home, Cory stands there along the street, making sure she's safely in her bedroom before he heads home to get a little bit of rest.

He's still feeling unlike he ever has before in life. His mind is wrapped around a bit of regret over what occurred, but his body is on cloud nine. The entire walk home, he's torn between the two as they battle for control.

Observing as Cory walks away, Tara stands there in her window, nervous over the worry about the change she knows is coming.

God, I was so stupid! Can't change that now, but maybe it won't be that bad.

After he's out of her line of sight, she changes into something comfortable. Curled up on the bed, she slides under the covers, falling asleep with a smile on her face, reminiscing.

Sneaking back to his house, Cory decides to take off running when the snow begins to fall again. His main concern now is keeping his promise to Tara. When he reaches his window and crawls back through, he quickly shuts it, gets undressed down to his boxers, and climbs into bed.

"Oh, man, I can still smell her," he says in a low tone as her scent lingers on the pillow.

With his eyes to indulge in the memory, he passes out until the late morning hours.

"Cory, son, it's going on eleven. Time to get up," his mother calls, cracking open his door.

Stirring from his pillow, he barely picks up his head, grunting at his mom.

"Ugh, go away, Mom. It's Sunday!"

She cackles for a moment. "Come on. Rick's done called twice for you. That means to get up and get moving, or else." She shoots him an evil glare as he flops back over on his bed.

Less than two minutes later, she sneaks back into his room with a pitcher full of cool water. From the edge of his bed, she lets him have it. The effect is almost instant when the water lands all over Cory. After he sits straight up, his mother makes a dash for the door, laughing the entire way.

"Not funny, Mom!" he yells, tossing the blankets off.

Grabbing his clothes, he quickly gets cleaned up and changes his bed linens. By the time he's getting ready to head out to the kitchen, Rick calls for him again.

"Cory, phone!" his mom yells from the living room.

"Coming," he responds, coming down the hallway.

Taking the phone from his mother's hand, he's quickly greeted. "Hey, Rick, what's up?"

"Yo, meet me at the point. We gotta talk!"

Cory, trying to keep a straight face, simply says, "Yeah, sure. Be there in a bit."

Rick hangs up, and Cory goes over to place the phone back on charge when he's stopped by his mother.

"I have something to ask you, and I want the truth."

"Uh, yeah, Mom." Cory is wide-eyed, facing away from her.

"Did Tara have a good time here last night?"

Cory's eyes transform to the size of an owl's when he hears that question.

"Uh, it was fine. We just talked. She was upset about her friend from back home giving her a hard time."

He can hear his mother huff.

"Do you think I'm that stupid, son?"

Cory tries to keep from cringing as he turns around. "No, Mom. I swear, that's all that happened."

She dips her head, giving him that "mom" look.

"Son, I love you, and I hope you all are safe. I will take your word for it, and your father doesn't know."

Cory sees that as a chance to flip the subject. "Hey, where is Dad?"

His mother is now the one avoiding eye contact. "He, uh, went back to the ER. He's still not feeling well. That's how I knew Tara was here, your dad was sick again, and well … yeah … anyway, young man, just, please, be careful."

Cory's feeling embarrassed, but in the front of his mind is the concern for his dad.

"Yes, ma'am, but anyway, Rick needs to talk to me. Care if I go talk to him?"

His mother nods her nod and waves him off.

Rushing out the door, he's just getting his coat on when he tugs on the car door. He speeds down to the river's edge, trying to figure out what has Rick has up his sleeve. When he arrives, Rick doesn't waste time, motioning him over to the Man-Van.

Cory doesn't get the chance to shut the van door before Rick starts giving him the third degree.

"Is it true? Did you and Tara do it last night?"

Stunned, Cory's jaw drops, saying it all.

"Holy shit. You did! Ah-ha, that's my boy!" Rick reaches over, smacking him on the shoulder.

"Yeah, we did, and it was great. My gosh, bro. When I touched her body and kissed all over it, uh, heavenly bliss was the feeling."

Cory is all smiles when Rick sees his best friend's world lighten up.

"See, I told you she'd be better than that bitch you was with before."

Cory can't help but agree. "Yeah, I just hope we didn't fuck up already. I really care about her."

Rick has some insight into that fact.

"Already got ya covered there. See she done talked to Kay, and your girl is nuts about you. She's worried you'll be disappointed if she says no or stops you one of these times and dump her over it."

Cory's reactions tell the tale. "Hell, no. I made her a promise, and I will keep it. She's been the best thing to happen to me."

Rick smirks, his arm still stretched over Cory's shoulder. "That a boy!"

Feeling better about it all, Cory thinks everything is settled.

"We good now, right?" he questions, about to reach for the handle.

"Nah, homes. I got some new info too, that I think you'll drop your jaw over."

"Oh?" Curious, Cory retracts his hand.

Rick sits there allowing the anticipation to swell. "So!" Cory barks out, making a strangling grip in the air with his hands.

Just as Rick opens his mouth, they hear another car pulling up as the tires come to a screeching halt.

"Who the hell …?" Cory mutters.

"It's, Frankie," Rick says, looking over his shoulder.

"Get out!" Frank screams, smacking the hood of his car.

Getting out, Rick leans up again his van while Cory runs around to see what's about to happen.

"Nice to see ya, there … George!" Rick says casually, sending Frank into a frantic frenzy.

"I am not George. Now go fix the rumor that I am! I'm not gay. If I were, then why would I have slept with his girl?" Frank argues, pointing over to Cory.

"Hey, leave Vanessa out of this. She's the past, ya unpredictable bastard."

Wanting to rub salt in the wound, Rick takes it to the next level.

"Who said that I was talking about her? I meant ya new one. You know, Tara. She was a terrific piece of ass last night."

That sends Cory over the edge, even though he knows it's a lie.

"Fuck you, ass hat! I know for a fact that she was with me last night!" Cory let's slip out, causing Frankie's face to take on a sarcastic sneer.

"Oh, now that'll spread around school—how easy that little slut is. She open for house calls? Say around noon?"

Frankie's forgotten that Rick is there with them. He charges over to Frankie, picking him up by the collar of his team jacket.

"Yo, take that shit back, and you ain't gonna say a damn thing, Georgie boy. I know for a fact you was with Lloyd last night too. I had to go make sure the heat was on at my father's church, and who did I see coming out of your house? None other than Lloyd, and I see ya two kissing when you walked him to your car to take him home."

Frankie's facial expression doesn't change, but his cheeks begins to glow a shade of maroon.

Cory picks up on the signals as his mouth drops low.

"Oh, damn, it's true! Then that's why you elected to stay off the team. More time to hide with Lloyd behind closed doors."

Frankie's eyes close, as he is riddled with guilt.

"Please, don't tell anyone and I'll keep my mouth shut. You have my word."

Rick puts him back on the ground. "Parents' pride, ain't it? I know Lloyd tells me all the time that *George* cares about him a lot."

Rick shakes his head, acknowledging it all.

The boys begin to feel horrible for Frankie, until he pops off again. "I'll still take a piece of Tara, though. She's hot, for sure!"

Not thinking twice, Rick reacts by knocking Frankie on his ass.

"Don't disrespect my boy or his woman. Now we can be cool and keep ya secret, or we can be dicks and have a talk with your folks for you."

"Understood. I'll back off." Pulling himself to his feet, Frankie throws his hands up in defeat.

The voice of reason comes from Cory. "Just get out of here. Rick, c'mon let's go."

Rick steps back and allows Frankie to get away.

They get into their own vehicles and take off for in separate destinations.

Rick heads over to his father's church to listen to the midday sermon, while Cory departs for Lloyd's classic late-70s model trailer. Pulling up, he sees the curtains move slightly.

"Good, he's home." Cory kills his engine and gets out, walking up to the door.

"Hey, Lloyd I know you're in there. Open up. It's me! I know you're in there."

The door latch flipping is heard, and Lloyd barely cracks the door. "Is he pissed?"

Cory shoves on the door and makes his way inside.

"Not really, but it's good to know it's true."

Lloyd's frown kills Cory, knowing it could ruin his hidden love life.

"It'll be okay. Hey, we're all seniors next year, and then we can all leave this dump. You can be happy and not have to hide."

Lloyd tries to smile but fights back the pain instead.

"He loves me, but his parents would kill him. I'm tired of always being the closet case in this town!" Lloyd cries out in frustration.

"Hey, you know you can always talk to me about it. I love ya, buddy, and you'll always be my boy. You're still one of my best friends, Lloyd."

Lloyd reveals his hidden secret. "I can't take it anymore, Core. I'm so depressed now from being curious guys' bitch to try shit with. I'm done."

Worry begins to settle into the pit of Cory's stomach.

"I'm not leaving you like this. C'mon, you're coming home with me." He takes Lloyd by the wrist, tugging at him to leave.

"No! I told you, I'm done. It's over. I can't do this anymore."

Cory's grip tightens ever so slightly. "I said let's go. If I have to call your mother, I will. I can't imagine how you feel, but it's only going to get better, I promise."

Lloyd's eyes dim, giving Cory the indication of how deep his depression runs.

"If you say so, but I guess I'll let you take me to my mother. I just want it to stop, Core." Lloyd breaks down, gripping Cory tightly, lowering his head on his shoulder as the tears fall.

Taken by surprise, Cory gradually puts his arms around Lloyd. "Hey, it's all good! Come on, let's get you somewhere so you can feel better."

Pulling away from his friend, Cory waits as Lloyd slips into his boots, and out the door they go.

"I guess you're taking me to my mother?"

Cory takes him by surprise. "Oh no, much, much worse, Lloyd. You're going to visit Tara with me, and I'll let her rip you apart.

Lloyd gulps hard, knowing Tara will rip him a new ass for acting so foolishly. "Please don't tell her about this. She'd kill me, for sure."

Cory teases as if he's going to tell her. "Well, then, Lloyd, it's been nice knowing you."

Lloyd's mouth barely dips open. "You asshole!"

That's all it takes to break his current mindset.

"There he is. Good to have ya back, buddy boy. C'mon, let's get going, and I won't say anything."

Lloyd fights to put on a straight face. The boys head out the door. Getting into the car, they head over to Tara's to see her folks' vehicles are gone.

"Guess she's not home. Oh well, maybe next time."

Cory lowers his head. "Let's see if she's home."

Lloyd fights against it. "If she is, then hey, a little ooh-la-la time with her boy toy!"

Cory waves it off. "Nice try, but there's more to her than just sex appeal.

"Aw, aren't you just the sweetest little thing!" Lloyd teases, batting his long eyelashes at Cory, clutching his hands together and twisting them.

"Hey, she's special to me."

Lloyd divulges a little more than he should. "I know, we talk all the time about you. She loves the way you touch her and how her past doesn't bug you. She's falling for you fast, my friend."

Cory smiles, feeling more confident. "Thank you. C'mon, let's go."

Popping open the doors, the boys stroll up to the door, hitting the doorbell a couple of times.

"Coming!" she yells from the other end of the house.

They listen as her footsteps get louder with each thud hitting the floor. Tara swings the door wide open, where she sees Lloyd standing in front of Cory.

"Lloyd, the most beautiful male to try on my gloss. How ya doin', bud? Wait, how did ya get here?"

Cory steps out from behind him. "Hey, beautiful, miss me?" he jokes, reaching out and taking her hand.

"Well, yeah, I think so, but … this handsome hunka man needs a makeover. Now get inside. It's freezin' out here." She takes Lloyd by the hand and escorts both boys inside.

Releasing Lloyd from her grip, she points over to the couch. "Take a seat. I'm going to make this fella here a prodigy."

She turns around, mouthing, "I know," to Cory as she disappears upstairs with Lloyd.

"Make 'em over good!" Cory yells, flopping down on the couch.

A few minutes go by, and Cory is still waiting around on the couch. He begins to slip into his own thoughts about the next game on the road. His attention snaps back to being on the couch when he hears Lloyd scream.

"Oh my gosh. I am so pretty!"

A few moments after hearing him scream, they come back down the steps. When he looks over to see Lloyd standing there, he's viewing him with makeup all over his face, highlighting his features of high cheekbones and eyeliner, making his eyes look bigger and brighter, causing the brown to stand out that much more.

"Wow, man. I gotta say, I like it," Cory says.

"Thanks, Core. You are too kind, but I know better. And, Tara, oh, sweet Tara, my angel of joy. You made me feel alive again by doing this. Now, if you'll excuse me, I'm heading to find my man. I don't care if he likes it or not. I'm tired of hiding my feelings for him!"

Taking charge, Lloyd bolts out of the house. He's out of sight before either Cory or Tara can make it outside.

"Guess you restored his confidence."

Tara shrugs her shoulders. "Looks that way, but now about me and you? Listen, last night was perfect, and you felt so damn good, but—"

Cory cuts her off.

"We don't need to overdo it, I get it. I-I uh, yeah, I agree, I can't ruin this between us."

Not willing to take the chance of her parents getting the wrong impression of them being at the house alone, Cory gives Tara a kiss, then breaks her grip and takes off to head home. When he arrives, he goes inside to get cleaned up and enjoy the rest of the day alone.

Even though from his appearance, it appears that everything is calm, Lloyd is raging with an intense inferno cascading from his broken heart. He makes his way down to the diner, where he sees Frank's Subaru sitting in the parking lot.

"Time to do this," he hums to himself, working up the nerve to confront Frank in public.

Marching through the door, he ignores his mother waving to him and goes straight up to Frank, sitting with his friends.

"Oh look, the drag queen is here," Joe blurts out, causing everyone to laugh.

"Hey, Blow Joe, go fuck yourself, okay, ya little scrawny ass clown."

The group of boys quit laughing as the mood shifts.

"Better watch it, homo, or else," Kevin threatens, cracking his knuckles.

"I'm not here for any of you, except for you." Lloyd points over to Frankie with his finger, beginning to shake.

Trying to act surprised, Frankie puts his hands in the air. "What did I do?"

That's when Lloyd makes his move, leaping into Frankie's lap. Everyone watching is shocked beyond belief when Lloyd presses his lips against Frankie's.

"What the fuck!" Frankie yelps, shoving Lloyd off after the initial shock wears off. "This is my man; this is George Carson. He's been visiting me late on weekend nights for quite some time, and I love you Frankie. Now, please come out and tell them that you love me, like you tell me all the time."

Frankie's eyes say it all when he dumps Lloyd onto the floor.

"You're crazy. I've never done anything with you other than make fun of your chubby ass. Me be with you? Yeah, that's funny. Now get lost or else," Frankie warns him, taking his foot and shoving him on the side of the head.

Pissed off, Lloyd springs back to his feet, slapping Frankie across the face and backhanding him, landing a shot on both cheeks.

"Fine, fuck you, then, ya piece of shit. I came to pour my heart out to you, and this is how you want to treat me. Fine!"

Lloyd turns around and stomps off with his mother following behind him.

"Lloyd, stop!" she yells, catching up to him. "I'm sorry, son, but you deserve better than that. I know it's difficult being different here, but let it go."

Lloyd's temper finally surfaces in an ugly fashion. "You know ... you know ... you don't know anything, Mom. I'm your gay son, the only openly gay kid in this entire town. It's not fair that I should put up with all this stuff. I'm tired of being alone and being picked on. Why can't anyone love me?"

Lloyd breaks down again, causing his mother to embrace her son to help soothe the pain.

"Then we'll leave if we have to, and I'll drive from Minneapolis or St. Paul. I'm done seeing you hurt like this, and I know your friends are tired of it too."

This sends Lloyd into breakdown mode. "No, we can't afford to move that far. It's only one more school year. We'll stay, but I have to go to college, Mom. I have to get away from RiverCreek."

"I agree, son, I agree. Now, I'll let Debbie take over and manage, and we'll go home and watch movies and binge on ice cream."

To put on a brave face, Lloyd nods when he lets his mother go. "Okay, Mom, that sounds good."

She hustles back inside for a moment, returning with her jacket on and her keys in her grip.

Later in the day, after the sun retires from the sky, Lloyd and his mother are resting on opposite ends of the couch when there's a knock on the rear door down the hall. Confused by who it could be, Lloyd's mother gets up to see who's knocking. To her surprise, she's greeted by Frankie, standing there, shivering.

"Hi, Ms. Trippet. Can I please speak to Lloyd?"

Her mother mode kicks in as her eyes sharpen with fury. "Why? To hurt his feelings again and break his heart?"

Lloyd comes to the door. "Oh, what do you want?" Lloyd asks, looking away.

"To apologize, you know what my parents would do if they discover that I'm bi. It's not easy, you know, hiding how I feel about you. Hell, I even gave up hockey to get spare time to spend with you."

Lloyd is unimpressed with his secret half's plea for forgiveness. "That is your choice, not mine."

Frankie stands there, confused as to what to do next.

"Well, please find it in your huge heart to forgive me. I do love you Lloyd—"

He's cut off by Ms. Trippet. "Not enough to come clean about being my son's lover. Now get lost, you little heartbreaking jerk. My son deserves better."

She slams the door in his face.

"You will find love, Lloyd. You were made special when you came into this world, and he's the trash in society not you. Now keep that chin up, my bouncing baby boy, because you will go out and see the world," his mother rants before they return to the living room to resume watching movies on the couch, enjoying each other's company the rest of the night.

CHAPTER 10

Bad News Night

About eight weeks have gone by since that crazy weekend. Things haven't calmed down between Lloyd and Frankie, as they battle it out in the shadow of night.

Rick and Kayla continue to dwell on the idea of getting more time alone since their relationship has heated up physically. Cory and Tara haven't had anything happen between them since that snowy romantic night.

Much to the surprise of their friends, when passion between Rick and Kayla isn't at new heights, they're battling over the littlest things. One Friday night, it spills over when everyone is hanging out down at the point.

"Hey, I wasn't done talking to you!" Kayla yells when Rick goes to walk away.

"Yeah, well go talk to someone who you like to flirt with and flaunt ya tits at!" Rick brawls, keeping his back to Kayla.

"Go fuck yourself! Fucking asshole!"

Rick doesn't let up arguing back. "Yeah, I bet you would like a good lay, wouldn't you. I see how you look at Nick at work. Want 'em? You can go have him."

Kayla takes off running after him, smacking him in the back of his head.

"I hate you, Rick!"

Hearing enough of her jaw jacking, Rick climbs into his van

and takes off. Out on the street, Kayla nearly gets hit by two others racing along the straight stretch.

"Yeah, you better run, bitch!" She stands there as the guilt and regret of arguing once again take control. "Come back … please …" she whispers, wiping away her tears.

Tara strolls up beside her and places her arm around Kayla's shoulders.

"He'll calm down and come back. He always does. Come on. I'll give you a ride home."

Kayla sniffles and walks over to Tara's Christmas present from her parents: a brand-new violet and gray Kia Sportage.

"He hates me, girl. I can't control myself, and he's so jealous it drives me crazy."

Cranking over the engine, Tara sits there for a moment, trying to think of anything to say. "I wish I could tell you what to do or say. It's not easy having to deal with this—believe me, I know. Just give him some time and space to cool down. Best I can tell you to do."

"I wanna spend the night over at your place. Last thing I need is Rick coming over, sneaking into my room, and wanting to make up for this. It hurts too much to keep going like this. I think we do need time apart."

Tara huffs, relating to the issue her best friend is feeling.

"Yeah. Need to stop and get you a change of clothes first?"

Kayla replies with a simple, "Yes" keeping her eyes locked on the edge of the road, staring out the passenger-side window.

"All right, let's do this, then. Girls night!" Tara announces, trying to swing the mood in her car.

They stop by Kayla's place. The girls quickly gather a few things she'll need for their night together.

"Don't forget your favorite movie, and when we get to my house, we'll order an extra-large cheese pizza and eat away our feelings."

Kayla does as best friend suggests and hurry back to Tara's. Relaxed on the couch, the girls use their time to chitchat, waiting on their food to arrive before they dive into Kayla's beloved chick-flick feature film.

"Well, I know you haven't discussed it much but tell me. Do you love him yet?"

Tara's face begins to glow a soft shade of rose.

"I don't know … my little secret."

The girls squeal at the top of their lungs.

"I can say this, since moving here, it's been so much better. I'm at the votec with Rick and Cory, and I have my own car now. Oh, girl, life here has been good so far. Now I have you as my bestie, and winter is almost half gone too. Now you know what that means."

They stare at each, counting to three using their fingers. "Bikini season!" They scream together right before the doorbell rings.

Rushing over to the door, Tara pauses for an instant to get the money from her purse. Once she opens the door, she hands the delivery guy a twenty-dollar bill. "Thank you, keep the change!"

She grips the box with both hands and playfully tosses it onto the glass coffee table.

"Dig in, girl, 'cause it is all ours!" Tara says.

Not wasting time, Kayla begins to munch on the pizza as Tara picks up the remote to hit play on the VCR.

"Tissue time," she says when the opening credits begin to appear on the screen.

Jumping and flopped back onto the couch, Tara digs into the pizza, forgetting about the world as they dive into a fantasy land of their own.

Not far from the girls' slumber party is Cory, driving around, trying to find Rick. He started at the bowling alley, then the movie theater, followed by cruising by his home. When he doesn't see his van anywhere, Cory's gut begins to turn to knots.

"Where the hell are you?" As luck would have it, Cory finally gets a glimpse at the tail end of the Man-Van.

"There you are!"

Sliding to a complete stop, Cory does his best to park as close as he can to the doors of Rick's fathers church. Once he's in the chapel, Cory sees Rick sitting in the final row of pews.

"Everything thing all right?"

Rick sits there with his hands in his lap. "Yeah, just trying to figure out why I screw up so much. It's not just Kayla, but man, remember when I said I was offered a scholarship to a Michigan College." Cory takes a seat beside Rick.

"Yeah I remember. We're all going that way together."

Tears forming in his puppy dog eyes, Rick divulges a secret he has hoped to avoid. "I lied about it. I applied to a few Michigan schools, but that's it. Other than Grambling, I don't have anyone else looking at me."

Cory sits there in silence.

"Sorry, Core."

Rolling anything that comes off his tongue, Cory tries to make the best of a bad night.

"Don't sweat it. We'll figure something out. If nothing else, get a camcorder and send schools your stuff."

A bright light goes off in Rick's mind. "Great idea. That would make it easier than only relying on Coach."

Cory nudges a bit. "Sometimes, I hit it right."

The boys share a laugh, trying to crack through the ice forming on the surface of the real issue.

"So what do I do about Kayla? How do I fix this?"

Taking a deep breath, Cory doesn't say a single word as the mood slips back to the way it was before.

"Thanks for listening, Core. You can split. I'm just gonna sit here for a minute."

Cory taps his thumb on the back edge of the pew as he sits there.

"Nah, you're my brother. I ain't gonna leave you here like this. You hurt, I hurt—simple as that."

Rick smirks and brings his hands together leaning into the pew. They sit there in silence for a while before heading out on separate paths, heading for home.

Once Cory arrives home, the surprises don't seem to end. After he gets inside and places his coat on the rack, his parents call from the kitchen.

"Cory, could you come in here, please," his father commands with something sounding off in his voice.

"Yeah, Dad, on my way."

His heart begins to pound harder when he notices his parents sitting at the table with their eyes locked on him.

"Take a seat, son. We have something to tell you," Mr. Dubois tells him, his hands shaking.

"Yeah, sure. Is everything okay?"

Trying to avoid eye contact, Mr. Dubois begins to deliver the bad news. "Well your mother and I have been trying to find a way to break this to you easily for a while now."

A look of fear creeps into Cory's eyes.

"You know I've been feeling sick for a while now, and well it's been hard to predict how I feel from day to day. Well, it's time you know that things are going to change around here."

"Is it cancer, Dad?" Cory gives a hard gulp in his throat, preparing for the worst.

"Not that bad, but it could be if I don't manage it better. I have diabetes, son, and my doctor has had a hard time helping me get it back under control."

A bit of the weight lifts from Cory's shoulders.

"I have to change my diet and pull back on the heavy duties at work and around here for a while, which means I'll need you to help pick up some of the slack. My blood pressure has also been elevated. That means I must be careful. If not, it could be bad news for me. We're monitoring my liver enzymes, hoping for the best in time." Mr. Dubois stops when he feels the signal from Mrs. Dubois—a light squeeze on his shoulder.

She steps in to speak, her voice is cracking from the stress of it all.

"That doesn't mean to quit hockey or anything else. You'll just need to do a few more things around here in place of your daddy doing it. Time to become more of a man—that's all," she says smilingly, trying to make the best of the news to their son.

"I got it, Mom, and Dad, I'll be my best. I promise."

Sensing he wants to get away from the table, Mr. Dubois excuses Cory. "You can go now, son. Sorry to scare you thinking it was something worse, but I'll manage. Telling your child that you're going to be stricken with something for life isn't easy. Night, son. Love ya."

Cory scoots his chair away, placing it back properly, and waves, making his way to his room.

Quickly walking to his room, Cory shuts and locks his door. His breathing becomes erratic as he worries about his father's well-being. "I can't do this. I gotta get out of here," he says, going over to his window and unlatching it. He's stopped when a knock comes softly from the other side of his door.

"Cory, may I come in, son?"

He stops to yank the curtains back together. He goes over to unlock the door.

"What, Mom?" he asks, standing in the doorway.

"Let me come inside, please."

Stepping aside, Cory closes the door.

"Your dad is scared; his hands and feet have been tingling almost nonstop or just flat-out going numb. His vision's even been affected to the point he's had to order glasses. So please don't think that was easy for him."

"I didn't think that at all, Mom. Don't worry. I'm going to help out more."

Taking a seat on his bed, his mother cups her hands over her face, breaking down again.

"Mom, it'll be okay—you'll see."

It's breaking Cory apart inside seeing his mother cry for the first time since his grandma passed away a few years ago.

Quietly walking over to his mom, Cory takes a seat beside her, putting his arm around her shoulders, trying to help her calm down.

"I've known your father since we were kids. I can't imagine losing him anytime soon."

Cory again tries to use reason. "He's the toughest guy I know."

He reaches for his box of tissues from his nightstand. Cory gives them to his mother.

"You're such a good kid. How did we get so lucky?"

Cory shrugs, trying to make her laugh with a goofy face.

Afterward she makes a deal with him. "Tell ya what. I'll keep your dad occupied so you can stay out late. Just don't go do something stupid or get me called to pick you up."

Cory nods, agreeing to her terms.

"Have fun, and keep your window unlocked so you can get in that way."

Cory and his mother get up, heading for the bedroom door. He hugs his mom one more time, then closes the door behind her. Cory stands near the door, waiting to hear his parents head into their room. Once they're in there, he gives it a few minutes to make sure the coast is clear. Sneaking out of his room, he can hear their radio on.

"Good thinking, Mom."

He makes a break for the heavy front door. Swinging it open, he looks back to make sure the suction from between the door and screen door doesn't get him busted.

After getting his coat on, he takes off for his car. He throws the shifter into neutral and pushes it back onto the street. Cory gets in and starts it up, pulling away as easily as he can without the turbo spooling up and giving him away.

Flipping his lights on, Cory cuts loose, entering the main drag of RiverCreek. When he comes to a stop at the light, he sits there revving his engine up, listening to turbo blow off in the freezing cold night air. His attention gets diverted to a set of headlights approaches the light beside him.

He rolls down the window and looks over to see Joe, sitting there, staring him down from his Eclipse.

"Wanna go?" Cory calls out, giving his car more gas.

"Better be ready to lose in that hunk of junk!" Joe cries.

"One lap. Once the light goes green again, down four blocks, make that left. Go until we reach the church. Then take that left to circle around it and use Delta Street to Bellevue Drive, then back to here."

Nodding to the route, Cory rolls up the window, prepared to go.

Waiting for the cycle to go back around, they feather their gas pedals. Cory gets into a dark frame of mind, ready to put Joe in his place. His left hand grips the steering wheel tightly while his other hand stays relaxed on the shifter. His breathing slows down to control his heartbeat.

The light flips, sending the cars squealing through first and second gears. Cory gives Joe a little bit of room, knowing that first turn is going to be icy. Joe's becoming overconfident, but as he makes that initial turn, he nearly loses control, sending his car into a light pole. Cory cracks up, taking the lead. Both cars, pushing their limits, can be heard echoing along the road.

Hitting the turn after the church, Cory's lead gets wider as Joe's fear of skidding again enter his mind being so close to the river, which causes the roads to freeze.

"C'mon!" Cory screams, looking in the rearview mirror. His determination carries him through the last stretch of the race.

Crossing back under the starting line, Cory downshifts, coming to a stop. He pulls over and doesn't see Joe anywhere.

"Hope he's okay …"

As he says that, he can hear Joe's Eclipse heading off in the opposite direction in defeat. "Ha ha, I knew my car was better!" he yells, throwing his arms up in victory.

Settled back into his car, Cory returns to cruising around and comes to a stop down at the point. No one else is there, so he stops there and leaves his car idling as he sits there and stares for a while at the calm river.

"Man, it's nights like this that make me glad I'm getting out of here."

Reclining in his seat back, Cory places his hands behind his head. Leaning a little over to the left, he begins to stare up at the clear night's starry sky, where he gets lost in his thoughts, forgetting about the time getting late.

The craziness has subsided but unaware of everything else, Tara and Kayla have retreated to Tara's bedroom for the night. They sit there painting each other's nails.

"I know it's supposed to be our night, but … what do you think the boys are doing?" Kayla wonders out loud, avoiding Tara's eyes.

"Probably out somewhere together being stupid. You know how those two are together. Missing Rick already, I take it?"

Kayla huffs after finishing up Tara's pinky toenail. "Kinda. He's an ass, but he's still my ass. He still loves me, and to be honest, I do like to make him jealous, but he takes it too far."

Tara scoots closer, keeping her wet nails straight on her bed. "Then stop taking it too far. Take control of him, take him by the shirt, pull him to you, kiss him, use a little tongue, and make him want you, girl."

Kayla is caught off guard; her face lights up with surprise. "Wow, that's hot!"

Tara gives her a little insight. "That's how I pretty much seduced Cory that night. I looked him in his eyes, deep and full of love, whispered sweet things to him, and placed my hand on the back of his head, pulling him to me; the rest was history."

Kayla's eyes light up with intrigue as she listens to her story. "Oh, wow, so you took control."

Tara dips her head with a twisted little grin. "Damn right, I did. Cory was going to stop and punk out on me, but I made sure he couldn't. He's ripped and hot as hell under those baggy clothes. Gives me cold chills thinking about it."

Tara shivers, sitting there, closing her eyes.

"Oh, girl, we gonna talk about this more. I want some tips and pointers. I wanna make tonight up to Rick, so c'mon what else you got to tell me."

The two girls giggle, staring at each other.

"Well, don't be afraid to be the one in control. Don't just give it up. Make Rick ache in pain. If you want, we can go shopping one day, and I will help you out."

"We'd have to go out of RiverCreek to do it. Everyone knows everyone here pretty much. Something you haven't picked up on yet. Say, maybe next weekend, go to Minneapolis for a girl's day out?"

Signaling yes with her head, Tara already has an idea of what she wants to do with Kayla to make her more appealing to Rick.

"Just keep him at bay after you two make up, and let me

handle that makeover. To even make it better, I'll have you come here next weekend and have him sneak in here while I sneak out to be with Cory."

Kayla likes that idea, and her eyes give away her excitement.

"Hell, yeah!" she squeals, then covers her mouth right after.

Tara laughs and does something unexpected. "You have some beautiful features, so let's get my makeup kit out and try a few new looks."

Tara places her hand softly along Kayla's cheek, brushing her hair out of her face.

Closing her eyes, Kayla likes the way Tara made her feel.

"I liked that," she admits, beginning to feel her cheeks get warm with embarrassment.

"That's the point. Teach these things to Rick yourself. Figure out what you like and go from there. Like I said, I can take control of things and make Cory do what I want. Make Rick do the same. Make him wait until he nibbles and kisses along your ears and neck."

Tara closes her eyes, visualizing it. "That's what I enjoy the most."

Kayla copies her movements, trying to envision the sensation in her mind. "I can't say I get it, not having experienced it," she whispers softly, pulling away from Tara.

"Make him. Tell him what you want. Like this …"

Kayla's suddenly thrusts on top of Tara, staring her in the eyes.

"Feel the want to go for more?" Tara questions, seeing her best friend's eyes change.

"Oh yeah, I can feel what you mean." She moans softly. "This is so hot." She begins to lean in, feeling a kiss.

"I don't think so," Tara tells her, flipping her over, taking the top position.

"This is for teaching purposes only." She leans forward, placing her finger over Kayla's lips.

"Shhh, and relax." Tara brushes the hair away from Kayla's shoulder, lightly teasing her.

Gasping from the sensations gushing throughout her body, Kayla tries not to squirm from the overwhelming new feeling.

"Oh God, no wonder you couldn't take no from Cory. Fuck … oh, stop, please, I can't take it, Tara."

Kayla shudders, trying to embrace the way her body aches for more.

"Now, shall we continue, or would you rather sneak out with me and go find Rick while I go get Cory?"

Sitting up and away from Kayla's torso, she watches as the urge takes its toll over Kayla. "We go find the boys! I got to try this on him. Oh, my God, you're good at that."

Tara smiles, getting off the bed, taking Kayla's hand and helping her up.

"Good, 'cause that is exactly how you should feel.

Going over to her bedroom door, Tara quietly lifts it up to keep it from creaking as she checks to make sure it's clear to sneak out from her bedroom window. Once it's closed, she locks it and goes over to her window.

"Before we go, remember how I got down so you can get back in just in case you beat me back here."

Kayla nods, then follows her out the window. Their primal urges continue to soar as they want to find Cory and Rick for a night of passionate pleasure.

CHAPTER 11

Taking What They Want

They're about to start running down the sidewalk when they hear the familiar sound of Cory's car approaching down the block.

"What the hell?" he says, rolling up to them. "Are you two crazy, being out here without a coat on?"

He begins taking his off to give to Kayla, since she's in nothing but a spaghetti-strap shirt.

"No, just trying to hurry to find you and Rick," She says, beginning to shake in the cold air.

"Get in the car and get warm. No way you're going there tonight. He's too upset—and get back inside, you two."

Once they get into the car, Tara tries to use the opportunity to teach Kayla a few new moves.

"We're sorry, baby. Can I get a kiss to help warm me up, please?" She bats her eyes over to him, giving Kayla the chance to see her moves in action.

"Come here then." Cory reaches over, pulling her over to him as close as possible.

She latches on to Cory, to attempt to crack through his resistance. Tara tries to push her luck when she takes possession of his arm, pulling his hand from the small of her back, resting it on her breast. Cory stops when he hears Kayla moaning a little too loud from the backseat.

"Oh, shit. I forgot she was there," he says, out of breath.

"I don't mind. I've seen you two kiss before," Kayla mentions, wanting to see how Tara can push his buttons.

"No, it isn't right to make you sit there and watch us."

Tara tries to keep going with suggestions. "Well, she can sneak back into my room, and we can go back to yours."

Cory takes control of the situation.

"No way! She's your guest, and you will not ditch her like that. Now, get back in there before we get into it."

She still tries to get her way. "But, baby, I need you. Don't you need me?"

Despite the impulse, Cory stands his ground. "You have no idea, but you got company. Goodnight, ladies. I'll see you later or at school. Don't make me regret this, Tara, please."

Not wanting to accept being turned down, Tara digs deep to manipulate his desires.

"But-but-but, Cory, I love you, and I want us to make love."

Shocked at hearing those words, Cory battles through the heat growing in his loins.

"We can't tonight, but damn it, you're good. I love you too, but not now."

Kayla even tries to push his buttons. "I can sit here and stay warm. I don't wanna come between you two."

That breaks through Cory's patience.

"I said no! Goodnight, ladies. Now get out of my damn car!" He lashes out, trying to contain his composure, not the heat of the moment

Disappointed that he could hold out, Tara tries to hold back her quivering lips.

"Don't do that, please. I'm sorry, I am, but it's not right to make her sit in the car."

Tara uses her sweet and innocent look to get her way. "She said she didn't mind, and she doesn't have to wait in the car. She can go down to the guest bedroom." Cory signals no and backs away, leaning up against his door.

"Night."

The girls get out, and Cory makes sure they go back through the window before he pulls away.

"Oh, I'm not taking no for an answer!" Tara growls, looking over to Kayla.

"I'll stay here. Go get him!"

Tara gives him time to get around the block. She climbs back through the window to go have it out with Cory. Kayla stands there until she sees Tara is out of sight and goes over to the bed. She begins to feel herself up and down, imagining Rick to be the one touching her body.

"Oh … Rick, don't quit …" she moans silently, using her hands to guide her body to crush her sexual requests pulsing in her veins.

Jogging over to Cory's, Tara meets him at his bedroom window.

"Don't think I'm taking no for an answer!" she says, grabbing Cory by his shoulder, turning him to face her.

"Get back to your house now! You can't ditch Kayla. That isn't right!"

Slipping her arms inside his coat, she gives him a look of purpose.

"Fuck you. I said I wanted you, and I'm here, so deal with it!"

Cory takes hold of her shirt with a new style to his attitude.

"You want it then get inside. Hurry up and get inside!" He reaches over opening his window with one hand.

She knows she's got her wish. Tara slides through the opening. The moment Cory pulls himself into his room, he gets his grip on Tara's shirt, yanking it over her head. She turns around after Cory unsnaps her bra. She removes it from her shoulders. Before it lands at her feet, Cory's already up close to her body.

He kneels, removing her yoga pants. He stands up, peeling his shirt off, making her shudder at the sight of his muscles.

"Lay down!" he orders her, working his way to removing his shoes, jeans, and boxers.

"Yes, baby, I'll do whatever you say."

A new notion, one he's never felt before; Cory's breathing becomes deeper as the empowerment sweeps over him.

"Shut your eyes now!" he instructs in a low tone, lowering himself down into his knees.

Guessing he's going to lower himself to kiss her, Tara is taken by surprise when she feels Cory kiss her inner thighs. Her hands on his head, she runs her fingers through his hair, realizing he has her where he wants her. Cory takes complete control when he moves from the crease of her thigh to working his way to orally tease Tara.

When the response of his actions races to her mind, Tara clutches her hands over her mouth trying not to moan or scream as Cory works his way over her body, making it tremble as she reaches her first oral orgasm.

After her body is ready on the bed, Cory prepares himself for more, taking out protection from his nightstand. When he's ready, he lowers himself down onto Tara's body, shoving into her body faster than he did last time. He doesn't waste time working himself into a steady pace. Able to control his breathing this time, he works his hips as they crash against Tara's body.

Wrapping her legs around his waist, Tara keeps her mouth covered with her hands to muffle her grunts. With each thrust, she begins to feel Cory swell up inside her, preparing to reach his climax. She removes her hands and reaches up, clutching the back of his neck.

"Don't stop. Please, don't stop. Faster, c'mon, faster!" she begs, breathing deeper as Cory begins to grunt, satisfying her request.

"Yes, oh, Cory, I love you," she says seconds before her body shakes with pleasure, causing her legs and hands to fall off Cory's body.

Soon he feels that her body surrenders to his. Cory pushes into her one more time before he comes to a stop, when his body sends everything he's experiencing through his explosion inside Tara's body.

"Was that good enough?" he asks, rolling off her body.

"That was what I needed," she says, lying there, trying to catch her breath.

"Me too. I've been wanting to do that again."

Tara twists her head to face his. "Anytime you want it, just say so. I'm all yours, I meant it. I love you, Cory."

She begins to rub his cheek.

Cory smiles then sits up. "Good to know. I love you too, and I mean it too."

Gradually working her way up to grab her clothes, Tara reaches over, kissing him passionately. Finally, able to get a moment away from her lips, Cory warns her, "Unless you want more, I'd suggest you stop now—or else."

Tara returns to kiss him, throwing her hips over his waist, sliding down to pick up where he left off.

"I'll take that as a yes," Cory huffs when Tara pushes herself into position, rotating her hips as she works her way to riding Cory.

Her hands firmly placed on his muscular chest, she takes control shoving down with force working her way to another orgasm.

Grinding her body hard for another ten minutes, she accidentally groans a little loudly when she explodes all over again. Her body tightens with intensity around Cory's shaft, which sends him into uncharted territory as he begins to tremor within Tara again.

"Wow, already, oh, fuck ..."

Her mouth shudders as one final small orgasm crashes over her body, feeling Cory expand and contract inside her.

Collapsed on top of Cory, their bodies collide with force. They nearly pass out together, embraced on the bed. The night is nearly halfway over when they let go of each other.

"Guess I should get back to Kayla."

Cory lifts himself up gives Tara a hand to her feet.

"Want me to walk you home?" he asks, bending over, slipping back into his jeans.

"Uh, of course, ya big lug." Tara stretches out to kiss him again.

Shortly after breaking the kiss, Cory reminds her they need to get moving.

"We can't keep kissing, or else it'll only result in more of the same."

She lifts her eyes seductively. Tara plays with him. "Not a bad thing."

Cory puts the brakes on immediately. "Yes, it is. I'm out of condoms. Rick's been taking them from me for him and Kayla."

Tara snaps her fingers.

"Well, that jerk, but who needs them. Pull out, baby."

That kills the mood right then and there.

"I'm easy, not dumb, sweetie. I couldn't if I wanted to, and I think you know that by now."

Tara motions her shoulders upwards.

"Oh, well, your loss," she teases, stepping back into the glowing light from the window.

"Get dressed and let's go," Cory says sternly, tossing her clothes to her.

"Fine." She exhales, frustrated at being turned down.

"Let's go," he says while opening the window and taking her hand to help her out.

Once they get around the corner from her house, Cory and Tara spot Rick's van parked along the edge of the curb.

"Well, guess they can always find each other," Tara let's slip out with a tiny giggle.

"Yeah, but oddly, there's no movement from the van, and his windows are too dark to see in there at night," Cory reminds her from the time they made out by the point.

Not risking the chance to interrupt them in the van, Cory gives Tara a boost back up to the roof. They both crouch down, making their way to the window. Cory stops momentarily when he reaches for the edging.

"Holy shit, I think we have bad timing," he states with a look of concern on his face.

Tara leans in to see what he's talking about. What she witnesses as her jaw drops wide open: there, on her bed, they get a view of Kayla lying on her stomach with her face buried in a pillow, allowing Rick to forcefully bury himself into her. He has his hands gripping her hips for balance since his pace is rough and rapid.

"They're fucking on my bed!" Tara cries out, clasping her mouth after she realizes she hasn't been quiet about it.

Cory pushes her away from the window so they don't get caught seeing their friends have sex.

"I think we'll chill right here for a moment," he suggests, slipping out of his coat, handing it to her.

"Damn it. See, we could've kept going, Cory!" she scolds him, smacking his arm in a frisky manner.

"My bad, my love."

While they sit and wait, inside the room, Rick is giving it his best effort.

"Yeah, Kay, oh fuck, yeah, baby," he groans, tightening his grip.

"You're going to kill me, Rick!" Kayla yells with her face firmly planted in the pillow.

"Good, you're mine to break," he reminds her while he picks up the pace.

Beginning to keep him tightening and twitching within her, Kayla pushes back, squeezing with all her might to help Rick to get off so she can end her misery in the position he has her pinned to.

"No, don't squeeze!" Rick grunts, feeling her tighten up, causing him to spasm.

"You bitch!" he cries out, digging his hands into her skin.

"Oh, fuck you, it hurts!" Kayla screams, still facing into the pillow.

Thinking it's finished, she pulls herself away from him, rolling over.

"You ain't done yet!" he growls, lowering himself, trying to kiss her as she pushes against him.

"No, I don't want ..."

Rick manages to get their lips connected, which forces Kayla to give in putting her arms around the back of his head.

Peeking into the window, Tara sees that they're just lying there, kissing.

"Good, they're done. See you, Cory." She waves, popping open the window.

Surprised by the window opening, Rick is nearly halfway inside Kayla when he stops.

"Oh, damn, I thought you was finished," Tara says when she notices his hips lowering.

"I am now!" he says, rolling off Kayla, hitting the floor softly enough to avoid a thud that would alert to Tara's parents.

"I'm sorry!" she mouths, covering her eyes so Rick can get up to get his clothes back on.

"I'm decent, and nice timing. Hey, wait, is that … no!" Rick notes, seeing Cory's coat still draped around her.

"Yeah, again, sorry."

Rick skips over to the window to see Cory making his way home. "Fuck, I need to go. My parents think I went to his place. Love ya, Kay. Bye!" He looks back, then rushes out the window.

Sitting there, Kayla covers her breasts. "Hey, could you um, ya know, hand me my clothes, please."

Tara is more than happy to fulfill that request.

"I am so incredibly sorry," she repeats, sitting beside Kayla.

"I'm not. I did what you told me to do. I took control, and then I gave him control. Even though that hurt like hell, I think it did the trick making up for what happened earlier."

Tara still refuses to look over at Kayla after she's dressed.

"Well, glad I could help," she retorts, folding her hand over her eyes.

In a surprising move to show her how much she's taken the advice to heart, Kayla kisses Tara. The action causes her to remove her hand when she feels their lips embrace.

"What was that for …" she begins, putting her hands to her lips.

"I wanted to do that earlier, but you backed away. You gave me the chance, and I took it. That's all I wanted, and see? You can look at me now."

They place a hand on each other's cheek.

"You little tease. Good job," Tara whispers, proudly able to flip the night around.

They hear the van start up and pull away.

"I take you had control and made Cory give in again?"

Tara tries to hide her smile. "Sort of. He got mad and took it all out on me. He, well, uh, did things differently, and unlike last time, it wasn't so fast since it wasn't his first time."

"Yay!" Kayla squeals with joy.

"I wanna know, how did Rick find you?" Tara beings to question, sitting there with her hands in on Kayla's thigh.

"Oh, it was too easy. He called your cellular, and since I picked up, he started to apologize, and well, I remembered what you told me."

Curious to what all occurred, Tara digs a little deeper. "So you said come over and let's do it?"

Kayla laughs, waving that notion off.

"No, I started to tease him by acting like I was touching myself, and he couldn't resist after I started moaning deeply into the phone.

"That's my girl!"

"Oh, it didn't stop there. When he got here, I was down to my panties and put him on the bed. I gave him a little lap dance and did something I've never done before, and well, you know."

Kayla motions using her hands.

"Oh my, did he like it?"

Kayla, in a hurry, acknowledges with a head shake. "Then I crawled up to his ear and told him to break me, and, well, he did."

The girls continue to go on about what each one did to seduce the boys. Still able to feel the connection from a few moments ago, Kayla surprises Tara once more with another kiss, as they experiment with each other. They giggle as they try new things.

A few blocks away, Rick parks by Cory's and runs to catch him before he gets back into his room through his window.

"Hey, Core, wait up!" he calls out, rushing to him.

"Oh, hey, hurry up it's cold!" Cory waves, waiting impatiently.

"Dude, what a crazy night, and your girl interrupted us, to boot," Rick informs him, helping Cory lift the window.

"Oh, my bad, man, she thought you was done, and besides, ain't like we didn't do the same thing here."

Rick nudges Cory in the arm before they climb into the house.

He shuts the window and stands there. The boys huddle around the heating vent.

"So I take it that the bed isn't a dry place to sit right now?"

Cory's eyes say it all when they shift in the direction of where they were on the bed.

"Oh, nice, bruh. Finally in the big boy club. Hell, yeah, welcome to the club."

Curling his lower lip and giving Rick a high five, the boys don't say anything else. They simply fix the bed, making themselves comfy before discussing it anymore.

"This is a whole new world for me. I wouldn't have ever thought anything could fix what happened tonight," Cory explains, remembering his dad's news.

"What happened?"

Cory begins to break it down.

"When I got home, my folks told me that my dad has diabetes, like, really badly. It's affecting my dad's hands and feet and stuff, man. My mother told me to get lost to go deal with it on my own. Then I beat Joe in a race, and then somehow, it was like Tara knew I needed something to distract me, and I took out how I was feeling on her body."

Rick sits there, stunned at the discovery.

"Oh, wow. Well, I do know this, from what Kay told me: Tara was showing her things to do to make me give in and then take control. So, really, I think that served two purposes."

Cory sits there letting it sink in. "Maybe, but whatever it was, I'm glad it worked. It's been a hell of a night—I know that much for sure."

Rick bounces his head in agreement. "Amen, bruh, but anyway, let's get some sleep and make tomorrow—or, well, today—a better one. We became real men tonight taking control of our women."

Cory takes it contrarily the wrong way of how Rick means over control.

"Yeah, you're right. Those girls belong to us, now, don't they?"

Rick pushes off the bed onto the mattress on the floor. "Damn right—to us and no one else. Oh, by the way, mind if I borrow yours to finish getting me off later."

Cory laughs sending a pillow crashing down, slamming Rick in the face. "Oh, that's it. You're dead, buddy boy!"

The boys wrestle around for a bit before calling it a draw.

"All right, all right, it's late enough. Let's get some rest," Rick suggests, trying to get out of the wristlock that has him pinned down on the floor.

"Cool, see ya in a few hours for church brother-man."

Rick yawns, saying, "Sounds good. Then we take the girls out to eat or something. Separately, though, ya know, to work into getting some more action."

Lying there, Cory doesn't make a sound as he tries to relax. When the roar of Rick's snoring travels through the air, Cory looks over to his other window, thinking about Tara as his eyes grow heavy and shut, sending him off to sleep.

CHAPTER 12

Hard-Hitting Playoffs

The regular season has ended for the RiverCreek Beavers. They've gained the number two-spot in the state playoffs, which take place in St. Paul. After they arrive in the city, the team, coach, assistants, and chaperones settle into their rooms, and the boys head off for practice.

"All right, boys, this is our year, our time, our championship to bring home!" the coach screams, trying to get the team excited.

"Yeah."

"Our time."

"Champions," the boys yell over top of each other, heading out to the ice.

Stopped by the entrance onto the ice, they get a glimpse of the team they'll be facing in the first of four rounds. Cory has already researched the entire bracket.

"The Minneapolis Minutemen, a private school. Take a good look, guys. They're smaller but faster than most of the teams here."

They make a hole so the opposing team can leave the ice. The Beavers take part in a stare-down as each team tries to get the early advantage in intimidation.

"You all aren't making it this year. Minutemen rule!" one of the taller players announces, getting into the face of the team captain.

"You're about to go home in body bags," Cory replies, stepping up and bumping chest to chest with the opponent.

After only a single scoff at the threat, the Minutemen player trots off for the locker room.

"Hey, bring it in!" Cory yells once everyone is out on the ice. "No mercy this year. No showing off. We do what we do best: hit 'em hard and score fast. We don't have Frankie this season, and we still came in tied for first, but we were forced into the number-two spot. It's our time, gentlemen. We've earned it. Beavers on three … one … two … three!"

"*Beavers*!" the team cries out, heading out to warm up for practice.

Taking time to watch parts of practice, Cory takes charge to make sure a new tactic works this time around as a surprise in the final game, should they make it there.

"Remember, speed is only part of the equation this time. Watch your hits. Don't be a puck hog. Defense stay ready with three. We've been practicing this all season," the coach calls out and stands in the box, observing the changes he's witnessed all season in Cory.

"You know, Leo, I wonder what's gotten into him? He's not the same soft-hearted player we've known. Look at him, taking charge out there. Tenacious and cunning. Something has finally pulled that fighting spirit out, and that might just be enough to take us the distance."

Leo, the assistant coach, lifts his head from the clipboard to view the practicing players.

"Yeah, Rob, you may have a point. I know he's been through a few rough patches over last few months. He might be using his pain to take it out on the ice. Sounds familiar to you back in the day."

The coaches stand there, allowing the kids to run the rest of practice. It gives them time not only to work hard but have some fun toward the end of their scheduled time on the ice.

"Five minutes left. Let's call it gentlemen. Time to get a good night's rest. We have the second game tomorrow morning. Come on, let's go RiverCreek!" The coach goes over opening the doors for the team to walk off the ice.

After getting cleaned up, Cory takes off to explore St. Paul. Alone, he walks along the sidewalks, soaking in everything he sees.

"This is what I can expect getting away from home. I forgot how big this place really is," he says to himself, gazing up at the high-rise buildings and corporations.

Something loud and roaring grabs his attention from the street. "Now, this I could get used to seeing."

He stands there nearly drooling at the sight of a tricked-out pearl-red Toyota Supra.

"Damn, that's pretty!" he coos, staring it down as it flies by him.

Heading in the same direction as the Supra, he gets a peep of another top-end import pulling beside of it, revving its engine a couple of times.

"A Nissan 300ZX. Holy hell—race, race, race."

His excitement supersedes his sense of exploration. Immediately, he sprints to the end of the block. He watches as they speed away down the straightaway from light to light, each roaring their way out of sight

"Awesome!"

After the exhilaration dies down inside of his body, Cory's stomach bellows, reminding him that it's empty. Returning to his stroll about the city, he comes across an option he doesn't have back in his suburban town.

"Wong Chow Fu Chinese Buffet," he reads on the door. "Smells good anyway."

Decided to check it out, Cory walks inside and pays for the buffet.

"Thank you very much. Enjoy buffet. Try new orange glaze chicken and duck. Very good," the cashier states as he takes Cory's cash.

Cory smiles and nods taking his tray over to his table. He walks over between the two extended food bars, where he fills his plate with as much as possible to sample a bit of everything.

There isn't anything his pallet doesn't enjoy; Cory overfills himself with three heaping plates of food. Letting his stomach settle, his mind reverts to thinking about Tara and how much she would've enjoyed the meal with him.

He drops a small tip for his server, Cory begins his wander prior to returning to the hotel. To head back up his room on the third floor, he takes the stairs, hoping to help burn off some of the excess bloating he's experiencing in his gut. Once through the door, he goes over flops onto the bed face first, passing out in no time.

It's the morning of the first and second rounds of the state playoffs. RiverCreek has arrived at the arena ready to make a deep run for the state title. Cory sends out a couple of players to scout the other teams to report back what they learn.

When it's their turn to take the ice, Cory leads the team for most of the game. He barely takes any time off the ice. He calls out plays each time they get possession.

"River route one!" he calls out, sending one defenseman and the left forward ahead of himself.

Passing the puck up to the defenseman, he signals that it's going to be a quick pass across the ice. When the goalie falls for the trick, Cory rips forward slapping the puck in mid pass sailing it behind the goalie for the goal. The play puts the team up three to one with half a minute left.

"Cory, off the ice!" the coach calls out, pulling Cory from the ice. "Great leadership out there, captain. Let them finish up the final few seconds."

Cory's breathing hard and sits without questioning the coach's decision.

Once the final buzzer blares, the team heads back preparing to face off against their archrival the next day. The team is full of energy, except for Cory, who's feeling being out on the ice most of the game.

"Come on, Cold Core, rest up and relax. We're all hitting the movies at St. Paul Mall. Get showered and let's go!" Joe explains, giving Cory a helping hand off the locker room bench.

"Thanks, Joe. Let me get a shower, and yeah, I'll join ya."

The spirit of winning is temporarily putting personal issues aside.

"Cool, dude. Hurry up!"

Cory rushes through his shower and quickly dresses back into street clothes. He rushes out to the caravan the coach has rented for the team.

"All right, boys, great game, but listen up. Our helpers have informed me that we were being watched too. Cory, tomorrow, you sit out in the beginning, and we have a surprise for everyone. Since I never turned in the paperwork, we have a surprise for the rest of the teams."

Popping up from behind the rear seat, Frankie makes his return to the team.

"Frankie!" the entire team shouts, pulling him out from behind the seat.

"Yeah boys, the coach talked me into coming back. We have college scouts here and well; I want that state title too!" he declares, coming to take a seat beside Cory.

"Hey, buddy boy, good to see ya finally become an animal. Relax, I got your back on the ice, Captain Core."

With a sigh of relief, Core leans back in the seat, knowing their odds of winning just increased that much more.

"Glad to have ya back, old friend."

Frankie grins, patting his teammate on the knee. "Let's roll, Coach!" Frankie cries out, eager to get to the movies.

The next two games, Frankie is not just the biggest surprise of the tournament. He's the biggest threat on the ice, even outperforming Cory's best efforts to remain top scorer.

In the semifinal game against the Twin City Dragons, Cory is beginning to feel fed up with Frankie's showboating.

"Frankie! I'm open, pass it!" Cory screams, sitting ten feet from the goal, distracting the goalie.

Taking the shot when he sees the goalie look away, the shot ricochets off the goalie's pads, giving the rebound shot and goal to Cory. He swiftly takes advantage of the opportunity to hit the winning shot.

Frustrated, Frankie leaves the ice in a hurry. The team crowds to Cory knocking him down onto the ice creating a dog pile. The boys are thrilled to be in the finals facing the Northome Norseman.

"We made it, guys. We're in the finals!" Cory shouts from the bottom of the pile.

"RiverCreek ..." the crowd chants, seeing them as the favorite facing Northome, the number-four seed in the tournament.

Slamming his gear down in the locker room, Frankie goes ballistic, punching lockers and kicking things around. The assistant coach follows him back that way and gives him time to cool down.

"Hey, Frankie, calm down, kid. You did well out there today. Forget about the fact that you missed the winning shot. Let it go. We're in the championship this year. You're not team captain anymore, so relax."

Frankie plops down along the bench, slowing his breathing to regain his composure. "Yes, Coach."

Coming into the locker room after the coach leaves is a tall, skinny man wearing a North Dakota State University polo and cap.

"Hello. Franklin Ford, I presume," he announces, trotting over to standing by Frankie.

"Yes, sir, can I help you?"

"Hi, I'm Peyton Walters, the athletic director for North Dakota State. You've been impressive last season and most of the tournament so far. I was hoping to discuss you coming to play for my school after you graduate next year."

Frankie is all ears as the he's about to be offered a full scholarship.

Back out on the ice, the team finally pulls themselves up. Once they're off the ice, a few of them are met by either coaches or athletic directors from small colleges with meet-and-greets. Cory looks past all of them when no one seems interested, making his way back to the locker room.

Unaware he's being followed, he turns the corner before his name is called out.

"Cory Dubois, team captain this season, averaging a hat trick during the regular season with at least one to two assists per game. Average playing time, twenty minutes or more. Beyond remarkable, young man."

Stopped outside the team door, Cory turns around to see a man just an inch shorter than him, standing there.

"Can I help you, sir?"

Grinning at him, the man approaches him in a business suit.

"Yes, I'm Gus Brooks, head hockey coach, Miami of Ohio University. I'm here to give you an offer to come play for one of the hottest teams in the country right now."

Unable to speak, Cory stands there, unaware his mouth is open.

"I know you have your senior year still left to play. I came here hoping to get you to say yes to a visit this summer. From what I seen over the last few days and the video tapes your coaches have sent me, I want you to play for my team. Here, I have packets and a letter of interest to hold your place for an official visit. All expenses paid for you and your folks. All I need is a yes and a handshake."

Releasing his stick to bounce on the floor, Cory extends his hand, nodding to the terms of the offer.

"Good, I'll be looking forward to hearing from your parents. Good luck tomorrow. I'll be watching, Captain Cory."

He hands over the packet of information and walks away. Cory bends down to get his stick and makes his way inside as the team comes around the corner.

He places the information in the top of his locker. Cory quickly gets cleaned up and picks up his packet and returns with everyone back to the hotel. Entering his room, he reads over the papers, excited about it the more he reads. Forgetting about dinner with the team in the banquet room, he stays in his room, thrilled to be realizing his dreams are going to come true.

Early the next morning, everyone gathers for breakfast. There's clink of a fork against a glass. The coach stands, preparing for a speech after clearing his throat.

"Good morning, young men. We're finally here. In a couple of hours, we'll be packed up, loaded onto the bus, and will be playing for the state title at noon. I couldn't be more proud of each and every one of you. A few of you have talked to or been offered scholarships to college. For you seniors, let me just say, we'll miss you next season, and best of luck. Make us proud transitioning to the next level. Enjoy the day, boys. If your family has driven up to see you play, then afterwards, you can leave with them. Get ready, boys. You're champions to me and our community already, but today, you play for yourselves."

Taking his seat, the boys dig in and devour their food. They sit around and wait to leave for the arena. When the time arrives, they load up. Nerves on end, the butterflies twirling around, the place is packed with people from all around the state coming to see the game. Chants for each team already vibrating throughout the arena.

In the locker room, RiverCreek is prepared for the fight of their lives. Unwilling to feel the fatigue and aching muscles from two grueling games, the team rallies to each other, combining their strengths one last time for the title.

"We got this, you all!" Joe screams over the collective clapping.

"It's our time, our title, our championship, for RiverCreek!" Frankie yells, turning red in the face.

"Do you want a vic-tor-ree! Do you want that trophy forever putting your names in history! Do you want to be remembered throughout the ages!" The coach screams, stomping with each statement.

"*Hell yeah*!" the entire team shrieks, following the coaches out when they wave them on.

Being stopped by the doors leading to the ice, the team waits to hear their name and number announced over the speakers; they each receive a monstrous applause roaring from the entire crowd.

"Hey, Frankie, Core, great season!" Joe compliments, giving his captains a pat on the back when he hears his name announced.

"Until next season, Cory, and tell Lloyd I'll see him soon, please," Frankie mentions.

Stunned by not only the statement, Cory and Frankie are called out together as team captain and former captain. The crowd rips to an even higher decibel. It's deafening to the players on the ice. The boys wave to the crowd, gliding up to center ice, hands extended high in the air.

Gathered along their box, the coach pulls everyone in close. "All right, this is our time, our day! Time to pull out your best performance yet. Every face off, mix it up, and hurry to do it. I'll switch you out to stay fresh and fast. Hit 'em hard, hit 'em first, and make every shot count. Don't be fooled—they've allowed two goals the entire time they've been here. Now get out there and show them who you are and why you deserve to be here.

"RiverCreek!"

The team chants, "RiverCreek" and the starters take their position on the ice.

The ref skates up with the puck in hand. "All right, boys, keep it clean and fair. Have fun, and congratulations reaching this game."

He drops the puck with Northome winning the faceoff. Cory, Frankie, and Joe hurry to get on defense, protecting the goalie. A quick slapshot is fired and nearly makes it inside the net but dings off the post.

Taking the puck into his possession, Frankie is alongside Joe, heading toward enemy territory. They easily skate by the shorter players on the opposing team. The defense stiffens up, blindsiding Frankie, and strips him of the puck. Joe reaches to try to steal it away but ends up face first on the ice for his efforts. The whistle blows for a high-stick penalty.

"Change it up!" Cory yells, holding up three fingers. Frankie and Joe both get off the ice to watch and learn how the Norsemen move.

RiverCreek loses the next faceoff, but Cory drives through the player going for the puck. After he knocks him down attempting to gain control, Cory charges easily down the ice, leaving him one-on-one with the goalie. From the games preceding this game, and waiting on a trick play, the goalie scoots out a bit.

Faking the shot Cory pulls the goalie to dropping to his knee-pads to block the shot. It's an opportunity for a power shot. Cory lets it fly, bouncing it off the pads, ringing the post and barely landing inside the net. The alarm goes off as the crowd pops over the play.

"Stay out there!" the coach screams, realizing they're in for a tough battle.

Frankie's been watching how the other team hunkers down, using leverage to get their way around his team.

"Coach, we need to focus on defense. They have speed and leverage on their side. If we can hold them off with three defensemen, we can handle them."

"Make it happen next time play stops. You and Cory lead the offense while Nathan goes out on defense, and stay near that goal, boys, hear me!"

The three players reply with in unison, "Yes, sir, Coach," prepared to get out on the ice.

Lined up for the faceoff, RiverCreek is given the puck when Northome doesn't even try to take possession. They tried to pull what Cory did, but the defense stands strong, crashing into each player, giving Caleb a lane down to try to score.

Circling around the net, he tries to trick the goalie when he switches direction. He's met by a Norsemen defender, who slams him onto the ice, taking the puck.

Passing it off to the team's leading scorer, they sail down the ice, speeding toward the goal. The Norsemen pull a trick they've used every game. The leading skater allows the puck to drift back to another player, who passes it quickly to another player directly across. Making it impossible to see the puck, they score, tying the game.

The crowd again brings an uproar across the arena.

Now is the time Frankie, Nathan, and Joe hit the ice, lining up the go on defense. Cory takes the faceoff only to get slammed on the ice again. The remaining four teammates protect the goal perfectly. When they get control of the puck again, Cory and Frankie try every trick they've ever used. Each time, it's broken up before they get within shooting distance of the net.

By the beginning of the final period, each team is worn down.

Exhaustion sets in and brings the pace down, but each side fights for control, with the score still tied at one apiece. Breathing hard, Cory decides to sit for half the period, trying to regain some strength. He's in noticeable pain when he hears a voice call out to him.

"Cory, baby boy. Hey, Cory!"

He twists his head to find the source of the voice, but it isn't until he hears hands pounding off the glass that he sees Tara standing there with a RiverCreek jersey on.

"I made it! We're all here. Now, get out there and win. I love you!" she yells, placing an open palm against the glass.

"Look who else made it!" she yells again. Lloyd comes up beside her, making a heart with his fingers.

Instantly reenergized, he sits there waiting for play to stop on the ice. After RiverCreek gets hit with another icing call, Cory takes his place on the ice. He speeds over to Frankie and whispers to him, "Hey, Lloyd came to see you play. Make him proud man. No judgements, either, but do it for him."

Frankie's facial expression transitions to pride in his eyes, as a wave of energy strikes him like as it did Cory.

"We got this …" Frankie states with anger in his eyes.

Heading up to take the faceoff, Frankie blocks his opponent's stick, sending the puck back to Joe. Together, with Cory behind them, the trio power through the other players, finally able to get a clean shot.

With every bit of strength left within him, Joe causes the goalie to mishandle the rebound. He leaps out to hold onto the puck, but Frankie comes up hitting the puck into a wide-open net.

"Yes! It's ours to win!" Frankie yells, looking up to see under two minutes left to play in the game.

The entire team goes on defense from that point on. When they get their hands on the puck, they take their time passing it back and forth, sending only two players up at a time. Everyone else pulls back. The Norsemen tries the same trick RiverCreek used with the entire team as a decoy on defense.

Nathan takes the shot, hoping to score with less than fifteen seconds left. Rushing back down the ice, Frankie and Cory double team to stop the advancement. Twisted around to try to run out the clock, they're both taken down with three seconds left.

"Three ... two ... one ..." the crowd counts down as a collective breath travels across the arena. The final desperation shot flies when the player hears the count of two seconds to go. The shot hits the end of the goalie's stick and it wraps around, spinning into the goal, but the referee waves it off, signaling that time has expired.

The RiverCreek players toss up their sticks and gloves into the air. They all realize what that calls means for their community.

"Holy shit they won! They won it all!" Rick screams in the stands, trying to rush down to the ice along with everyone who travelled from town.

Frankie and Cory meet on the ice eye to eye and nod. They smile and share a hug in victory as their mutual respect for their talents on the ice supersede their personal issues.

"Congrats, Cold Core!"

Shaking his hand, Cory sends one back. "You too, Frankie. Have fun when you get home. It's spring break!"

The boys are tackled by their friends.

"Time to party tonight!" Rick informs Cory, shaking him by the jersey.

The celebration continues, with players and coaches being interviewed as they come off the ice. The team quickly showers, and the ones who need a ride back home gather in the caravan. Rick catches Cory and pulls him out to his Man-Van, as he has plans for a surprise to kick off spring break in style before heading home.

CHAPTER 13

Spring Break to Summer

Sore and stiff from the playoff tournament, Cory climbs into Rick's Man-Van. He's pulled inside when Tara reaches out taking his battered and beaten body. He can't even cry out in agony before she plants a prolonged kiss on his lips.

"Oh yeah, now that's sexy!" Kayla taunts staring back at them.

Groaning from her squeezing his body, Cory breaks away from the kiss to sit upright in the seat. "Ugh, I hurt all over. Sorry sweetie, but I took a beating this weekend."

Tara instantly releases her grip, sliding back against the arm rest. "I didn't know, I'm sorry."

"It's fine love, just got to be gentle for a few days. The entire team is feeling it, but damn it was worth it."

Rick roars up, yelling out the window.

"Yeah, state champs' baby! Team captain right here, Cold Cory Dubois, leader, lover, and best friend people. Right here in the RiverCreek Man-Van! About to go out to the Disgraced Thru Grace concert!"

Cory's confused by the last part of the announcement. "Who is Disgraced Thru Grace?

Rick rotates his eyes to speak.

"Oh man, they're touring with F.O.W.L., which uh is Freedom Over World Leaders. F.O.W.L., they're a radical 90's gangster rap group that never signed to a major label. Figured I'd treat everyone to the show. Tickets were cheap and we're front row. Plus, Disgraced Thru Grace is a new rock band that's doing the fair tour with them."

Listening to Rick explain about the group, they listen to one of their CDs on the way to the fairgrounds for the concert.

After parking over in the grass, the kids get out, marching along the gravel road. They stop at the gate, where Rick pulls out four tickets, handing them over to security.

"Thank you. Enjoy the show, kids."

Rick hands each of them a ripped ticket stub after they walk onto the open field. The front row is standing room-only down by the elevated stage. The crowd gathers swiftly, causing the noise to be louder than any of them expected.

Shortly after the lights turn on, a voice emanates from behind the stage.

"Ladies and gentlemen, thank you for attending today's show. Please give a round of applause for the opening performer. Straight out of the Dirty South, from Atlanta, Georgia, he is known for stirring up havoc on a microphone. Give it up for J-Faktur."

The crowd gets loud as a Caucasian young adult male with brown and bleached-blond hair, wearing an Atlanta Thrashers jersey with baggy Paco Jeans, walks out on stage.

"Hello, St. Paul. Sup? Y'all ready to get this party started and outta control?"

The crowd roars louder when the first beat begins.

"Hey, uh, yeah, uh let me get a feel of the spill. Here we go, it's a thrill to seal the deal of the rap game, so I'm here to build my name, making y'all think that I'm insane. I'm just OC that's outta control, being straight with ya, ya know. Gonna put it down in this town with a sound like ya never heard when ya listen to my words. Hitting the road with my band expanding my brand, can't keep my head in the sand cuz I gotta plan. Gonna set the stage ablaze at the sound of my name. It'll make ya go. Outta control, don't ya know."

Rick begins to get into the song, waving his hand in the air. "He's pretty good huh, Core," he shouts over the beat.

"Yeah, not too bad. Sorry, I'm not that into it yet, I feel like hell, man, but thank you for this."

Rick gives him a thumbs-up gesture, returning his attention to the stage.

After the song is finished, J-Faktur removes his earplugs to address the crowd.

"Y'all like that one? That was 'Outta Control,' one of my newest hits. Anyway, it's great being here and having a great time. Just got in town to watch today's hockey finals. Anyone of y'all see that wicked fucking game?"

The crowd pops back with cheering and booing. Rick begins, pointing to Cory trying, to get the performer's attention.

"Hey, you here in the front, was you there?" he asks finally, seeing Rick waving his arms.

"Hey, y'all, chill for a minute. Let this man speak."

Rick barely gets out, "My boy here is the team captain of the winning team."

Motioning that he could just make out what he says, there's a surprise announcement that follows.

"Captain, you say. Well, how about I give you and your friends a chance to really enjoy the show from the best seats in the house. Backstage with me? I love hockey, and it would be my honor to talk to a future pro player. Security, guide them back!"

The four of them are left speechless as they wait for security to escort them back behind the scenes.

"All right. Let's make some noise!"

The next song begins when the kids get backstage.

"Hey little man, congrats on the win!" One of the F.O.W.L. members calls out, watching in the wings of the stage to see how the crowd reacts.

"Hey, Zamaal, he's got two songs left. Get everyone ready!"

Rick's reaction is priceless when he sees the other three members of the group gather by the curtain.

They wave to them before they take off for the stage. Once they're out on the stage, Disgraced Thru Grace come out next to gauge the crowd and give the foursome watching from the other side a thumbs-up and a wave.

"Holy shit, I got to see them up close." Rick squeals, bouncing up and down on his heels.

"Chill, Rick!" Kayla says, pushing on his arm.

The kids wait around for the opening act to finish, introducing and interacting with the crowd so they can chat with him for a bit.

Backstage, J-Faktur waves them all over.

"Hey, thank you for bringing us backstage," Cory begins to say, feeling privileged.

"Nah, it's nothing y'all. I seen that game today, and wow, talk about some hard-hitting, almost nonstop action. I thought f'real that it was going to OT when that shot got off."

Cory admits something out loud. "I thought so too at first, but when the buzzer went off and the light didn't flash to signal a goal, I knew we had it."

Extending his arm, J-Faktur shakes Cory's hand. "You all got a ton a heart to keep going like y'all did. I see ya here with ya gal and whatnot, standing tall. Hell, yeah, son, I figured you was beaten to a pulp. Another reason why I brought ya backstage. Relax and have some fun. Need anything, let security know."

He pats Cory on the back and mentions one final thing before he leaves.

"It was excellent, but please, y'all, make yaselves comfy. Stand here to view the stage and enjoy the show. I got me some um, business, to handle. I just wanted to tell you up close congrats on the 'W' dawg. Peace, y'all."

The four of them wave goodbye to him, seeing him stride to his trailer with an escort on each arm. He looks back and winks, picking up his pace.

After the show is finished, Rick stands there waiting to meet the group.

"Holy shit, what a show!" the lead hip hop artist claims, taking his earplug out.

"Yeah, that was a show."

They turn to see Rick standing there with a smile not even a stick of dynamite could destroy.

"Sup, little homie. Gotta pen handy?"

Rick pats around, trying to find anything in a pocket.

"Here, kid." Dakota from Disgraced Thru Grace hands over a piece of paper and a marker.

The group take their time signing each of their names, causing Rick to act like an excited child on Christmas morning. They hand over the autographed paper, and the band gets a good glimpse of Kayla coming up getting her clutches on Rick.

"That ya girl? She's fine homeboy. Gotta love a white blond chick. And what deep chocolate brown eyes you have, miss. Y'all be careful out there in the real world. Ain't so nice seeing a mixed couple."

Rick takes his advance with a grain of salt.

"We will do, sir, thank you!"

They stand there and watch as the ensemble of artists walk away, leaving them there to wait around for Cory and Tara to return from listening to the Southern rock band that's getting into their first song.

"Hey, I have something to tell you later," Cory says, trying to break the news about getting an offer to visit Miami.

"Can it wait? I just wanna enjoy this." Tara struts up to him, hiking up her shirt, showing off her flat stomach.

"Right now, I wanna give my champ the kiss he deserves." She pins his sore body up against the wall, giving him a seductive kiss.

Grunting when his back slams against the wall, Cory pulls her away. "You gonna have to wait for a minute, doll. It hurts to even move right now."

Her hand against his glides down the side of his face. She smirks and helps him off the wall. They return to where Rick and Kayla are still waiting for them.

"Come on, you two. Let's hit the road. Gotta haul back to town," Rick calls out, waving them to get a move on.

With a sigh in frustration at not being able to get his exciting news out in the open, Cory tries to hide it by acting distraught.

"The Man-Van looks different with your back seat actually put back in it," Cory mentions when they approach the van.

"Yeah, well you need a ride home, and your folks didn't think you'd want to be seen with them."

The four of them crack up laughing and climb inside.

"I know one thing: it'll be nice to get home and soak in a hot tub full of Epsom Salt. Oh, yeah, I have something I need to tell you all." Cory tries for a second time to spill his news, but Tara ensures that it's not to be discussed.

"It can wait, babe? For now, let's enjoy the ride home. This place is beautiful without snow."

Cory huffs, with more frustration building within him. Relaxed in his seat, Cory buckles himself in and finds a way to get comfortable enough to fall asleep after about twenty minutes.

Waking up when Rick pulls over, Cory is surprised to be home already.

"Hey, Cory, wake up, man. You're home."

Sitting up wiping the droll from his chin, Cory looks around.

"What, home already? Didn't we just leave? Hey, where are the girls?" he babbles trying to gain his senses.

"Well, I dropped them off over at Kay's. Come on, I'll help ya pack ya stuff inside."

The boys head inside to toss Cory's belongings in his room. Locking eyes on the bed, Cory stumbles over flopping face first and passes out immediately. After a few hours, when he finally reenters the world, Cory gets up to the smells of food emanating from down the hallway.

Walking stiffly into the kitchen, Cory gets his sights on Tara, standing there with her back to him.

"Hey, you didn't have to come over and cook. I can make something to eat on my own.

Startled, Tara jumps holding her hand over her chest. "You jerk! You scared me, oh, good Lord, Core. Anyway, yes I did need to cook. Your parents are out enjoying a night to themselves and, well, reheated leftover pizza just ain't dinner."

Up against the doorway laughing, Cory finally notices that his girl is standing in there in an apron and her bra.

"Looking pretty good, baby girl."

She ducks her head down a bit, smiling. "Wanted to give you something special. Ya know, to have for dessert later."

"Oh, not tonight. My body is way too ravaged and smashed to fool around. I love the thought, but we can't."

Tara returns her attention to her food on the stove. "I understand, but hey, at least you liked the view."

Cory surprises her with what he says next.

"I love that view, and I love you."

He walks away, which leaves her speechless.

The rest of their evening after dinner is spent on the couch watching classic movies.

"Did you mean it?"

Cory looks over to her with a confused glare in his eyes. "Mean what? I haven't said anything since dinner."

Tara explains what she means.

"Exactly, you said I love you and walked off on me. Did you mean it? You know I've been burned before, so don't lie to me."

That strikes a chord with Cory.

"I would never lie about that. You know I was cheated on lots of times by—" He stops when a knock comes from the door. "Who in the world ...?"

Motioning for him to stay seated, Tara answers the door. The instant she opens it, her eyes can't believe who's standing there.

"Oh, hi, there, I'm looking for my boy toy, Cory. You must be the side slut, Terror Ho Bag."

Without even thinking, Tara hauls off, nailing Venessa directly in the nose.

"You bitch!" Venessa screams, grabbing her blood-soaked nose.

"Get out of here or else your jaw is next."

Cory tries to rush the door to get between them, to play peacemaker. "That is enough, Vanessa. All you do is cause trouble. Go sleep with Frankie or someone else and leave us alone."

He slams the door in her face and checks on Tara's partially swollen red knuckles.

"Are you okay?" he asks, examining her hand.

"Yeah, just sore. I promise, I'm fine." She smiles as he takes her hand, kissing each knuckle.

"Well, then, let's get back to our movie."

They return to the couch cuddled up and eventually fall asleep, until Cory's parents arrive and send Tara home. His mother places a blanket over him to let him remain asleep where he's comfortable.

Using the last day of the weekend to rest, Cory's spring break is spent working with his father over at the garage. He details cars after they're repaired. It is one way he works for the extra money to save for items he wants to install on his car.

Together with Rick, on days he isn't busy with try outs for the track team, they work feverishly for tips. Each vehicle they work on together, they flip between the exterior and interior.

During the week for Tara and Kayla, they work together at the store. While Kayla maintains her position at the register, Tara is the working customer service desk and also does the movie and video games rental services.

Knowing the kids head back to school soon, their parents give them Friday off to spend together to enjoy a picnic down by the point where they all hang out.

Parked and walking down to the edge of the water, the double couple prepare for a bit of fun.

"Hey Core, grab that corner and straighten it out, please and thanks, sir," Rick mentions.

When Cory leans down, Tara takes advantage and jumps on his back, sending them both crashing to the ground where she begins tickling him.

"Okay … okay … okay … you win!" Cory cries out, barely able to breathe.

Standing there with the cooler in her hands, Kayla nearly falls trying to get the bulky oversized cooler onto the blanket.

"Thanks guys, I got this," she barks, out of breath, resting against the cooler.

"Sorry, honey bunny, I was gonna go back and get it."

With a roll of her eyes, Kayla curls her lips. "Now you tell me!"

Scooting over to rest up against Rick, Kayla flops her head against his chest. "I love sunny days like today. Just so peaceful and nice to relax in the sun. Hey, Tara wanna sunbathe after we get back?"

Removing the lid from the picnic basket, Tara looks up with a simple "yes," then reaches inside, taking out the paper plates and cups.

"Hope y'all like fried chicken, potato salad, coleslaw, cornbread, and baked beans."

Bewildered by the selection, the three of them gaze over to Tara.

"Say what, I don't think I've had any of that together," Rick admits, observing each container now in the middle of the blanket.

"Trust me, she's a great cook," Cory says, waiting for the lids to open as Tara starts to blush.

"If you say so, brother man."

Rick takes his plate from Tara's grip, along with a plastic spoon, getting a sample of everything she mentioned. He stares at it and lifts it up to his nose, shutting his eyes to inhale the home-cooked goodness.

"Mmm'mmm, now that smells good," Rick admits before he tastes it.

With the first bite, Rick's taste buds are overwhelmed when the sensations explode on his tongue. "Holy shit, that's the stuff right there!"

Extending his hand, he waits for Tara to give him a high five.

"Thanks, handsome," she mumbles with a smile stretched over her face.

While they bask in the sun, the kids eat and joke around for a while. It isn't until they hear the crack of thunder coming that they realize the fun must come to an end.

"Guess that means it's time to head inside," Cory says, pointing out over the horizon, where the dark clouds begin to blow in the musky scent of the approaching storm.

"Yeah, looks like a good one too. Girls, go ahead and get in the cars. Core, let's hook and book it."

Helping Tara to her feet, Cory begins tossing everything together, cramming it into the cooler, and runs it up to the Man-Van.

"Better hurry. That storm isn't coming in slow," Kayla tells Cory, keeping her eyes locked on the growing darkness overhead.

"Sure thing. Just gotta get the blanket and trash."

Running back to Rick, the boys quickly put the last of it all in the middle of the blanket to tie the corners together and haul ass back to their cars.

Rushed into the Celica, Cory starts it up trying to get home before the rain hits. After the second crash of thunder roars down from the sky, Rick picks up the first lightning strike from the corner of his eye.

"Wow, it's coming in fast," he whispers, slamming the side door shut, then climbs over the blanket to get to the driver's side.

Wasting no time, Rick fires up his van, racing Kayla home.

"Looks like we made it in time," he comments, pulling into her driveway.

"Yup, hey wanna come in for a little while, or at least until the storm passes?" she asks, gently playing with his arm.

"Sure thing, sugar. Got anything in mind?"

Playing hard to get, Kayla looks away. "Guess you'll have to wait and see."

Rick reaches over, pulling her in for a kiss. Once he's made his point with his lips, he puts his forehead against hers.

"C'mon and show me. You know you want to."

Only able to giggle at the thought, she escorts him inside. Just as she closes the door, the rain makes its presence known, pounding against the house.

"Made it in time. Now, come on, let's head to my room," she orders, taking charge over, Rick wanting to make the most of an opportunity on a rainy day.

It's another opportunity that they make the most of as they continue their new intimate game, riding out the storm as it spends a few hours hovering over town.

CHAPTER 14

Summertime Surprises

Summer vacation is in full swing by now, and Cory has forgotten all about trying to tell Tara about his upcoming trip to Miami of Ohio. His parents are excited to head out of town, so much so that they've planned what they will do while Cory is escorted around the university by the coach and the athletic director.

"Hey, Cory, are you packed up and ready to go?" his mother calls out from the living room.

"Almost, Mom. Just gotta zip my bag and I'm good."

She's getting more impatient, tapping her foot on the floor. "Hurry up or we're leaving without you!" she teases, feeling excited to leave town.

Knocking on the edge of the screen door, Tara catches the end of their exchange.

"Hi, Mrs. Dubois. Going on a weekend getaway?"

Waving her to come inside, the news is about to blow Tara away. "No, it's the trip to Oxford, Ohio, for Cory's official visit to the college for a scholarship offer. Didn't he tell you after he won the state title?"

She gasps quietly to herself. Tara tries to hide her shock.

"Oh, yeah. Guess I forgot, but hey have fun, and I'll see y'all when ya get back. Bring me a postcard!"

She spins around, heading out the door, barely missing Cory, who is finally coming out from his room.

"Someone here, Mom?"

"Just Tara forgetting about your visit. She said she'll see you when we get back. Now come on kid and let's go!" She motions him toward the door, locking it behind them.

Fueled by pure rage, Tara stands there with a sarcastic smile, waving as Cory and his parents fade away in the distance.

"Oh, you poor bastard, you're gonna pay for lying to me!" she grunts, nearly grinding her teeth.

Cruising to Kayla's to blow off some steam, Tara pulls up to see Kayla lying out in the sun.

"Hey, girl, what is up?" Kayla calls out, looking over to her.

"Oh, I'm pissed! Cory is going to visit a college he never told me about."

Confused, Kayla tips her sunglasses away from her eyes. "Say what? Where's he going?"

After slamming her car door, Tara mumbles, "Miami" as she leans against the door.

"What are you going to do when he gets back?"

Tara places her index finger to her lips. "I guess I'll have to deal with it. I'll tell you this: if he thinks he's going to lie and keep things from me, I'll beat his ass. My ex did that to me, and I will not go through that ever again."

Sitting up, Kayla gets to her feet to take her towel inside and throw on some clothes.

"Hey, come on inside. I'll get dressed, and we'll go see if Rick knew anything about this. If he did, I'll kick him in the balls."

Tara shoves off her Kia and struts into the house.

"I hate being lied to more than anything!" Tara reiterates, trying to keep herself fired up.

"Don't blame ya, girl."

After getting back into regular clothes, the girls head out to find Rick. On the way there, they both immediately notice the Man-Van sitting in the church parking lot.

"There he is. Pull in and I'll go get him. I won't cause a scene in the church," Kayla explains, cracking her knuckles, prepared for an all-out verbal assault if Rick admits to knowing about the trip.

"Go get 'em girl. I'll ask all the questions," Tara says, pissed, a scowl frozen on her face.

Taking her time inside, Kayla baits Rick, acting as if nothing is wrong in the slightest bit. Once she's able to convince him to come outside with her, he's ambushed when both ladies pounce on him.

"I want the truth, Rick. Did you know about Cory going to Ohio?" Tara begins.

"Yeah? How come you didn't tell either of us about the offer he has?" Kayla interjects.

"Is he giving up on Western Michigan? Is he going to throw me away like some piece of trash?" Tara badgers Rick at the same time.

Not able to get a word in edgewise, Rick's eyes tell the whole tale. His head goes back and forth as the girls continue their assault.

"Well, spill it! What's the damn deal with Cory keeping this from me?" Tara yells, almost ready to slap Cory's best friend.

Hearing Tara swear on holy ground forces him to put a halt to it all. "Woah, right there. Swear again on church grounds, and you're gone! You can badger me all you want, but don't you dare ever swear on my father's property!"

He places his finger directly in Tara's face.

"Get your hand out of her face!" Kayla yells, slapping his hand away.

"Don't ever hit me again. You're both lucky we're on holy ground, or else I'd tell you exactly what I think of both of you right about now. Now, stop acting like crazy lunatics and leave."

Both girls look at each before they haul off, slapping Rick across the face.

"Don't you ever insult us like that again," Tara scolds, putting her hands on her hips.

"Look, I thought Cory told you. If he didn't then he had his reasons, but leave me out of your all's drama. Other than that, I have to help my father. Later."

Rick turns around, walking away.

"Yeah, go ahead and run off. You're just like every other guy in this shitty-ass town!" Kayla screams, angry at Rick for not being on their side.

"I said don't cuss. Now leave before I call the cops for trespassing. Last warning—I mean it," Rick says, shaking his head as he walks back into the church.

"Jerk face!" Kayla screeches, kicking a rock across the parking lot.

Tara takes out her keys and motions Kayla to get into the car. "That's fine. If that's how they wanna play it, then we can do it better. They wanna ignore and keep things from us; then we can ignore them and make them come crawling back to us."

Over the next two days, Cory is blown away with his visit to Miami University. From the weight room to the feel of practicing with some of the team out on the ice, he feels completely at home. Meanwhile, his parents are out enjoying the Miami Valley with the sights and attractions. None of them are aware of the events building pressure back home. The entire trip, they forget about RiverCreek as they enjoy Ohio. Their final night, they even try a local delicacy—a pizza place called LaRosa's Pizza.

When they arrive home and unpack, Cory can't wait to find Tara and explain every detail of the trip. Snatching the cordless phone, he dials her house but only gets the answering machine.

"Well, shoot. Maybe she's at work," Cory says, hanging up. He then dials her cell phone number. It rings twice before she picks up.

"Fuck off, liar!" she barks into the phone, then hangs up, leaving Cory confused.

"What did I do?"

Concerned over her attitude, Cory quickly grabs his car keys. Heading out the door, he forgets to tell his parents goodbye.

"Hey, be home by dark. I mean it!" his father yells to get his son's attention.

In his car, Cory speeds around town, trying to find Tara. He checks by her house, her mother's store, and even by the point where everyone from school has gathered. Cory doesn't see Tara anywhere.

Now, his own frustration building, he struggles to put together what he's done wrong. Cory doesn't regard the speed limits around town. He's down by Lloyd's place when he finally notices Tara and Lloyd heading in the opposite direction.

"About damn time!" he says over the turbo blowing off when he downshifts, swinging his Celica around in the middle of the road, nearly colliding with another oncoming car.

Power shifting to catch up, Cory doesn't hesitate to pass Tara and Lloyd, cutting them off, nearly causing them to crash into his car. With a renewed sense of anger, Tara gets out, slamming her door shut.

"Are you really that stupid? You nearly hit us, you stupid idiot!"

Cory stands there with a scowl, accompanied with heavy breathing.

"Really, you wanna yell at me again when I've done nothing wrong. I'm starting to think you've done gone off the deep end!"

Tara's eyes grow wide under her sunglasses.

"That's the second time this week I've been called crazy. I'd rather be crazy than be a secretive lying asshole like you."

When the pieces come together, Cory's expression doesn't change at all.

"You're mad because I tried to tell you before about going to check out a college? Every time I tried, you changed the subject. Then you are nuts, you crazy bitch."

"I'll show you crazy if you wanna see crazy!"

She reaches into her Kia Sportage and pulls out a tire iron, ready to fuck up Cory's car. This forces Lloyd to become the peacekeeper.

"Stop it! Both of you are saying things you don't mean. You two are supposed to love each other, and this isn't the way to fix things."

Lloyd gets between them, extending his arms to keep them apart.

"No, I'm done being treated this way. I'm through with you Cory and every other guy treating me like this. Don't ever bother me again, ya selfish prick."

Cory's mouth gets the best of him before he realizes it. "Up yours, ho bag! You're no better than that tramp Vanessa—just another pretty face trying to fuck your way to a better life."

Tara's mouth dips open with crocodile tears forming in her eyes.

"Cory, that's enough! Take it back right now. You love her, and you damn well know it. She's a wonderful woman to have. Now you both need to cool it before you say anything else you will regret."

Hearing enough, Cory waits until Lloyd looks back to Tara as she sniffles, trying to keep her tears from free flowing down her cheeks.

Turning his back proves costly, as Cory places his hands on Lloyd, shoving him directly into Tara and sending them both onto the blacktop.

"Go have her make you a real man, Lloyd."

Cory gets back into his car, dashing around the corner.

"Son of a bitch. What the hell is wrong with you two?" Lloyd says, helping Tara back to her feet.

"He ain't getting away with this!"

Getting into her car, Tara doesn't wait for Lloyd to climb back into the passenger's seat. She tries to chase Cory to continue their scuffle.

"Hey, at least take me home!" Lloyd screams, standing in the street.

"God, this place blows," he says, flopping his hands down to his side as he walks to meet his mother at the diner.

Cory gains some distance from Tara, making his way back to the point with everyone else. He throws his car shifter in neutral and rips the e-brake. He power slides into the parking lot, squalling the tires until he comes to a complete stop.

"Yeah, Core, way to make those tires squall, buddy boy!" Joe calls out, cupping his hands around his mouth.

Minutes after getting out, he vanishes into the crowd. Tara pulls up, blocking the Celica from getting away.

"Cory, you motherfucker, where the hell are you?" she screams, looking around, trying to find him.

"I'm not finished with you yet."

She begins shoving people out of her way, knocking some of them to the ground in her heated search.

"He's over here!" she hears Kayla call out back toward the other side of the parking lot.

"Thanks, loud mouth. Like I need to hear them argue. It's bad enough I'm still pissed over how you disrespected my father's church."

Breaking away from his hand, Kayla reignites their feud.

"I'm still pissed at you too, asshole, so don't start with me."

Rick tries to walk away when Kayla runs up, shoving him in the small of his back.

"Come on, pussy, fight back!" she cries, pushing Rick's buttons.

"Stop it right now. I'm not doing this. I love you, but you need to calm down. Take that thing there with you while I talk Cory down." He points over to Tara, trying to defuse them.

"I'd rather get hit by a car than listen to you ever again."

Kayla walks away backward, flipping both Cory and Rick the bird, unaware of a race that's in progress. She slips on some loose gravel along the edge of the road. She panics when she and everyone else hear the blaring horn. Rick rushes to get to her when he realizes she's too scared to move out of the way.

She's almost back to her feet when she's suddenly struck by a blue Subaru WRX. She's tossed from bumper to bumper, landing hard on the pavement, rolling several feet and bouncing less with each roll.

"Kayla!" Tara shrieks in terror as Cory and Rick dash over to her.

"Don't move her yet. We need to support her head," Cory orders, rushing to help Rick roll her over since she's face down on the road.

"No, no, no, please be okay. Someone call 911 now!" Rick pleads. Everyone is in a total state of shock when the WRX doesn't even stop or turn around to check on Kayla.

"Whose car is that?" Cory cries after helping Rick roll Kayla onto her back.

"Rick, *Rick*!" he screams, holding onto her head.

"Go get help. Take Tara with you. Hurry!" Cory demands, knowing it's not looking good.

Cory looks down to see the damage inflicted by the car. Kayla is cut up from head to toe. Her face is busted open. She's barely moaning before she begins to gurgle, coughing up blood from her lips.

"Hey! Go get her help now!" Cory repeats, trying to keep Kayla from moving her head.

Realizing she's in bad shape, Cory stays behind when Rick and Tara go for help. It feels like time stands still as Cory talks to Kayla to keep her still.

"It's okay, Kayla. I got you. Just don't move. You're going to be okay." He knows better, though. She's already coughed up blood.

She's beginning to gag with each cough, trying to get her breath.

"Hold on, Kayla. Help is coming. You can't give up," Cory tries to soothe her, fighting back his own emotions to keep her from panicking.

Moments later, everyone can hear the echo of sirens approaching.

"Fuzz, everyone run!" Joe calls out, causing a stir of panic when reality enters the crowd again.

Not budging at all, Cory stays where he is with Kayla as Joe kneels beside him.

"That was Frankie's new car. I can't believe that he would hit her and keep going," Joe reveals, covering his mouth in shock.

Cory can't seem to wrap his mind around Frankie being that careless.

"Joe, get out of here. If she dies, you don't wanna be here to see that."

"No, I can't leave you here like this. What can I do to help?" Joe takes Kayla's hand, talking to her. "Hey, Kayla, don't leave us please. I never told you this, but I've had the biggest crush on you for a long time now." His eyes fill with tears as he pulls her wrist to his face, lightly kissing it.

"It's not good. Please leave, Joe. You don't want this burned into your mind forever."

Joe shakes his head, refusing to go. Kayla begins to go into convulsions for a when the paramedics pull up with Sherriff Dubois behind them.

"Cory, what happened?" she questions, seeing Kayla's blood covering his hands and shirt.

"She got hit during an argument with me and Rick and Tara. I think it was Frank's car that hit her. He didn't stop, Mom."

Looking down at Kayla, she knows it's only a matter of time. "Boys, leave now, both of you."

She slips on a pair of latex gloves to assist the paramedics.

"Fellas, you're going to have to rush it. She's fading fast," the sheriff advises, looking into Kayla's eyes.

"I said leave. I mean it, Cory! You and Joe both get out of here."

Cory gets to his feet as she begins to shake again, darker blood spitting up with her coughing. The paramedics hurry to get her strapped to the backboard. After placing a brace around her neck and loading her onto the stretcher, they rush her to the back of the ambulance. Once they're about to pick up the stretcher, they hear Kayla give one final deep gasp as her chest stops moving.

"Bag her and begin compressions!"

The boys hear them as they stand there with Sheriff Dubois.

"No," she sighs, pulling the boys close to her body.

"Mom, no ... she's ..." Cory stutters, wiping his eyes.

"I'm so sorry, son."

Cory begins to break down in tears when he hears Rick and Tara pulling up behind them. Unable to move, they stand there facing the ambulance when the other two creep up and see the expressions on each of their faces.

"No ..." Tara whispers, seeing Cory and his mother crying.

Suddenly, one of the paramedics peeks around the edge of the ambulance. "Sherriff, we need to see you."

He looks at the ground when he calls for her.

"*No*!" Rick shouts, falling to his knees. "God, no, don't take her from me!"

Following the paramedic into the rear of the ambulance, Sheriff Dubois places her hand over Kayla's eyes, closing them for the last time.

"Go with an angel to face God, you sweet beautiful young woman. I guess it's my job to call it now. Time of death: five minutes after noon. She's singing with the angels now."

Sheriff Dubois places her other hand over her eyes, trying to control the pain. She's unaware that Cory has been secretly following her and listening on the other side of the rear door.

Turned back to his friends, Cory dips his head as he walks back, shaking it from side to side. Walking up, he puts his arms around Tara, pulling her in tightly, trying to comfort her. She grips him with all her might, unable to control her grief.

Joe is walking up to the ambulance when he sees the sheriff hop out of the back.

"Mrs. Dubois, I know who hit her. It was Frankie for sure, ma'am. I can't believe he would keep running."

With her hands on his shoulders, she locks eyes with him. "You'll be required to testify that in court. I'm going to arrest him now, so head down with Cory and the others to the station to make your statements."

Joe signals that he understands and walks away.

"Cory, Tara, Rick, all of you get down to the station now. There's nothing else you can do here. I mean it, get down there or else you'll be in serious trouble. I'm bringing in the driver of the car for charges."

They can't move, still stuck in a moment of shock.

"I said get moving!" she commands, pointing to their cars.

Heeding her warning, the kids climb into the Man-Van where, Cory reveals what he knows.

"Frankie's going to pay for this."

Rick can't accept that Kayla is gone. "She's alive, I know it. She can't be gone."

Tara places her hand on his arm. "I wish that were true, Rick, but Cory, what do you mean Frankie will pay. Did he hit her?"

Cory acknowledges with a simple head nod.

"He's dead," Rick grumbles, dropping the van into gear to head for the sheriff's station.

Nearly an hour goes by before Sheriff Dubois arrives with Frankie in handcuffs. Without thinking, Rick rushes him, spearing him with all his strength. Before he can begin a physical assault, two deputies get their hands on Rick, pulling him away.

"Get him in a cool-down cell, now!" the sheriff orders, picking Frank off the floor. "You're being formerly charged with manslaughter, reckless driving, and failure to control your vehicle, causing bodily damage," she informs him, tossing him into a cell after she uncuffs his wrists. "Did all of you get a report filled out?" All four eyewitnesses reply, "Yes" before she waves them away. "Go home. Cory go get your car and go home. I am sorry to say kids, she's gone. If you need anything, I am a phone call away."

Fighting back the tears, Rick stands there, walking out of the cell.

"I'm good. Let's go," he says in a shaky voice.

"Mrs. Dubois, can you please take me home?" Tara asks, not wanting to see Cory covered with Kayla's blood.

"Yeah, I'll have Deputy Lewis here run you home. If you need anything, please don't hesitate to ask or call, day or night."

She walks over to Tara, embracing her as the boys have left the station.

"She's in a much better place now, but if you'll excuse me, I need to be there when her parents identify her body."

Tara is unable to let go, burying her face into the sheriff's chest. "I don't wanna let go yet …"

"Lewis, could you go to the hospital morgue for me please. I can't leave her like this. And someone needs to be there for the Spencer's for support.

"Yes, Sheriff, it'd be my honor to assist since you were close to everyone involved."

Closing her eyes Mrs. Dubois instantly goes from sheriff to comforting parent, holding Tara in her arms, letting her cry until she can't cry anymore.

The fallout from this event is only about to begin.

CHAPTER 15

Broken Hearts

Just days after her tragic death, Kayla's funeral has RiverCreek buzzing. It's the headline for the news station as the case develops. News stations from all over the state have arrived to report on the case.

Rick has become a ghost. No one has seen him since dropping Cory off at his car. Worried, his parents have requested a missing person's report to be issued from the sheriff's office. He doesn't resurface until the morning of the funeral.

Unable to go inside the church, Cory sits on the hood if his car. He's sitting there in his suit, ignoring the humidity that is causing him to sweat like crazy. He's sitting there trying to get the images out of his mind when he notices Rick pulling into the church parking lot.

"Hey there he is." He slides off his hood, making his way back to Rick. "Where you been, brother?"

As he keeps his face forward, it is clear that something has happened to Rick.

"You ain't my brother. My brother wouldn't have allowed her to die. It's all you and that bitches' fault."

Rick plants an open palm in Cory's face, shoving him away from the van.

"Dude, what the hell?"

Rick doesn't budge at all. "He's dead, just wait. I will kill

Frankie, and if you get in my way, I will take you down too, white boy."

Rick starts his van again, backing out onto the road and pulling away.

"Rick, stop!" Cory can only stand there, unsure of what to do. Still feeling as if he's lost his grip on reality Cory rips off his jacket, flinging it on the ground.

"I can't handle this anymore. Tara's pissed at me, Rick's gone, Kayla's dead—what else could go wrong?"

Cory bends over, picking up his jacket and returning to his car. He tosses it into the back seat. After unbuttoning his dress shirt, he throws it into the car as well. He's standing there in his gray slacks with a black muscle shirt, pounding his fist against the roof of his car.

Barely able to hear a racket of banging outside, Tara quietly leaves after the preacher finishes his sermon. She can't watch the pallbearers march up around the closed casket.

Unable to breathe, Tara gets outside to see Cory striking his car. She goes up to him. It's the first time they've talked in days.

"Hey, are you doing okay?"

He just stands there, unable to speak.

"Listen, I'm sorry, and I miss you. I love you, and I am so sorry about all this. It's tearing me apart, and I can't take you hurting." They stand there in silence.

"Please say something to me. I can't take this. I lost my best friend, and I'm losing you too. My heart is killing me, Cory. Talk to me!"

She latches onto him, trying to get any kind of reaction out of him.

"I can't do this," he mutters, stepping back to open his car door.

Standing there as tears fill her eyes once again, Tara can't move as she listens to Cory start his car and pull away.

"Come back," she stammers, beginning to shake at the onset of a panic attack.

As he races around the empty streets, Cory drives like a man possessed, trying to shake everything he's feeling, from the pain of losing his friends to the constant replay of Kayla being run over. His mind is nearly at the breaking point when he almost crashes head-on into a telephone poll.

He throws his car into neutral as he sits there, trying to catch his breath. He can't feel his hands when his panic attack strikes him. Unable to breathe, Cory pops his door open, falling to the pavement only to roll around for several seconds.

He's nearly to the point of blacking out when he feels a set of hands grabbing him.

"Come on Cory, you need help," he hears as Lloyd picks him up.

"I-I-I-I-I can't breathe." He huffs, trying to suck in air.

"I have ya, Cory. Calm down. Just relax. You're safe."

Lloyd gets him over to the sidewalk, where Cory collapses again.

"Hang on. I'll get you help." Lloyd runs, banging on windows. "Call Sheriff Dubois. Her son needs help ASAP!" he calls out, trying not to panic.

Clutching his chest, Cory feels as if he's about to experience his heart explode. "I'm sorry, Tara. I love you. Forgive me. Please, forgive me. Marry me …" he rambles, losing focus as everything begins to fade to black.

He's brought back to life by the use of smelling salt. After opening his eyes, he's greeted by his mother sitting beside him with Lloyd standing behind her.

"Mom … what happened?" Cory pulls himself up, resting his hand against his forehead.

"You blacked out, son. Lloyd found someone to get ahold of me, and thank goodness. You need to see a doctor. You haven't been the same since that day."

Taking her hand to get back on his feet, Cory stands there, holding his head, feeling it pound as his vision slowly pulses back into focus with each heartbeat.

"I'm fine, Mom. Just need to be alone for a while."

She places a hand on his shoulder. "No, son, that's the last thing you need right now. Lloyd, would you care to stick with him for the day, please."

With a nod, he goes over, snatching the keys from Cory's pocket. "You're with me. C'mon, let's go talk."

The boys walk away with Lloyd putting his arm around Cory for balance. Sheriff Dubois stands there, feeling a heavy burden over herself, unable to protect her son from the pain he's experiencing.

"Don't do anything stupid, Cory. That's all I ask. I couldn't bear losing you." She wipes a tear from her eye.

The clouds continue to hang over the town like a bad omen as time ticks with no sound.

A couple of hours later, the two boys have found their way back to the point. They're surprised that everyone from school has once again gathered. This time, it's for a memorial tribute to Kayla. Each of them places a rose where her dried blood stained the road.

"Hey Cory, hey Lloyd, I got each of you a rose to place in case you showed up," Tara explains, handing each of them a white rose.

"Thank you, Tara," Lloyd says, gently taking his to place it with all the others already resting on the heated pavement.

"Cory, please talk to me. It's killing me seeing you like this. I still love you."

She goes to touch his face with her hand when he jerks away, closing his eyes as he kneels to drop his rose softly.

"I can still see her eyes looking at mine. I can hear her gasping for air. How do I get over that?" Cory says softly in a struggle to keep Kayla's stare from flashing in his eyes.

Lloyd and Tara both come up behind, kneeling with him.

"It'll take time, man. You did your best. You was able to be there," Lloyd explains in his attempt to comfort his friend.

"It's all my fault. If I had just listened to you, none of this would've happened," Cory replies.

Slowly leaning forward a bit more, his left hand balances the tilted weight while his right hand stays over his eyes.

"It's just as much my fault too. I'm sorry I was so stupid. Please, don't blame yourself. Come here, baby. It will be okay, I promise."

Tara gets on her knees, pulling Cory to her, wrapping her arms around him.

"Let it go. I got you." She sobs as Lloyd and everyone else come close to help comfort the two of them.

"We're all here for both of you," Joe calls out from somewhere hidden in the crowd.

"Yeah! Frankie ain't getting away with this one. We all saw him keep going!" a female voice cries out in anger.

"You're the man, Cory!" one of this other teammate's yells, throwing his fist into the air.

"For Kayla. We will never forget!" his teammate announces as everyone else reaches an arm out, extending them toward the heavens.

Feeling the support of everyone around him, Cory's pain begins to ease a bit for the first time in days. "Thank you, everyone," he says, pulling away from Tara.

"Hey, Cory, come on, we'll head to my place. Gotta keep my promise to your mom," Lloyd says, hoping to get him away from the scene of the accident.

"Mind if I tag along?" Tara asks, looking down at Cory.

"You're my guest, so yes, you can come," Lloyd replies before Cory has a chance.

Lloyd gives Cory and Tara a helping hand to their feet; the three of them glide over to her car.

"I won't stay long. I just want to make sure you're going to be okay."

Lloyd waves her weak excuse off.

"You can stay as long as you need to stay with us. I'll order us a couple of pizzas and just relax."

Tara smiles looking over at him. "Thank you," she whispers when they begin to pull away.

After the trio arrive at the trailer, the three of them get inside to the A/C escaping the blazing humidity. Cory is still hanging his head low as he flops down on the couch.

"If you don't mind, I'll order food and leave you two alone to talk," Lloyd suggests, heading back to his room.

"You don't—"

Tara is cut off mid-sentence.

"Shut it! You two need each other, and I know you love each other too. Now, knock off this foolishness and fix this. I love ya both like family. Now, work it out."

Taken by surprise, Tara sits there staring at Lloyd, motioning for her to turn her chair around to face Cory. He doesn't budge until she does just that and reaches out to him.

"Hey, hey, look at me, please. It's killing me to see you like this."

Cory sits there motionless.

"Can you tell me this much. Do you still love me?"

Cory acknowledges her with a nod.

"I love you too, so can we fix this please?"

He shakes his head no.

"Why? I want to be with just you—no one else. You're who I need, Cory, and you need me. Especially right now, don't make me come over there."

Watching him sit there and breathe, Tara tries to scoot across to him quietly. "I mean it. I'll get you."

She rushes onto his lap, pinning his shoulders to the back of the couch. "I got you, baby boy!"

He keeps his head low without uttering a single word. Frustrated with his attitude, Tara places her hands firmly on each side of his head, yanking his face to meet hers.

"You're better than this!" she tells him, planting her lips on his.

Signs of life begin to return when he takes his arms to hold Tara's body, pulling her in close. She moans, feeling his touch against her skin as he shifts his arm under her blouse. The intensity soars, causing the room to fade away.

With her eyes closed, all Tara can see around her is the heat of the moment as the fiery colors swirl all around them. As she's connected to Cory, her body weakens from the anguish, filling with passion all over again.

The two of them are oblivious that food has arrived. Lloyd takes an entire pizza pie back to this room, allowing them to reconnect.

God, I hope this fixes things, he tells himself in his mind and closes his door to drown out the noises coming from the living room.

Tara can't hold out any longer. She's feeling the sensation overwhelming her body's desire to take Cory once again.

"Can I have you?" she leans in to whisper in his ear.

"I don't have anything on me to be safe."

Unconcerned over his words, she whispers, "Worth the risk. I need you."

Listening to her say that, Cory takes her from sitting on his lap and tosses them down on the couch. Unable to control his actions, he immediately begins to remove their clothes.

"Are you sure?" he whispers one final time.

Resting up against Tara's body, ready to let him penetrate deep into her body, she gives him an answer.

"Just do it!" She pulls him into her, making herself shudder as he begins to thrust.

Lloyd hears the commotion growing as both of them groan louder. He turns on his radio. That isn't enough when Tara begins screaming.

"Bloody hell, Cory, don't kill the poor girl," he comments to himself, cranking up the tunes even higher.

Burrowing her fingernails into Cory's back so deeply, she draws droplets of blood, which rise to the surface of the broken skin.

"Yes, Cory, goddamn, you feel so much better this way," she grumbles, squeezing her legs around his forceful hips, plunging with everything he has into her body.

He's lightly biting her neck when he feels his own release being pushed past the point of no return. Allowing his instincts to take control over his actions, Cory picks up speed, pounding harder into Tara's lower region, sending her into a frenzy of pleasure combined with pain.

"Cory," she expels, squeezing around his penis with all her might, sending his body the signal to release deep inside of hers.

"Tara," she hears him say, releasing his grip on her neck with his final push into her body, shoving with everything he has, sending wave after wave of semen into her womb.

Lying there together in a lake of sweat, Tara tenderly rests her arms over Cory's shoulders. She tries to catch her breath when it dawns on her exactly what happened minutes earlier.

"Oh, my God, did we just seriously do that without protection." She gasps, opening her eyes wide.

"Yes, we did. Do you regret it?" As she pushes Cory off her breasts, fear takes control.

"Us doing this, no, but taking the chance we just did, fuck, yes. I don't want kids yet. Oh, God, get off of me!"

Tara pushes and shoves her way from under Cory, landing hard on the floor.

"It'll be fine. The more you worry, the more it could happen," Cory advises, rolling over and slipping on his boxers and pants.

"Fuck you, all right. You're not the one who would have to carry a baby. God, how can you can be such an asshole?"

Getting dressed in a rush, Tara leans in, slapping Cory across the face. "Glad you're not worried."

Cory swiftly gets to his feet. "If you ever get pregnant by me, I will be there, and I will take care of both of you."

Humiliated, Tara reaches out, lightly kissing the red mark on Cory's cheek. "I'm sorry, but my past seems to keep haunting me."

"I'm not him. I'm me. I can't be both. Either accept me for who I am and love me or go back to what you know."

Hunkering her head low, Tara stands there upset.

"Let your past go," Cory says, moving to the side, heading for the door. "Tell Lloyd thank you for me—for everything. I love you Tara, but I can't do this if you're gonna treat me like this."

He takes off out the door after picking up his keys from the coffee table.

"Cory, wait," she pleads, reaching out to stop him.

"I love you," he states, going out the door without looking back.

Hearing the front door open and slam closed, Lloyd comes out to see Tara standing there. "Everything okay?"

She doesn't budge. "Yes, and Cory said thank you for everything. I have to go too, Lloyd. You've been a real sweetheart." Tara turns around to face him before she leaves.

As Tara gives him a peck on the cheek, he sees the anguish in her eyes.

"What'd he do now?"

She shakes her head before she speaks.

"Nothing. It's on me again. I'm so stupid to not see how different he is, and I've ruined it all over again." Hiding her grief, she takes off, slamming into the screen door and running away.

"This is why I gave up finding love here," he says, standing there alone in the middle of the living room.

A few weeks go by, and relief comes when Tara's period hits. Excited for once when she feels the familiar pain of cramps, she calls Cory to share the news.

"Hey, Cory, it's me. Wanted to tell you we're good from that day at Lloyd's."

He sits there at his desk in his room just as nonchalant as that day. "I knew it would come. Anyway, how are you doing?"

She's relieved to hear him sounding more like his old self.

"I'm good. I miss you. Can we go talk or out to eat sometime soon?"

He turns her request into something different.

"Actually, I was about to go looking for Rick. He's still missing, and his parents are worried. You can tag along if you want. I'm heading to Minneapolis to see if he's anywhere we've been up that way."

Not thinking twice about the chance to spend time with him, she jumps at the opportunity.

"Yeah, I'm on my way." She closes her phone and escapes for her Kia.

Arriving at his house, she sees him waiting on the edge of his hood. "Hurry up. We got a lot of traveling to do," he instructs, sliding down to get into the driver's seat.

"Let's go!" she says, closing the passenger side door.

"We will, but first come here!" he orders, taking her by the shirt between her breasts, pulling her in for a prolonged kiss. "I'm sorry, forgive me?" he wonders out loud as he releases his grip.

"Always and forever," Tara tells him reaching back to buckle herself into the seat.

"Good, I needed my space, and I feel so bad about hurting you."

"Water under the bridge, my sweet Cory."

She smiles, feeling every bit of weight lifting from her shoulders.

"Good, let's go find Rick. He hasn't been seen since the funeral," Cory reveals with a gleam of hope.

Tara's expression goes from smiling and happy-go-lucky to concerned. "Let's go see if we can find him and bring his ass home."

They're about twenty miles away from RiverCreek when Tara sees the Man-Van parked at a vacant parking lot. "Cory, turn right!" she screams, pointing over.

"Good eye, beautiful" he says, nearly missing the turn.

"Let me approach him. The last time we bumped into each other, it was a mess," Cory says, unsure about how things will go this time.

"Be careful, please." Tara gulps hard, her heart rate rising.

Leaving the car door open with the engine running, Cory creeps up to the edge of the van. He peeks into the rear hatch, where he sees Rick passed out cold. All around him there's an arrangement of beer cans. Pounding on the glass, Cory stirs him out of his drunken slumber.

"Rick! Wake up!" He continues to pound until Rick extends his hand, flipping Cory his middle finger high in the air.

"Fuck off, white boy!"

"That's the last time you're going to call me that, you son of a bitch," Cory says. He opens the hatch and yanks Rick from the van by the wrist.

Fearing the worst is about to happen, Tara takes out her phone from her purse, calling the sheriff.

"Mrs. Dubois, we've found Rick. We're out by this old store. Uh, I think it says Hex on the side. Please hurry."

Mrs. Dubois' radio can be heard in the background. "I'm on the way. I'll radio the station near there. I know exactly where you are."

Cory kneels, trying to keep Rick conscious. "Time to go home, Rick. We're all worried about you."

Rick opens his eyes, clutching Cory by the throat. "It's your fault, you sorry worthless prick. If it wasn't for you and that bitch, Kay would still be here."

Watching from the Celica, Tara gasps when she sees Rick get to his feet, still choking Cory. Cory uses his hands to break the grip from around his throat and shoves Rick back into the edge of the rear of the van.

"It was an accident, and I've done beat myself up over it more than you ever could."

When he hears Cory state that, Rick reacts with his own hands. "Yeah, beat your ass—that's exactly what I'm gonna go."

Balled up his fist, Rick swings, nearly connecting with Cory's jaw. Natural reaction takes control of Cory as he steps in, swinging on Rick, connecting against Rick's exposed ribs.

"Not this time, Rick! I've tried to talk to you and wanted to help, but now I'm just gonna hurt ya."

Cory front kicks Rick, connecting a solid blow into Rick's junk, forcing him to the ground. "I'm done being nice!" He steps over Rick, kneeing his side several times until he hears the echoes of sirens approaching and backs away.

Within a matter of moments, three state troopers pull up and see Cory standing near Rick's fallen and battered body.

"Son, back away now," one of the officers orders, placing his hand on his weapon.

"Yes, sir. My mother is the Sheriff of RiverCreek. We were out looking for Rick here. When we found him, he attacked me first sir." Confused by the statement, the state trooper speaks up.

"What do you mean we?"

Cory points back to his car where they notice Tara sitting in the seat.

"Miss, come out here please," they call out, waving her over to them as Cory keeps his hands raised over his head.

"Could you tell us exactly what happened here?"

Startled, Tara looks over to Rick, still seething in pain on the ground.

"Yes. I seen his van, and when we pulled up, my boyfriend

went to check on him and help him come home. That's when Rick, the guy on the ground there, attacked Cory, my boyfriend. He was just defending himself, I swear."

Two officers step between the boys.

"Young man, come with me please. Your mother is on her way here. She called our station to relay your position. We'll hold you two here until she arrives. Now, as for your friend, I can smell the alcohol from his vehicle and, he's going with us before we can release him. Son, public intoxication is a serious offense in this state. How old are you?"

As he groans in pain, Rick lifts his head with his eyes still closed.

"Almost eighteen, worthless, racist pigs," he calls out, unaware of how much trouble he's about to land in.

"Excuse me, I know you're not referring to me being an Asian police officer," the first officer on the scene says, turning around and kneeling toward Rick.

"Son, I'm the same race as you. I wasn't dumb enough to screw up my life," he tells him, trying to ease his worries.

"White boy there killed my girl. He killed Kayla!" Rick screams.

Concerned over the comment, the officers stand and point to Cory. "Don't move!"

"She was struck by a car racing a few weeks ago! I tried to save her, I swear. Look it up," Cory cries out, placing his hands in the air once again.

They help Rick to his feet, locking his hands together behind his back with cuffs. The officer near Cory comes over and has him do the same.

"Turn around. We're detaining you until Sheriff Dubois arrives and clears your story."

Cory follows their instructions as they place cuffs around his wrists and sit him in the back of the cruiser.

"Miss, please go sit on the hood of the car," one of the officer's orders, pointing to the Celica.

Tara does as she's told until Cory's mother arrives.

She rushes over to the state troopers. "Release my son

immediately. He was doing me a favor searching for Mr. McGuiness."

The trooper signals over to his officers to release Cory. "Sorry, old friend. Mr. McGuiness there accused your son of killing this Kayla girl—"

Her reactions say it all. "Remember the girl I told you my son watched die a little while back? That was Rick's girlfriend. He is drunk, so release him to my custody, and I will take him back to sober up. I'll pull his license and release him to his parents. You wanna tow his car, be my guest."

Ronald takes her request, calling in for a tow truck while Sheriff Dubois transfers Rick into her cruiser.

"Thanks, fellas. I'll see ya around," she calls out once Rick is placed safely in the backseat of the cruiser.

They release Cory as he's prepared to return to RiverCreek.

"Stay out of trouble, young man," he's told when the cuffs fall from his wrists.

"Yes, sir. Bye." Cory rushes back to his car, waving for Tara get in.

"You had me worried!" she yells once the doors are shut.

"You and me both. Let's get home and find out what's going to happen."

Together, they make their way back to RiverCreek, where tensions have been running high since the day Kayla passed away. The community is on edge, wondering what's going to happen when Frankie's trial gets a confirmed date. The outcome is the hottest subject on everyone's lips. Even news reporters speculate on what will happen once a verdict is reached.

CHAPTER 16

The Trial and Outcome

The kids' senior year is well underway by the time a judge is ready to begin the pretrial process. Rumors spread rapidly that it'll be Judge Klifton, a well-known name in law and politics. This judge is a country club member who is extremely close to Frankie's family.

One day after school, Tara is home researching the details about the judge with Cory sitting behind her.

"Says here that he's an easy-going guy. Typical country-club-donating older white judge who's been accused of allowing the rich side of town to get away with quite a bit in the past."

Rolling his eyes, Cory's misgivings are clear. "Figures. Best lawyers from his dad's firm in Minneapolis, and now a family friend hearing it all. He's going to get off Scot-free!"

Her gut instincts churn when she listens to him rant. "I hope you're wrong. Kayla deserves to have him put away for life, if you ask my opinion."

Trying to move past the court stuff, Tara leans back in her seat. "Hey, let's go get something to eat. I'm starving. Besides, we've been cooped up over this way too much lately."

Cory runs his fingers through her hair. "Yeah, babe, you're right. Let's go. Oh, and hey, Kayla will get justice. I know it. I feel it."

Tara smiles as she gets to her feet.

"Let's take my car this time," Tara suggests.

Cory signals okay with his hand. He transitions his signal for Tara to lead the way so he can watch her shake her ass down the steps.

"Enjoy the view," she says, knowing exactly why he's a few extra feet behind her.

"Always have, always will."

She blushes, taking her keys from the hook by the door.

By the time the news story breaks concerning the case, the cold air from Canada has begun dropping the temperature in RiverCreek.

"Good evening, residents of RiverCreek. This is Gayle Anderson, reporting live from the steps of the courthouse. We're about to learn details concerning the Ford case in just a few moments. Hopefully, we will get an idea of when proceedings will begin."

Seconds later, the sheriff and the lawyers come bursting from the doors leading from the courthouse. They approach the microphone, and Sheriff Dubois introduces the gentlemen.

"Ladies and gentlemen, thank you for your patience. From the pretrial proceedings, we have a bit of information to pass along. For starters, the press will not be allowed inside the courtroom. The families of those involved will be present. When the verdict is handed down I will read it to you then but not beforehand. That is all, other than announcing that the case will head to trial on October 1. Thank you."

The short press release travels swiftly around town.

"Hope he fries in hell!" Rick says, watching it live behind everyone else, trying to get questions to the sheriff and each of the lawyers.

A collective sigh cascades through RiverCreek as the times passes before the opening arguments. Frankie has since been released to home confinement, with a private tutor sent from the Board of Education. Rick has his own agenda, casing the house on occasion, hoping to find a way to get his hands on Frankie.

"I'm going to fucking kill you," he whispers every time he walks by there as a red fury blurs his judgement.

On October 1, the lawyers push their way by the reporters coming from as far away as California and New York, each reporter trying to gain access to any new information.

"Excuse me, sir, please, a word about what's about to happen privately," Gayle Anderson shouts over the roar of the crowd.

The lawyers are met by deputies helping escort them away from the circus of reporters.

"Thanks, boys. I never imagined this little town would get this kind of exposure," Frankie's attorney says, wiping his brow with a handkerchief.

"Come on, they're waiting," the deputy states in an annoyed tone.

Waltzing into the courtroom, the deputies close the doors, standing guard outside as the proceedings begin.

"Good morning, counselors I trust everyone is ready. Sheriff Dubois, if you would like to make an opening statement for the record, I'll allow you the time you need."

Once she's to her feet, the sheriff approaches the bench and stops a few feet from the podium.

"Thank you, Judge Klifton. I'm here today, along with the paramedics and autopsy reports that indicate what happened physically to Kayla Spencer. Since my three key witnesses weren't allowed to testify, I must be their voice of reason. One of these witnesses was my own son, Your Honor. Over the course of this trial, I will prove why Franklin Ford deserves to sit behind bars for a good portion of his life."

"Thank you, Sheriff. I look forward to hearing your testimony. Counsel for the defendant, do you have a statement ready at this time?"

Standing from his seat, Frankie's lawyer patiently waits for Sheriff Dubois to take her seat.

"Yes, Your Honor, my client has admitted his wrongdoing to the family of Kayla Spencer since the time of the accident—which is exactly what is sounds like, an accident—that took the life of a dear, sweet young lady. We won't hide the fact that speed played a part in this case, although his car was doing as the driver wanted. Miss Spencer knew the danger that day of walking near the edge of the road."

Kayla's father isn't able to contain his emotions when he listens to Frank's lawyer spout off about his daughter.

"Hey, asshole, that's my little girl, and she's not here to defend herself. Shut the fuck up about shit you don't know about. You weren't there to see it happen."

Frankie turns around in his seat, popping off before anyone else. "Neither was you. Now shut it before I come back here and knock your teeth down your damn throat."

Pounding the gavel, Judge Klifton takes control of his courtroom.

"Order! Order! Both of you, pipe down before you're held in contempt. Thank you, Counsel. Time for the prosecution to stake their claim in this case."

"Thank you, Your Honor. From today through the final day of this trial, I will cross-examine not just the sheriff and Mr. Ford here, but we will dig up the exact causes of this case and attempt to ensure that no one else will suffer the fate this poor young lady had to endure."

As hours turn into days, the prosecuting attorney attempts to build his case. It's the in the middle of the second week before Sheriff Dubois takes the stand.

"Witness for the prosecution, Your Honor. I'd like to call Sheriff Dubois to the stand."

After making her way to the stand, she settles into her seat, then places her hand on the Bible, swearing to tell the truth as she knows it.

"So, Sheriff, how long have you served this community?" The prosecuting attorney asks.

"Nearly eight years as sheriff. Before that, I was a deputy for the three previous sheriffs."

Pacing back and forth, the attorney comes up with his next question. "In your own words, please describe to the best of your ability the accounts of the day in question. Why do you think Mr. Ford ran over Miss Spencer that day?"

"From what I've been able to gather from reports, most of the students from RiverCreek High that were there that day. There was some arguing going on that caused Frankie here to lose his cool once again. As he does, he settles things with a race, since his family has the means to afford the best cars."

"Ah you see, Your Honor, he knew his car was a means to an end of an argument. Given that fact that he knew he could go fast and acted inappropriately makes him guilty. I'm certain you've broken up several races over the years, correct, Sheriff?"

Rolling her eyes toward the ceiling, she recollects her memory.

"Yes, a few, some that nearly had people get injured from reckless driving."

She's stops at that point. "Any before that day involving Mr. Ford?"

"Absolutely, sir. He's wrecked his own car before, rubbing paint with my son's car and a few others as well."

Now pointing over to Frankie, the attorney raises the volume of his voice sharply. "Exactly, careless and thoughtless over the concerns of others. He's created property damage before moving on to running over innocent bystanders."

"Objection, Your Honor! There have been no reports of any of these accusations."

The judge shifts through his papers. "Sustained. Stay on point, Counsel."

With his hands in the air, he continues his questions. "So, according to your own personal observations, Sheriff, please lay out the events that happened when you received the distress call."

"Well, my son's girlfriend, Tara Rose, called in. Panic was in her voice. She was rambling on that Kayla had been struck by a car and that the driver kept going without signs of returning to the scene of the crime. When I arrived behind the paramedics, I witnessed my son keeping Kayla's head still. I watched her fade away as she coughed up more and more blood. When I helped get her fastened to the gurney, they placed her in the back of the ambulance, where she died minutes later."

"When did you discover that Mr. Ford was the driver of the car that had struck Kayla Spencer?"

Sinking in her chair, she closes her eyes, holding back the pain. "His best friend, Joseph Winters, informed me, off to the side, that it was Frankie driving."

"That's all I have, Your Honor. Thank you, Sheriff."

That gives Frank's attorney the opportunity to tear her story apart.

"Yes, Sheriff, thank you, but now I have a few questions for you."

"Go ahead, sir," she says, curling her lips, which have begun to feel dry and cracked.

"Your son, Cory Dubois, is he a trained medical professional?"

Resting hands in her lap she replies, "Almost. He's been studying surgical technology at the votec school since this past January."

Acknowledging her response, he moves on to the second part of his question. "Does he have a current verified certification for CPR or trauma treatment? Did he have to move Kayla Spencer's body in any way that day that could have caused her further internal injury?"

"I'm certain he was cautious. We've talked about how to move an injured person if it ever happened."

He sees the limelight in her words and takes his opportunity to break her apart.

"Exactly true, but what gives you or him the ability to move a patient before qualified, trained personnel arrive? Could he have done more damage when he flipped her body into position? Could that be the very reason why she choked to death on her own blood?"

As white as a ghost in her seat, she has no choice but to answer the question. "It is a possibility, but he's a smart kid. He was calm and collected when I arrived. He's got his sights set on becoming a surgeon." Her statement is exactly what was needed to discredit her son's actions.

"He's in high school still, isn't he? No real medical training. No CPR certification, just gut instinct that could've been the deciding factor in what caused this young lady to die. She was denied treatment before she had received proper treatment from trained professionals licensed to do so."

"Objection, all speculation, Your Honor!" the prosecution attorney yells, rising to his feet in a hurry.

"Overruled. Sheriff, thank you for your testimony. You're excused from any further questions."

Taking a deep breath, she makes one final statement on her own. "You may try to discredit me, sir but this young man knows what he did, which is exactly why he ran to his father to protect him. He's guilty by running off knowing he was about to face justice."

Again, striking several times with his gavel, Judge Klifton points it over to Sheriff Dubois. "That is enough! You are excused from these proceedings from here on out. Bailiff, escort her from my court immediately."

On her way out, Kayla's parents' mouth, "Thank you" as she passes by them. She dips her head to let them know she accepts their gratitude.

One by one, everyone from Frankie and Kayla's parents build character about their kids. The paramedics who responded to the accident even testify. Even letters from the students both kids go to school with are eventually brought in as evidence given the amount of attention to help each side of the argument.

Every day after school, Rick would stand off in the distance, waiting for anything to come from the courthouse. Tara and Cory stand across from him on the other side of the street, staring at him, and occasionally motion for him to join them.

"He still hates me," Cory tells her, trying to get his attention one afternoon.

"He's hurting, baby boy. I miss Kayla too, but I have you to lean on."

Tugging on her shirt, Cory makes his point. "He has me too. I tried to save her. Doesn't that account for anything?"

Able to listen to them, Gayle Anderson turns around to approach the couple. "Excuse me, young man. Did I just hear you say you tried to save the young lady's life?"

Cory nods as they try to get away. "No, please, tell us your side of the events before the verdict comes any moment now."

"Look, lady, all I have to say is this, and this alone. Frankie deserves to rot in jail for a long time. He knew what he did was wrong, and he ran like a coward when his car ran over Kayla. He could see that she tripped in the road and did nothing to avoid hitting her."

Her cameraman catches it all on camera. "Thank you. That's all we need."

Rick sees it all unfold; he rushes across the street, taking the camera and smashing it on the sidewalk.

"Hey, bitch, you ain't twisting my boy's words around to make it how you want it to sound."

Stunned, they all stand there and stare at the destroyed camera.

"You're gonna pay for that!" she yells, looking back to him.

"Bill me," he states, crossing his arms.

Suddenly, the other reporters begin to chatter loudly as they see the lawyers coming from the courthouse.

"This is it. Go grab another camera!" Gayle shrieks, pushing on her cameraman.

"Thank you, ladies and gentlemen of the press, for patiently waiting. We have reached a verdict in this case, and before we read it aloud, there's a young man here who would like to make a statement to the entire community of RiverCreek."

Frankie is waved out to take his place at the podium. Once he clears his throat, he takes out a prepared statement.

"Thank you, everyone, for coming here today." His voice is shaky when he begins his speech. "I am so thankful for everyone involved being honest and truthful over this matter. Like so many others, I am more than ready to put this terrible tragedy behind me and move forward with my life. It saddens me deeply to have caused such pain to not only Kayla's family but to my own and others close to us. Our community will never be the same. It is with a heavy heart that we lost such a bright, beautiful life. She will forever be remembered in our hearts and memories. I will always honor her name and spirit. Thank you."

He goes to leave when reporters begin pouring out questions and comments.

"Did your lawyer prepare that phony statement?" Gayle Anderson asks, rushing to get the closest to the podium.

"Actually, yes he did. Listen, what I did was horrible, and I wish I could take it back, but I can't."

Stopped before he makes his next point, Frankie sees Rick approaching him with tears in his eyes.

"Frankie, I just wanted to say I forgive you!" he yells out over the roar of the crowd.

"Hey, young man, are you friends with my client?" Frankie's lawyer calls out from the podium.

"Yes, we know each other."

He sees it as a chance for a photo opportunity; he motions for Rick to be brought up to them.

"Ladies and gentlemen, as we await the young man to join us, it is my pleasure to announce that other than probation until my client turns twenty-one. Along with the suspension of his driver's license, he has been found not guilty on the charge of second-degree murder. Thank you."

Frankie smiles, standing there with his lawyer, wanting to put this entire ordeal behind him.

Once Rick joins them at the podium, the crowd overhears Frankie say, "I'm sorry about Kayla. I know you loved her, and she was a beautiful soul."

Rick shakes his head, agreeing to what Frankie admits with open arms to embrace in a sympathy hug.

"Bring it in, man. I forgive you," Rick states in a calm but eerie tone.

Taking one hand to shake Frankie's hand, they come close for a hug. That's the chance Rick has been waiting to jump at. When he slips his hand away from Frankie's, takes a Glock 9 millimeter from the front of his belt, and fires almost the entire clip into

Frankie's torso and gut region, spraying blood everywhere as the bullets pass completely through Frankie's body.

The crowd panics and scatters when the first shot rings out. Frankie's head slumps on Rick's shoulder when Rick halts the deadly assault. Rick bounces up to where he can get one last shot off, putting it between Frankie's glazed-over, lifeless eyes.

"Motherfucker, I got you!" he proclaims in victory over the mic.

Cory sends Tara running away from the area as he stands there.

"Rick, no!" he screams, unable to move.

"Sorry, Core, but this is the only thing to make it right. Now run before I have to shoot you too."

Rick points the gun at Cory as he stands there in fear with his eyes shut tightly. Police officers from inside the courthouse storm Rick, tackling him to the ground before he can pull the trigger.

"Get off of me. I'm finished! Let me go, pigs. I'll kill you all!" he shouts repeatedly as he's rolled onto his stomach with cuffs placed tightly around his wrists.

"I'll finish you all off! Cory, Tara, Joe, Kevin, Margie, you're all dead when I get free! This isn't over, not by a longshot, you sons of bitches!"

Cory hasn't moved when his mother comes up to him. "Cory! Cory! Are you hurt?" she asks, shaking him back into reality.

"Yeah—I mean, no. Mom, did he really just do that?"

Unfortunately, she must tell her son, "Yes, Cory, and doing it like this with all these cameras and witnesses, he's probably going to be locked up for life. Go home. This isn't for you to see."

Seeing how he can't move just yet, his mother waves over a deputy.

"Sean, take him to find Tara Rose and take them to my house, please."

Her deputy takes Cory gently by his arm to a cruiser as they go track down Tara a few blocks away.

"Tara Rose?" he calls out, pulling up beside her.

Out of breath, she says, "Yes, sir," placing her hands on her knees.

"Get into the car. By order of the sheriff, I am to drop you both off at her residence."

By the time they're dropped off, Mr. Dubois rushes out to check on the kids.

"Are you two okay? I saw the news and your mother called. How could they be that stupid not to think anyone would go after Frankie?"

Cory looks his father in eyes, needing something made perfectly clear. "Did he kill him, Dad? Did Rick just murder Frankie?"

Without hesitation Mr. Dubois lowers in his head as if he were in prayer. "Yes son, he did, and your mom will be here after she clears the scene. So come on inside now, both of ya, and try to relax. Tara, I've called your mother, and she's fine with you staying here until she closes the store."

"Thank you. I don't wanna be alone right now."

He takes them into his arms, bringing them into the house. A few hours later, Mrs. Dubois comes home covered in Frankie's blood. She tries to sneak inside without being seen, but she fails when she bumps into Tara sitting at the kitchen table.

"Oh my God. Is all that Frankie's blood?"

"Yes, darling, it is. He's gone, and Rick's in deep too. Don't tell Cory. It'll break his heart. How are you doing with all of this? First Kayla, then you two broke up for a little while, and now this. You walked into the hornet's nest."

Tara soaks in everything. She puts her head down on the table, exhausted from it all.

"Hey, sweetheart, go lie down on the couch until your mom gets here. I'm going to get cleaned up, and I'll come out and sit with you."

"Thank you," Tara says, gradually peeling herself from the table and dragging her feet to the couch, where she stretches out using her forearm to block out the light.

It's past eleven o'clock when Olivia pulls up to the house. Knocking lightly on the door, she's greeted by Mr. Dubois.

"Hey, lady, wish I could say this under better circumstances, but I can't. She's been out cold for a few hours now, and she's tore up. Cory is too, so maybe we should hold them from school for a few days."

"I agree. Her father will be home in a few more days and taking his vacation. I'll have him stay with them. He's great at getting them to open up. Cory loves talking to him, especially about cars."

After they exchange a hug, Olivia goes over, picking up Tara in her arms. With her arms around her mother's neck, she nestles up to her shoulder.

"Thanks for keeping her safe."

Mr. Dubois holds the door. "You're more than welcome. We love having her here. You got a wonderful girl there."

The chaos hasn't settled down as the events reach across the state and country, when reporters cover what they experienced in remote broadcasts.

The tragedies have once and for all placed RiverCreek on the map in a negative fashion. Everyone watches replay of Rick's actions—at least what can be shown on TV. These actions that will weigh heavily on both Tara and Cory as time passes after that day.

CHAPTER 17

Unplanned Madness

When the sun rises in the morning, Cory wakes up to the sun high in the sky.

"What in the world?" he says, looking over at his clock. "After nine. Holy hell, I'm late for school!" Cory rushes to get ready when his mother taps on his door.

"Cory, honey, are you decent?"

"Yeah, Mom. I'm good."

She opens his door, seeing him at his dresser, picking out clothes.

"Hey, stop, you're not going to class today. I've done called your principal and explained everything, and he's given you and Tara the rest of the week off."

Cory stands there, unable to process what he's told. "Huh?"

After taking a seat on his bed, she pats it for him to join her.

"You witnessed what Rick did, and it took its toll on you and Tara both. You watched two of your best friends either get killed or commit murder. Your mind ain't gonna be focused on school. Tara has been given the same time away from class to get your minds to settle down. I don't care if you go get her and relax around town, but stay away from the courthouse and the reporters."

"Yes, Mom. We'll probably just hang out and relax then."

Seeing that he's going to follow through with her instructions, she gets up to leave. Before she closes the door, Cory manages to say one last thing.

"Mom, why did Rick do that, knowing he would be caught right there?"

Unsure of what to tell him, she wings it. "Sometimes we do things without caring what happens to us. I hate seeing him go through this too, but there's nothing I can do about it. I love him like a second son, and it's tearing me apart to see him sitting behind bars."

She closes the door, going back to her bedroom, fighting the urge to cry. Cory, meanwhile, takes a shower and leaves to head over to Tara's. When he arrives, he sees her looking out the window, keeping an eye out for him.

"Looks like she's waiting on me."

Strolling up to the door, he twists the knob and heads inside to see her in a nightgown.

"Thought we'd try what we did at Lloyd's to get it out of our system," she admits, feeling embarrassed about him seeing her in the silky white gown.

"Oh, wow," is all he can muster, going to her, picking her up, and placing her legs around his waist.

"All this for me. I'm touched," he says, carrying her up the steps to her bedroom and shutting the door with his foot.

She's already yanked his shirt off, feeling his chest and stomach muscles. "I need you," she murmurs in his ear as he slips her out of the gown, exposing her bare skin to his.

"I can't take not being with you," he replies, slipping his jeans and boxers to the floor.

They kiss for a few minutes, until Tara flips him onto his back. She takes control, sliding down enough for him to shove into her body, making her stride back and forth. He ravishes her body with chills, sinking further onto Cory's hardness.

Fuck, yes, Cory. This feels so good!" she lets out, picking up momentum.

"Don't stop. I'm almost there," Cory tells her, tightening his grip on her hips, helping her grind.

"Not yet, not yet!" she moans as she feels him explode within her body. "Ah, damn it. I said not yet, Cory."

She stops, bringing herself down to lie on his chest.

"You don't love me just because we do this, do you?"

Cory plays with her hair. "I'd love you the same even if we waited. We can stop if you want."

Pulling her head up to meet him in the eyes, she says, "I don't think so."

She scoots up, kissing him again, causing his body to react as the passion between them builds once again.

"Good," he tells her, rolling on top of her, sliding down to work her up by kissing over her breasts.

Arching her back, she places her hands on the back of his head. "Oh, yes. This feels so damn good, Cory! I can't wait. Take me again, now!"

Cory is more than happy to fulfill her wish, plunging deep into her without warming up.

He's ramming into her like a man possessed.

"Yes, yes, yes, that's it, harder," Tara pleads, grabbing her headboard to keep it from banging against the wall.

"Cory!" she screams at the top of her lungs, squeezing when her body can't handle anymore, sending her sexual desire into hyperdrive.

"Oh, Tara." Cory exhales again, shoving into her, releasing a second wave of semen into her body.

"Again?" she questions, looking at him as her vision unblurs.

"Oh, yeah, again."

She moves over so he can get comfy beside her on the bed

"You're more than I deserve," Cory says, pulling Tara over to him, resting her head on his shoulder.

"You're my rock. I'd be lost without you, Tara." She curls up closer to him, closing her eyes, falling asleep she listens to his heartbeat.

A few hours go by before they wake up to the sounds of the elementary school bus dropping kids off along the street.

"Oh, wow. We've been asleep for a while," Tara says mid-yawn.

"Yeah, guess we better get dressed before your mom gets home."

"Oh, she's closing the store so we have all day to ourselves." She takes her hand, resting it on his cheek, turning his lips to meet hers.

Running his hand up the side of her body, he's forgotten that they're naked. When he rubs her breast, he breaks away from their kiss.

"If we don't stop, we're gonna end up doing this again."

Tara smiles. "Good. I can't get enough of you today." She throws herself over his body, working her way down his to his hips.

"You know we're taking a big risk, right?" he mutters, holding her hips firmly.

"Worth the risk, ain't it, handsome? We got lucky before, and I like our chances. You said you'd be there, and well, I don't wanna waste time going out to buy those damn condoms. Besides, it feels so much better without them, don't you agree?"

Cory releases his grip. "Oh, yes, but it's your choice, because I don't wanna stop."

Tara takes that as her cue to take her hand, guiding Cory's manhood into her for the third time in a few hours.

"Ugh, just be a little easier this time. Guess I'm feeling earlier catch up to us," Cory says as Tara goes slow and easy.

"Yeah, I'm feeling it too," she replies with a bit of pain in her eyes.

He lies there, letting her ride him for nearly fifteen minutes before he finally begins to feel himself swelling up to get off again.

"Almost there. Don't stop," he calls out, leaning his head back onto the pillow, preparing to let go of the pressure building within himself.

"I can feel it. Come on, baby, let it go," Tara cries out, keeping up her stride until she feels the familiar sensation of Cory blast inside of her.

She's dizzy when she stops and falls onto her side.

"I can't go anymore; you've nearly killed me," she says, closing her eyes, feeling her body tell her to quit.

"Agreed. Let's get cleaned up and go get something to eat."

Helping each other to their feet, the couple make a dash for the shower down the upstairs hallway.

"Shower together?" Tara suggests, getting out two towels from the closet.

"Sure, that's a first for me." Tara hands him a towel, looking him in the eye.

"Me too. Sounds exciting, doesn't it?" She raises her eyebrows, teasing him to follow her into the shower.

When she adjusts the water temperature, Tara pulls the curtain back, getting in first. "Water's good and hot now."

She sticks a hand out, reaching for Cory.

"Ooh la-la, sexy lady." He takes her offer, joining her under the waterfall style showerhead.

"Oh, that feels amazing," Cory says when the water hits his body.

They once again revert to making out under the water, using their passion to forget about the world. They remain under the water long enough that the hot water disappears, causing Cory to break away.

"Holy shit, that's cold!" he yells, arching his back.

"Oh wow, guess we're finished then."

They get out and dry off before heading back to the bedroom. Tara goes through her drawers while Cory slips back into his clothes quickly.

"In the mood for anything specific?" he wonders out loud, not feeling anything special

"I'm good going to the diner and spending some time there."

Cory bends over, tying his shoes. "Sounds good. But, uh, are we going to do this every day?"

Stopped dead in her tracks, Tara feels a shivering cold impression in her spine.

"We can if you want to. You know, I'm not going to stop you."

On the bed, unsure of what to say next, Cory turns his head, nudging his shoulders. "I have no complaints."

Tara smiles over at him, sending him a wink.

They say very little of anything on their way over to the diner. When they arrive, they find an empty booth. They're greeted by Lloyd's mother.

"Hey, kids, it's good to see you out together. What can I get you today? It's on me? Lloyd will be here in a bit from school."

"I just want a sweet tea, cheeseburger with tomato, mayo, and lettuce, and onion rings," Tara orders, looking at the menu.

"Ugh, I'll have the black bean burrito with salsa and a Pepsi."

Their orders are written down and placed in the window.

"Tara, are you okay?"

Cory's eyes read what he's thinking loud and clear.

"No, like when we were going through town, everything that's happened just hits me. It's eating me inside. I don't know how much more I can take."

Able to rest his head against the top of the booth, Cory understands how she feels. "I know. All I can see are the images of blood—Kayla's and Frankie's blood going everywhere. It makes it hard to breathe at times."

Tara notices that Cory's hands have begun to tremble slightly. "Hey, calm down. You're with me. Calm down my angel. It's okay."

His breathing begins to speed up with shallow breaths.

"Mrs. Trippet, I need you!" Tara screams, trying to help Cory regain control.

Diverting her attention to Cory, Mrs. Trippet takes off from behind the counter to assist Tara with Cory's panic attack.

"Cory, Cory, Cory, it's okay. You're fine, sweetie. It's Lloyd's momma. Come on, follow my voice and slow your breathing down. You're gonna scare Tara to death if you don't calm down." She looks back and points to a pitcher of water sitting on the counter. "Tara, get that and a clean rag for me, now."

She rushes to get what's requested. Tara rushes back, dipping the clean hand towel into the ice water. "Shhh. It's okay, Cory. It's almost over."

She rings it out folding it up, placing it on his forehead.

"He's gonna be fine. Panic attacks are a pain. Lloyd used to get them when he came out about being gay. Poor boys. Life here hasn't been kind to them last few years."

"Sorry, I wish I could control that better," Cory says once he's able to quit shaking.

"It's all right, sweetness. You've had a rough time for a while, but you'll be fine. Just think about something that makes you happy. I'll check on your food. I'm here if you need me for anything."

She hands Tara the towel, going back to her post by the service window. Dabbing it on Cory's forehead, he can see the concern in her eyes.

"I'm sorry. I guess I'm not as strong as I thought I was."

Clearing her throat, Tara continues to pamper him. "If you wasn't, you would've cracked like Rick and hurt someone by now. I won't let you not be okay, baby. I love you too much to let you not be okay."

After a few more deep breaths, Cory sits there coming back fully to his senses. "I love you too. I just need to get away from here."

A few minutes later, Lloyd walks through the diner door and sees them sitting there.

"Hey, you two playing hooky today?"

Tara waves him over to explain the deal. "Nah, after seeing Rick shoot Frankie, we've been excused for the week."

Lloyd's facial expression says it all when he covers his mouth with his hand. "Oh, wow, you were there? Like, up close and personal in all that craziness?"

Cory focuses his attention to give Lloyd the details. "I watched as Rick's bullets tore through Frankie's body, spraying blood every which way from Sunday."

Dropping his jaw down, Lloyd sits there unable to speak.

"Yeah, then he pointed it at me, and that's all I remember, really."

From the counter, Mrs. Trippet listens and can feel the vibrations of pain coming from the table.

"No way! Rick wouldn't hurt you. You've been best friends

since, like, first grade. This isn't RiverCreek anymore. This place has become a madhouse."

The three of them sit there, chatting for a while, even long after the food is done and gone. Hoping this will be a positive way for them to release their issues between each other, Mrs. Trippet keeps an eye on them even during the dinner rush.

That's the pattern that follows over the next few days. Cory would get up, get dressed, and meet Tara by her front door. From there, they would spend time having sex for a few hours, then relax before heading over to meet Lloyd at the diner to help them escape their personal hells.

The following week, the couple returns to school to looks of sorrow and shame from their fellow students.

Over time, Cory's panic attacks ease quite a bit—until one night several weeks later, when they're out with Lloyd heading to the movies. As soon as they park, Tara takes off like a bullet from the car, heading for a trash can.

"She okay?" Lloyd says, seeing her bent over, puking into the trash can.

"I don't know. Maybe she's caught the virus that's going around. She's been pale and quiet all day."

Not sure what to think of it all, Lloyd opens the backdoor of the Sportage, worried about Tara.

"Stay here. I'll go find out. If I get sick, no big deal. You, though, don't need to come down with anything before your first game."

Taking his advice, Cory hangs back killing the vehicle's engine, taking the key from the switch. He stands there watching Lloyd approach Tara with caution.

"Hey, are you okay? Didn't catch a nasty bug, did you?"

Lloyd keeps his distance at first, using his jacket sleeve to cover his nose and mouth.

"Nothing contagious, Lloyd. I think I'm pregnant. I'm late, and this isn't the first time I've thrown up, either."

Lloyd turns to look at Cory. "Really? Oh, shit girl, what are you two gonna do?"

"Cory doesn't know yet. I couldn't hold it in this time. Oh, God Lloyd, I feel like I'm about to die."

When she begins to puke again, Lloyd frantically waves Cory over. When he stops beside Lloyd, he whispers into his ear.

"I think you got her sick with your love stick, brother man. She thinks she's pregnant—"

"What!" he yells, his voice echoing across the lot. "Tara, really, please tell me he's yanking my chain."

Able to push her body away from the trash can, she gives away the answer with her eyes.

"You've got to me fucking kidding me! Seriously, what are we going to do? I have my ride to Miami, and you got accepted into culinary school in Michigan."

"I don't know, Core. I'm scared as hell. My parents will kill me."

Cory tries to think about what to do when he feels his hand begin to shake. "Not now," he says, tightening his hands, trying to stop them from shaking.

"No, no, Cory I can't handle both of you going down at the same time. Listen to me. It's going to be fine. Your parents will help you all out. This isn't the end of the world. Maybe she's just sick. Flu can cause pregnancy-like symptoms, I think, so relax."

Cory begins to take control of his breathing the way Lloyd has showed him.

"Yeah, yeah, you might be right. I got this," he says, closing his eyes, keeping himself in control when a solution creeps into his mind.

"That a boy. Now go comfort your girl, and let's just forget tonight and go get a test."

With his hands on her shoulders, Cory assists Tara back over to her vehicle, putting her in the back seat to lie down rather than sit up.

"Just relax. We'll head to Wal-Mart, and I'll buy a test."

Speeding through traffic to get to Wal-Mart, Cory and Lloyd run inside, picking up a pregnancy test and trying to check out without anyone seeing what's in his hands.

"Ah, did someone make a bad decision around homecoming time?" the clerk teases, scanning the item and placing it in a bag.

"No, my sister—it's for her—and since she's only sixteen, well, you know, just being careful," Cory says, hoping she'd buy the story.

"Well, tell your sister if she ain't, to get on birth control. Don't wanna screw up her life. Have a good night, gentlemen," she tells them, giving Cory that look that she can see through his bullshit.

Walking with a quick pace, the boys go to Lloyd's trailer, since it's the closest location for Tara to take the test. While Cory waits impatiently in the living room, Lloyd sits with him, going over baby names.

"Hey, if it's a girl, you could name her Chloe or Sophy."

Cory flips him off. "Not funny at all man. Hey, between us, if she is, I might enlist. I can finish college that way, and they can have my benefits and stuff."

Lloyd gives Cory's idea a standoffish glare.

"Nah, man, they'd need you here. Your parents would—"

He's stopped when Tara comes out, carrying the test crying.

"It's yes … I'm sorry …"

Cory can't believe it until he sees the test strip indicator give off two blue lines.

"Fuck!" he yells, taking Tara in his arms.

"We'll be all right. If anything, you can go to school first, and then I'll go after you."

Tara's at a loss for words, crying harder when she drops the pregnancy test on the floor.

"Hey, guys, I could keep it for a while. I don't have plans other than continuing to save up for a car and then worry about college. Since I'd consider myself an uncle to this baby, it would be my honor."

Cory ignores everything around him as he holds Tara closer.

"I don't love you any less. Matter of fact, I love you more. We'll figure this out, together, but do me a favor."

Tara collects her composure long enough to say, "What?" Cory kneels right then and there.

"Marry me, Tara. After we graduate, we get married and make this right."

Still too worried about what to tell her parents, Tara shakes her head no. "Not like this, Cory. I'm sorry. I gotta go."

She takes off out the door, shoving Cory on his ass.

"Tara, wait!" he shouts, trying to grab her hand.

"Give her some space, Cory. Not everyday life keeps throwing you one curveball after another."

"Lloyd, I love her, and she's carrying my child. I will make this right."

Giving Cory a hand to his feet, the boys stand there looking down at the test.

"I believe you, man, but right now, let it sink in. She's not going to be able to control how she feels. I mean it, though—I'd be willing to help you all not put your lives on hold. You can't afford to lose that scholarship."

As he thinks it over, Cory's mind is made up. "I got this, but you don't know how much I appreciate everything you and your mom have done lately."

Lloyd latches onto Cory. "You are family, so it's what we do. You've been by my side even when others looked at me and mocked me for who I am."

"I love ya, Lloyd. We've grown up together. Gay, straight, or both, you're a good friend, and I'd still whip ass if someone crossed you the wrong way."

Lloyd releases Cory and guides him to the door. "Good luck telling your parents."

That statement forces knots to form in his stomach. "Yeah, wish me luck. Later, man."

On his way home, Cory gets passed by his mother's cruiser a couple of blocks away. When she sees that it's her son walking in the cold night's air, she pulls over to wait for him to climb inside.

"Why are you walking?"

With a prolonged deep breath, Cory breaks down and calls his mom by a new name.

"Well, Tara ran home to tell her parents something important, and well, I need to tell you something too … Grandma."

He hunkers down, waiting for a slap to the back of his head.

"You're kidding me? You two with a baby at your age! Oh my God, son, how could you? Your father is going to die of a heart attack."

She lifts her foot from the brake pedal, they round the block, making it home within a matter of minutes. By the time they make it inside, Mr. Dubois is sitting in his chair, staring down his son.

"Do I say congratulations, or should I be worried?" he says, tapping his foot on the floor.

"Yeah, Olivia called. Son, as disappointed as I am, I'm also excited. I get to see a grandbaby before I die."

"Dad, I … it wasn't … I got nothing, Dad."

Barely able to pull himself from his chair, he approaches his son.

"It'll be the greatest feeling in the world when you hold that child. Love it, son, as I have loved you. We'll work it out. This isn't the end of the world, just your childhood. Get to bed while your mother and I come up with something to help you out."

Heading back to his room, Cory shuts and locks his door. He places a towel at the base of the door. He gets online to fill out an online form for the military to see if they have jobs in surgery.

"There you are, surgeon's assistant, pretty much a surgical technician. Perfect!"

Cory types in a fake phone number. He submits his information with plans to head to St. Paul to learn more about his options from the recruiters, feeling this is his best option to keep everyone else from placing more on their plate than they can handle.

CHAPTER 18

Cory's Decision

Rather than drive to school the next day, Cory takes off to St. Paul, convinced he's making the right decision for his child and Tara.

"I got myself into this. I can fix this one myself."

Gulping forcefully, he pulls himself from his car and heads into the recruitment office.

"Morning, young man. What can the United States Army do for you?"

Wiping his feet on the mat, he tries to speak clearly.

"I, uh, found out I'm going to be a dad, and I want to provide for my child and my child's mom."

After he listens to Cory's opening remark, the recruiter introduces himself.

"Well, I'm Staff Sergeant Porter. You made the correct decision coming to talk to us. We'll make a real man out of you, one your child can be proud of in these dangerous times—since the September 11 attacks. Let me ask you, son, any special skills or talents the army can use in a young man like yourself?"

In the seat at the edge of the desk, Cory brings up the online form.

"Well, I put all that in the online form last night."

The recruiter laughs. "Those go to a centralized location. We hardly ever see them. So what did you put on there for your preference?"

"Surgeon assistant. I'm already studying surgical technology now. I'll be certified in January and finished with my core classes with school."

As Sgt. Porter writes it all down, he begins his recruitment speech. "Well, first, I need your name, social insurance number, age, and any legal issues you might have. We'll get you scheduled for the ASVAB test, and then we'll ship you off to the Military Entrance Processing Station, or MEPS, where you will have every opportunity to select that dream job. Plus, we also offer regent opportunities to earn your degree to become an officer, to earn even more money."

The fact he can still earn his college degree makes Cory eager for the chance to join.

"I'm, Cory Dubois. I just turned eighteen not long ago, and there are no issues. My mother is a sheriff in RiverCreek. They don't know that I'm here."

Writing everything down on his notepad, Sgt. Porter assures Cory his secret will be safe.

"I won't say a thing to anyone. You're of legal age, and hey, you want to provide for your old lady and unborn child. I can respect that; I have three of my own, and they're a treasure. Tell ya what—write down your social security number for me and we'll get you into the system. Come back up here in two weeks, and we'll get your test out of the way."

Cory agrees to the date, extending his hand. "Sounds good. I'll see you then, sir."

He gets up and is about to walk out when he stops and picks up almost one of every pamphlet near the door.

"Oh, yes, certainly, take all those you want and read them over. I'll see what I can do about getting you into the medical job you want. Not too many apply for that or have an idea of what they wanna do before they talk to the job specialist."

Cory develops a smirk that his recruiter doesn't see when he walks out the door. "Good, I'm not giving up too much. Guess it's time to get to class."

Cory drives just over the speed limit to make it to school before lunch.

Pulling into his parking spot, he goes into the votec building and down to the lunchroom, where he sees Tara sitting alone.

"Hey, lady, how you feeling today?" He takes his seat with a Pepsi Blue in his hands.

"Like roadkill ran over twice. I didn't know a person could puke this much. Where were you this morning?"

Lying through his teeth, Cory plays it off. "Overslept, and my parents took off early this morning. I think my dad had a doctor's appointment. His condition isn't improving that much."

Tara takes a swig of his soda. "Ugh that stuff is disgusting, but I hope he feels better soon. Anyway, I've been thinking, maybe I should go take care of this at the women's clinic. We can't raise a kid at our age."

After he hears that, Cory tries to keep from going off the deep end.

"I'll be damned if you do that. Listen, I have this figured out. Just agree to marry me, and we'll be fine—I promise. We can elope, and I will have us a place in almost no time. We can do this, Tara. Would I do you wrong?"

She rests her head against his shoulder and assures him she knows better.

"No, but I'm scared, Cory. This isn't as easy as it seems. What if I get fat and stay fat? I won't be as pretty."

Huffing for a second, Cory puts her nerves to rest.

"You'll always be Tara, my Tara, to me. You are beautiful now, and you'll be beautiful after too. Now let go of the fear. That way, you won't hurt the baby. Let me handle this for us."

Yawning out of nowhere, she returns to her answer.

"The answer is still no, by the way. I'm not agreeing to anything until I know we're going to be fine."

"Give me a few more weeks. It'll all be worked out by then—I promise."

She pulls her head up, looking at him. "What did you do?"

Cory shrugs his shoulders.

"Nothing yet, but until you agree, I'm not saying how I'm gonna make sure we'll be fine."

Tara begins to get a little prissy.

"Don't do anything stupid. I can't handle that; we've been through enough already. Last thing I need is to lose you too. I'd die if you were taken away from me."

Cory eases her fear. "I'm not leaving you, I promise, but I am making sure we're going to be okay. Now agree to marry me, damn it."

Giggling, Tara gives him a straight-up reaction.

"Buy me a ring and put it on my finger, dumbass."

He takes her hand, looking her dead square in the eyes. "I can't buy the most expensive one yet, but I will get you one if you agree right here right now."

She turns into a shy timid school girl, still giggling uncontrollably.

"Get the ring and ask me again."

Taking the hint, Cory takes his place beside her again.

"Be honest. Have you been thinking about any names yet?"

Pulling out a small notepad, Tara reveals a few selections.

"I like Samantha and Carly a lot. I've also considered Kayla too, but then I wanna cry thinking about her not being here for this."

To comfort her the best way he can, Cory puts his arm around her shoulders. "I understand completely, but what if we have a little boy?"

She has one name written down. "Cory Jr., or CJ—that's what I want if we have a little boy."

He sits there, allowing the possibility to sink in his head. "CJ, yeah, I think I like that too. Either that or maybe David, or maybe even Ethan. A little girl—I like Claire or Catherine."

Tara gives him a look of discontent.

"Uh, I don't freakin' think so, big boy."

Her reaction causes Cory to laugh loudly, as it echoes in the corridor. "Fine, we'll go with your names then. Anyway, bell's about to ring. We need to get to class."

Playfully frowning, Tara tries to convince Cory to wait until the bell. "Just another couple more minutes. Please, baby. I didn't get to see you this morning."

Cory shakes his head no, reaching out and taking her hand to lead her down to her culinary lab.

After escorting her to class, Cory begins his stroll over to the other side of the building to his only core class needed to graduate early.

"Ugh, almost over, almost over," he repeats, heading into biology class.

In his final class that extends into after school with the adult educational classes, Cory hits the books hard, wanting to ensure he will be prepared when he goes to sign up for the Army in a few weeks.

Got to get this right. No second chances. This is for the baby. Our baby, our future, time for us to escape RiverCreek once and for all!

Feeling a new lease on life, his motivation takes control of his mind during class. He becomes a new man knowing what's at stake. While in the study lab, he uses the time to go over how to hide, turning down the scholarship offer. He needs to figure out how to keep this from his parents, knowing they'll disapprove of his decision.

The next two weeks fly by for Cory. Over that time, he's pushed to do what he has planned even more when Tara gives him a copy of her first ultrasound. When he walks into the recruiter's office again, he has the picture in hand.

"Well, there he is: Cory Dubois. You ready to tackle this test and make your life worthwhile son?"

Determined he's doing the right thing, Cory nods, looking at the ultrasound of a little blob on the printout.

"Yes, sir. I got my motivation right here." He tightens his grip, feeling ready to take on the entire world.

"Let's do it then. You'll be right here in this office for a while. As soon as you're finished, we'll get your score and see if we can get you that dream job."

Amped with adrenaline, Cory follows his recruiter in the office, taking a seat to read the instructions on the screen.

"Need anything? Water, soda, a prayer request, anything at all?" his recruiter asks before leaving the testing area.

"Nope, I'm ready to go."

Giving Cory the go signal with a finger gun gesture, he closes the door as Cory dives into the ASVAB for the next two hours.

He finishes up the final test, a timed portion to challenge an individual under pressure, Cory flies through as many questions as possible. Once the test locks, when time expires, he gets up and returns to the office to wait for his results.

"How ya feel about how ya did?" he's asked as he standing by the door.

"I did the best I could do is all I can say. I'll let the results speak for me."

Sgt. Porter chuckles a bit. "I like that attitude. Give me a minute to pull up exactly how well you did."

Closing the door, Cory can hear him typing on the keyboard until he's called into the test room.

"Cory, come take a gander, and let's go over your options."

Listening to the tone in his voice, Cory's nerves stand on end, sending his blood pressure through the roof while he walks over to the screen. Sgt. Porter turns the monitor around to reveal his results.

"I'd say you did pretty damn well, kid. You scored in the ninety-third percentile, guaranteeing you a job in any field you want for the army. Congratulations!"

Cory nearly faints when he hears his results. "So does that mean I can be a surgeon assistant?"

"Hell, son, you can become a surgeon with scores like these. Don't settle yourself so low. We'll send all this up, along with my recommendations, and get you on your way. That kid is going to be bragging on you to his friends when he gets older."

Cory shakes his hand, excited about his future.

"Oh, I need one more thing. In order for your old lady—and I use that term loosely—to receive your benefits for her and the baby, I need her social security number too. That way when the baby is born, the army can add the baby automatically."

Cory has one more important thing hit his mind. "Do my parents qualify for any of my benefits? My dad is struggling with his diabetes, and I'd like to get him better help, if I can."

That strikes a personal chord with Sgt. Porter. "Absolutely. I lost my mother to that last year actually. I need their socials too, and I promise I will make sure he receives the best benefits possible. You seem like a straight-up young man. I'm glad to see people like you still willing to join," Sgt. Porter says and exchanges one final handshake with Cory before he leaves to rush home.

"Oh, when do you need me to come back?" Flipping through his calendar, Cory waits by the door. "Let's say December 19—that way, you don't miss school again."

A single nod is all Cory uses to signal as he reaches for the door.

He hides his excitement until he gets into his car. "Yes, yes, yes! I did it. This must be what I needed to do. Otherwise, why would I have done that well? Oh, I can't wait to tell Tara!"

Doing his best to rush back to RiverCreek, he can barely contain his enthusiasm.

He arrives minutes before the bell rings. He hurries down the hallway to wait for Tara. When the chimes begin releasing the students go to their next class, he stands there waiting to see her.

"Hey, babe, I got some great news," he begins, anxious to get the cat out of the bag.

"I don't care, this is the second time you've skipped class lately. Are you doing something behind my back?"

His hands shaking with excitement he begins to explain. "Yes, but it's not bad I swear—nothing like you would think."

Tara leans to her side waiting to hear him explain. "This better be good."

"I've been talking to an army recruiter for a couple of weeks now, and I took my test today and I scored high—like, really, really, high—on my tests. I can go in and work my way to becoming a surgeon in time, and my classes here matter. Plus, you and the baby get my benefits the minute I sign up."

Standing there speechless, Tara drops her books. When Cory bends over to pick them up, she hauls off, slapping the taste out of his mouth.

"You idiot. Did you not remember what happened back in

September 2001? Really, you think the army is what I want for you, for us? You would have to go over there and fight or something worse. We've lost people we care about lately. Do you think I could take it if you got killed because you think that is your only way to support our child?"

This isn't what Cory was expecting at all. He was hoping to be hailed as a conquering hero.

"It makes sense, with the benefits, a guaranteed check, a way to provide for us. I'm not thinking about myself; I am thinking about our future. I'm ready to do this. I'm ready to marry you and do what's right for our family."

Her eyes closed, she can sense this is a losing battle. "Fine, if this is truly what you want, then do it. Just don't die, please! You're too important to the two of us in this world, outside your family."

Cory blows her away with his next statement. "You are my family. We are meant to be together forever."

Tara begins to break down and rubs the spot where she hauled off and hit Cory. "I'm sorry I hit you. It scares the living hell out of me that you could get hurt or killed."

"I understand, love. I'll be safe in a hospital far from the action, I promise. Tell you what, if they don't give me the job I want, I'll walk away."

Tara holds her stomach, preparing to run off. "Sounds good. Sorry, I gotta go."

Cory nods his understanding with a look of concern on his face. "Glad it's not me throwing up all the time."

Remembering he still has Tara's book in his hands. He takes off behind her, waiting outside the ladies' bathroom for her to come out.

"Here, you might need this for class. Wiping her mouth with a paper towel, Tara throws it away, taking her books. "Gee, thanks, love. I feel like death all over again. Anyway, I guess your parents don't know about this."

"Not at all, and I'm going to need your social to put on my record too. That way, you and the baby receive my benefits when I ship off."

Still holding her stomach, Tara returns to the restroom, where, this time, Cory can listen as she's not quiet, throwing up again.

When she returns for a second time, she's late for class when the tardy bell rings. "Great, late for class. God, this sucks!"

Cory rubs the small of her back for comfort.

"Yeah, let's get moving. I'm sorry you're going through this. I wish I could do something about it."

Tara shows she's feeling better being able to pick on Cory. "Well, it is mostly your fault. You had to go and make it feel too damn good, asshole."

They share a laugh together as he escorts her to class, carrying her books.

Once he arrives, tardy for his crossover class, Cory takes his seat, daydreaming at times about the possibilities that lie ahead for him, Tara, and the baby. That's all he can think about for weeks as his appointment for the Military Entrance Processing Station creeps closer.

Using the excuse that he's staying over at Lloyd's, Cory takes off for St. Paul the morning of his appointment. He sets off early, well before the sun peeks from the base of the skyline. Cory arrives nearly twenty minutes before the recruiting office opens.

When he sees Sgt. Porter arrive to unlock the door, Cory gets out ready to get a move on.

"Morning, sir. I'm ready to get this done!"

Sgt. Porter is startled when Cory comes out of nowhere. "Oh, dear God, kid, you got me good. Glad to see you. Van will be here at nine to pick you up. You're going to Minneapolis to our Minnesota MEPS. Remember, you don't have to pick an MOS you don't want."

"M-O-S?" Cory repeats, confused.

"Oh, yeah, that stands for military occupational specialty. Your job code, here's the job you want—it's called 68 Delta. Operating room specialist. I know it doesn't sound like what you want. Trust me when I say it's exactly what you're studying. I asked a friend of mine who's an army doctor."

Cory lips the job code a couple of times. "Thank you, Sgt. Porter."

Inside out of the cold, the two of them sit and talk until the van pulls up, honking to get their attention.

"All right, Cory, best of luck and I'll see you when you get back." He gives Cory a firm handshake before he leaves.

"See you soon enough." Cory takes in a deep breath, dashing for the waiting van.

Through the entire process, ranging from physical to psychiatric evaluation, Cory flies through it all to finally meet the jobs counselor. He patiently sits there as the top selections chosen are read to him aloud.

"Excuse me, sir, but I know the job I want."

Paused from the monotone reading voice, the jobs counselor rolls his eyes over to Cory.

"Okay, and what job would that be, because you're no general, kid."

Resisting the urge to be a smartass, Cory tells him exactly what job he wants. "I want 68 Delta—operating room specialty. I'm about to earn my certificate in surgical technology, and this is what I want to do."

Once he types in the keywords, the overweight middle-aged white civilian government worker waits for his system to pull up Cory's selection.

"Yeah, it says here you're qualified even without it. So is that what you really want?"

As he taps his fingers together, already annoyed, Cory reaffirms his answer. "Yes, sir. If I didn't, I wouldn't tell you that, would I?"

Smacking his lips a couple times, he prints out the contract with the requirements Cory must abide by in order to accept the job.

"Here you go. The terms are this simple. You sign up for six years. You attend Basic Combat Training in South Carolina. From there, you go on to our medical training facility in upper New York state for six months. Then you'll have the choice to stay stateside or go overseas when you enter the final weeks of your medical training. Just sign on the dotted line, and you're all set," the job counselor explains, obviously bored with his job.

Cory looks over it all to make sure it's correct. "I can handle those conditions." He signs the contract without hesitation.

"Good luck. You leave for BCT on February 1 of next year. Please send in the next applicant, and you have a nice day."

Glad to finally be finished, Cory walks away to the front of the station, where his ride is waiting for him.

"Ready to get moving there, kid?" the driver asks, twirling the keys on his index finger.

"Let's roll!" he calls out, ready to get home and finally tell his parents.

Arriving back at the office, Cory goes in smiling. "I take it you got the job?"

Cory smacks his hands together. "You're damn right, I did. I leave February 1, which means I won't miss a single game this season."

Stunned, Sgt. Porter is curious. "You play sports? I mean, I could tell you're in shape, but that's awesome. That means you could do a pre-PT test and earn a higher rank like P2 or maybe P3. Besides, I might even show up and try to recruit some kids."

Cory shrugs his shoulders. "Go ahead. I'm certain some wouldn't mind escaping RiverCreek, like I am."

Standing there for a moment, neither of them say anything.

"Guess I should get home. Time to tell my parents that I'm in the army."

Sgt. Porter has nothing to say other than "Best of luck. I'll come by from now on to check in, and we'll go run and train and stuff."

Cory waves leaving the office so he can head home to share the news. On his way home, it begins to snow heavily, putting down more than an inch before he pulls up to the edge of his street.

Once he's parked and closes his eyes for a minute, he's preparing for World War 3 when he walks through the door. Gradually working up the courage to get out of his car, he pushes the door open, planting his feet firmly on the fresh, dry, fluffy snow.

Here we go, he tells himself, walking up to the front door.

Slowly twisting the knob, he pushes it open to discover Tara is there waiting for him to arrive home.

"How did it go?" she asks him with his parents sitting right there.

"I got it. I went in there determined to get the job I had in mind, and I got it. I leave February 1, so Mom, Dad, I did it. I joined the army."

They both smile and reveal their own little secret. "We know, son. We've known for a while. The information you filled out on the internet came in a while ago. We've been waiting for you to come tell us."

He stands there, finding it hard to understand that they've already accepted his decision.

"We're not thrilled about it, but your mother and I are proud that you stepped up to handle your responsibilities. That's our boy, putting the world before yourself."

Cory witnesses his dad wiping away a tear from his eye.

"Thank you, Dad. That's what I needed to hear."

Tara sits there with Mrs. Dubois, unable to speak. They hold hands, being able to read each other by speaking with their eyes.

"Mom, Tara, this is what's best for us. I love you, and hey, I have something for you. Consider it an early Christmas present."

He goes over, taking her hand and getting down on one knee. With his free hand, he takes out a ring box.

"Tara Marie Rose, I love you more than life itself. Will you marry me when I get home?"

Shaking her head yes, Cory takes the ring from its case, but before he can slip it on her finger, his mother motions for them to stop.

"Wait. I'll be right back."

She hurries to her bedroom and returns holding her hand out to her son. "I'd be honored if you asked her with your great-great-grandmother's sapphire engagement ring. It's nearly a hundred years old."

Cory is at a loss for words. "Take it, son. Put it on her finger."

Reaching out taking the ring into the palm of his hand, Cory positions it at the end of Tara's ring finger.

"Again, will you marry me?"

Tara's voice is shaky by this time. "Yes, yes, I will. I'll always be yours."

He slips the antique ring over her knuckle.

The rest of the evening, Cory, Tara, and his parents celebrate together as they try to enjoy the obvious emotions riding high throughout the house—instead of the typical fear every parent feels when their child is going to leave home for the armed forces.

CHAPTER 19

Dear Cory

Ever since he made it perfectly clear that he'd be leaving in a few short months, due to graduating early, Tara has kept her feelings bottled up inside. She's torn up, believing that Cory has given up on his dreams. Every day, she puts a fake smile on the outside while her soul screams in agony on the inside.

On the flipside of things, Cory feels empowered and raring to go. He's training harder in the weight room after practice. He's even playing less time on the ice to make sure he doesn't get injured before he leaves. He's up before the sun every morning to run three miles in the frigid winter air to expand his lungs. Pushing himself to the extreme pays off, as Cory's physique becomes more cut, with lean, toned muscle.

One morning during his run, he takes a detour from his normal route, heading over to see Tara. Walking up the steps, he knocks on the door, waiting for her to open it up.

"Come on, Tara. I'm freezing in my sweat," he says, beginning to feel a chill setting in on his damp skin.

Knocking loudly again, he stands there clutching his arms with his hands rubbing them together, bouncing in place. Eventually Tara comes to the door, holding her robe closed.

"Hey, sorry. My morning sickness hit hard this morning. Come on inside. I could use a head rub."

She moves aside, allowing Cory to finally get out of the cold.

"Thanks. I was doing good until I stopped running. Go lie down on the couch and I'll rub your head. I hate that I can't make you feel better."

Slinking over to the couch, Cory helps Tara get comfy when she stretches out, groaning as her body feels everything changing.

"This sucks! After you leave, my mom is taking time away from the store to be here more. She's finally come around to enjoying the fact that she'll be a grandma—although she's not very happy about you taking us with you to the base."

Cory glides his fingers through Tara's smooth, silky brown hair.

"I know, but at least I can try to get us based somewhere near here. It'll all work out—just wait and see. Hell, I can't believe I leave next week already."

Tara frowns, squinting harder with her eyes closed. "No, I'm not ready for you to go yet."

"I'll write every day, I promise. By the time I get finished and find out where I'll be placed, you'll have the baby, and we'll have our own little family. It's going to be great—I know it."

Tara's not as enthused. "How can you be so sure? How do you know it's going to work out like you think or plan?"

Pausing mid-stroke through her hair, Cory explains the best way he knows. "Faith. It's a feeling I have, and this feels right for us."

Yawning when Cory resumes his duty of rubbing her head, Tara is out cold within a matter of minutes, lightly snoring from exhaustion. Giving her time to get in a relaxed deep sleep, Cory lifts her head from his lap. He places a throw pillow in his place so he can head back home to finish his run.

He locks the door on his way out. Cory lifts the hoodie cover over his head again as he takes off, sprinting home. The snow crunches beneath his shoes. He strides along, ignoring the burning sensation expanding in his lungs due to the temperature dropping with the wind blowing from the north. He spends the rest of his morning at home, resting his aching muscles.

Arriving for his final game on the ice, Cory is called immediately by the coach.

"Hey, Core, can I see you in my office, please."

Puzzled by the coach calling for him in private, Cory puts his pads back into his locker and heads into the office.

"What's up, sir?"

His coach points for him to take a seat.

"You leave soon for the army, right? You need to rest between now and then. Stay in your regular clothes and help me coach the game. You're done as of today. We hate to see you go when our season hinges on this game. All I can say, though, is that I understand and wish you the best of luck. I hate seeing you kids grow up and graduate, but in your case, it's been an honor and pleasure and to watch you grow into a bright and talented young man," the coach says with a look of concern in his eyes.

Cory takes the advice of his coach to rest and relax, which helps him make calls during the game.

Heeding the advice of his coach, Cory takes the next week to rest up. He uses his time to go around town to gather up memories to take with him, to keep pieces of his past still fresh in his mind.

He even goes back to the point where Kayla died, standing there where she pretty much died on the pavement.

"This is for you, Kayla. I miss you and wish you was still here." He kneels on both knees, removing his glove, kissing his hand, and placing it down on the icy pavement in honor of his late friend.

After he finishes his tribute to Kayla, he drives over to the courthouse, where he once again kneels where Rick shot Frankie.

"Guys, this is also for both of you. You couldn't escape this hell, but I am, and I'll always remember the good times we had." He places his fist where Frank's blood stained the concrete, dedicating a moment of silence to everyone devastated by the actions that occurred that day.

Going back to the places where the pain is still fresh for everyone residing in RiverCreek, Cory uses this pain as fuel for his internal inferno to remind himself why he can't fail.

Time isn't kind for everyone dreading the day that Cory is set to leave for South Carolina. Unsure of when his recruiter will be by to pick him up to drive him to the airport, Tara arrives early, already in tears before she even gets through the door. Seeing her upset is enough to make Mrs. Dubois break down with her.

Sniffling, his mom begins shuffling through old photos again. "When did you, my little boy, grow up?"

Tara joins her looking over the collection of holidays, school photos, and newspaper clippings from his hockey career.

"Oh, he's always been a little cutie." Tara sobs, putting a tissue to her nose and blowing it with force.

Cory and his father sit at the kitchen table, trying to make the best use of time through small talk. "Remember, don't be a smartass, and we'll be there when you graduate. It's going to be lonesome around here, son, but I am proud of you."

"Thanks, Dad. I'm gonna miss you all too, and I'll write every week. Tara, I can't wait to get back so we can get to our own place on base."

Twisting her head to see him from the corner of her eye, she smiles an obvious fake smile. "Yeah, can't wait."

They all jump when Sgt. Porter comes knocking on the door.

"Come in," Mrs. Dubois shouts, clutching her hand over her heart, feeling her anxiety evolve into fear of the unknown from this moment forward.

"Hello everyone. I'm Staff Sergeant Porter. I believe you're all here to wish Cory good luck."

"I'm not ready to let him go yet," Mrs. Dubois shudders to say as her lips being to quiver.

"He's in excellent hands, Momma bear. He picked a safe job, and you'll be proud of him."

She wipes her eyes, getting to her feet to hug Cory one more time. "It doesn't matter if he's eighteen or twenty-eight—he's still my baby."

Cory walks up hugging her farewell, whereupon her crying increases in intensity.

"It'll be okay, Mom—I promise."

Next, Cory turns to Tara, who's still sitting on the couch, trying to hide her tears.

"Don't I get a hug?"

She gets to her feet slowly, trying to buy a few more seconds.

"I take it you're the mom-to-be. Cory was right when he said you are an absolute beauty. Congratulations on the baby. I know Daddy here is glad to have it happen."

Tara shoots Sgt. Porter a dirty look that he doesn't take to heart; he sees that same look every time he ships out a recruit.

"Sir, make the best man possible out of him. He's got a real good head on his shoulders," Mr. Dubois says, coming up and putting his arms around both Cory and Tara.

"You have a brave young man here, sir. We'll make a better man out of him—you have my word. Cory, come on, time to go if you want to make your flight to Fort Jackson."

He takes a step back away from Tara. Cory goes over, taking his travel bag with him. As he walks out the door, excited about his new adventure, he doesn't look back when the butterflies begin to fly in his stomach.

Placing his bag in the front floorboard of the Jeep, Cory gets in, trying not to look back at his parents and Tara, who are standing in the window watching him leave.

"Give it time. It won't hurt as much. I remember when I left for basic training. Just takes time and adjusting, Cory." He pats him on the shoulder. After placing the shifter in drive, they slowly pull away.

"There he goes, ladies. It'll be, what, about five or six months before we see him again?" Mr. Dubois says, supporting his wife on one shoulder while Tara leans on the opposite shoulder, unable to control themselves.

A couple weeks fly by, and Cory is almost to the end of the first of three phases during his course of basic training. Red Phase, the toughest portion of it all. One evening, when mail call comes through, it is about to change the nature of Cory's life.

"All right, gentlemen, mail call! Alderson, Adkins, Bailey, Peterson, Hammond, Miller, McCoy, Dubois …"

Hearing his name, Cory drops his Smart Book to receive his mail.

"Thank you, Drill Sergeant," he says, taking a couple of envelopes being held out in his direction.

"You're welcome, PFC Dubois. Hey! See that, maggots? He said thank you. Means he has manners, something most of ya mommas didn't teach your fucking dumbasses. Now straighten it up next time, or else. Is that clear, maggots!"

In collective group, everyone in the bay provides the typical response: "Yes, Drill Sergeant!"

Time to read the letters from his parents first. Cory gets some relief when he discovers that his recruiter kept his word, ensuring that Mr. Dubois would receive better medical care.

> Dear Cory,
>
> It's Mom and Dad with some wonderful news, son. Your dad is getting the medical care we couldn't afford on our own. He's seeing a doctor who listens to how he feels and does not just try to treat a few symptoms as they come up. He's feeling so much better, and he's active again. I can't tell you how good that makes me feel. Tara is doing well too. She stops by all the time to check in, and we adore her to death, son. You couldn't have done any better. We miss you so much, but we know you felt as if you had to do this for yourself, as well as the baby and Tara. Take care, and we can't wait to see you.
>
> Love, Mom
> Cory,
>
> Hey, son, it's great to hear that you were picked to be platoon leader. You'll go far at anything you do, and there's no stopping you once your mind is made up. Guess that's your mom's side taking charge there—haha—anywho, I ain't got much to say, other than you've made us so proud and I can't wait to have

you home. Your car is parked at the garage for now, and it will stay there until you get a base somewhere and I can bring it to you. Not really much else to say other than take care and learn all you can.

Dad

Placing the letters back into the envelope, Cory places them under his pillow. Now carefully taking his time, he smells the perfume Tara sprayed on her letter when he opens it, picturing her lying on her bed writing it.

Dear Cory,

Hey, handsome, I miss you so much, and it's so cold here without you. It's weird going to school and not seeing you there. I've gotten so used to you being around, that it feels like a piece of me is dead while you're gone. I don't know what all to say tonight. My mom and dad say howdy and get home soon. They miss spending time with you too. Dad misses talking cars with you, and Mom misses joking around with you on how bad you are at pretending to know anything about her college football. I miss holding and kissing you. I feel like I'm going to die without you here. Every time I see headlights driving by, I run to my window, hoping it's you, but then I get sad all over again when I remember you're far away from me. Come home now!

Love you now and forever,
Tara

Folding the letter back together carefully along the creases, Cory slides it back inside the envelope and places both letters in his locker.

"Hey, Cory, you have first fire watch tonight at 2100 hours sharp," his battle buddy, Private Alderson, calls out, writing down the schedule on the dry-erase board.

"First watch—heard ya loud and clear, Brad. Thanks for the heads-up."

Cory gets his notepad and pencil ready. He heads over to the table positioned near the entrance to the latrine. Once lights-out occurs, he moves the notepad into a better position so he can use his hour-long watch to write home to everyone.

> Dear Mom and Dad,
>
> I'm glad to know that everything is going well. So happy to hear you're doing better, Dad. I've been thinking about requesting for a medical unit in Kentucky or Wisconsin to be somewhat close to home. If not, I'll be sent to Germany. It's been rough, but it's about to get a little easier when I transition and move into White Phase, where we'll have more classroom lessons and learn more about battlefield structure. I can't wait to see all of you at graduation before I go to New York for a year there. Write back soon. Love you, Mom and Dad.
>
> Hugs,
> Cory

When he's finished, he rips the letter from the pad, folding it in half and placing it in the back of his notepad so he doesn't lose it. Once it's safely tucked away, Cory gets his army-issued L-shaped flashlight to make his round down every row, making sure everyone is asleep and accounted for in their bunks.

Back to his station, he sits there for a minute before he begins to write Tara's return letter. Making sure he's not about to be disturbed when he hears a couple of drill sergeants outside doing their own perimeter walkthrough, Cory begins his second letter.

Hey, Tara,

God knows I'm counting down the days until I get to see and hold you again. This is definitely harder than anything else I've ever done before. I sit and wait every day for more letters, so please write as much as you can or want. Thinking about you and our future makes me fight harder every single day. Most of the guys here use politics to rationalize why they're here. I have you, which is much better than saying, "I'm here to kill terrorists." I'm here to preserve life—that's what our drill sergeant told us when we got here on day one. I hate being away from you, and I'm sure you'd laugh if you saw me now, being bald and all. No more styled hair. Hell, no more hair at all, lol, which is weird, considering we still have to have shampoo and conditioner. Anyway, give my best to your mom and dad, and always the baby. My time to write is short tonight, but know I am always thinking about you, and I love you, oh so much.

Love, Cory

Placing his pencil down, Cory hears a double tap on the desk when the next person up for fire watch arrives at the desk. "You're good, Cory. See you in the morning, man."

Cory double taps on the desk, the signal for shift exchange. He gets up and heads off to bed.

After he gets his letters out and sees that he hasn't received any mail for a couple of weeks, he tries to phone home when his platoon has their day for a three-minute call, but no one picks up anywhere he calls. Pissed that his phone time has been wasted, Cory heads back into the bay, where he waits for mail call later that evening.

"Private First Class Dubois, you're first up for letters from home. Come get it while it's hot and fresh!" his Drill Sergeant teases knowing he's had it rough, barely receiving any mail.

"Thank you, Drill Sergeant." Taking the single letter over to his bunk, Cory debates even reading it considering the funk he's feeling.

He decides to go ahead and read it since it is from Tara, Cory rips it open carelessly, hoping it'll kill his bad mood.

> Dear Cory,
>
> This is going to be the hardest thing I have ever written, said, and done in my life. First, we're sorry you haven't heard from us. My father was in a high-speed crash in his truck, out near California, and my mother has been out there waiting to see if he will make it or not. It doesn't sound good from what she's told me. Also, your parents have been letting me stay with them since my mom's been gone, but all that might change when you get further down this letter.

After that part of the letter, Cory's heart drops into the pit of his stomach when a gut-wrenching blow assaults his body.

> I've cried so hard for so long over this, and it's going to be unbearable to tell you. Cory, please don't hate me, but I lost the baby not long after my last letter. I noticed some blood, and when we arrived at the hospital, it got worse. I miscarried, and it's nearly killed me not telling you earlier. Your parents have been so good to me since then too. I have cried myself to sleep every night since, and it gets harder when I look in the mirror and I see myself. I hate myself. I must have done something wrong. I am so sorry, and I don't blame you if you hate me forever. I hate myself more every day. That being the case, I have to do something else …

Cory's nearly in tears when he flips the letter over to continue reading on the backside.

> I want you to move on from me. Go travel the world and enjoy the experience of a lifetime. I've told your recruiter, and he's taken care of everything. Again, I am so very sorry about all of this. You deserve better than me. I'll always love you, and no one else will ever take my heart the way you did.
>
> Goodbye,
> Tara Marie Rose

At the bottom half of letter, Cory notices the tear stains. "Son of a bitch," he blurts out instantly, getting his Drill Sergeant's attention.

"PFC Dubois, my office, *now*."

Cory swings his body off his bunk, following the instructor to his office.

"Shut the door and take a seat," he's told when he stands in the doorway.

"Yes, Drill Sergeant." Cory does as he's told, taking a seat.

He notices something odd. His instructor takes off his drill sergeant campaign green hat. "All right, kid, talk to me as your friend and not as your teacher. Something's got you tore up. You're normally level-headed. What's wrong?"

Cory retrieves the letter from his pocket and hands it over. As the drill sergeant takes his time to read it over, he sits there watching.

"Wish I could say this is a first to read. It sucks, and I apologize that you must feel that rage, son. Explains why your mail and phone calls have dropped off. It's perfectly fine to let out how you feel in here right now."

Tightening his face to keep from a breakdown, Cory shakes his head no. "I'm good, Drill Sergeant. I wanna get through basic and my medical classes. Do I have to go home for hometown recruiting?"

"I can see if I can get it waived if you'd rather get straight to your permanent duty station."

Cory doesn't even consider weighing out his options.

"Please, I want to get there and forget about her and RiverCreek—leave it in the past, where that shit hole belongs."

After a sigh, he realizes he can't do much more other than grant Cory's wish to skip going home.

"I'll make the call and get the form filled out. Go on back out there and try to relax as best ya can, Cory. Again, if it holds any meaning, kid, I'm sorry. I've listened to you brag about it since the day you arrived."

Cory simply gets up going back to his bunk, ignoring his friends the rest of the night. He writes one more letter, allowing his emotions to get the best of him.

> Mom and Dad,
>
> They changed my orders. I won't be walking at graduation. I'll be shipped directly to my school in New York. When I get there, I'll let you know when to expect a graduation date from there. Also give Tara a message for me, please. Tell her that I am sorry about her dad and I hope he pulls through. Other than that, she can go fuck herself and she should never bother me again. Until that day we see each other again.
>
> Your son,
Cory

After sending his letter out, Cory directs his focus on finishing up basic training. When his graduation day comes and goes, he's flown to JFK Airport, where he meets up with other soldiers coming from all over the country to attend classes at the Army Medical Personnel Training Academy.

His year goes by in a flash, without writing home or even a

phone call to check in on his parents. Cory can't find it within himself to let go of the rage over being ignored for so long. Near the end of his training program, when he meets with his career advisor, he expresses his desire to be shipped overseas to Germany.

When he receives his orders, Cory packs up, not even considering contacting anyone back home. He tosses the few pictures he's kept with him in the trash on his way out the door to board his plane, heading for Europe, where his next adventure begins.

He's struggled to remain numb since the letter from Tara. His anger and frustrations intertwine with guilt and pain from being told he's no longer to be a father. His heart feels as if it's been ripped out, as a large part of his soul crumbled the day he read those words that Tara miscarried. All Cory can do is look forward, ready to tackle the world and continue to fight to forget about RiverCreek and Tara.

CHAPTER 20

Six Years Advanced

It's been six years since Cory refused to return home, turning his back on his past. After signing a new contract a year earlier to continue his medical training, he's had to make the transition from working in a traditional M.A.S.H. hospital to a larger more secure military field hospital, now called a cash, or C.S.H.

Cory's worked hard and is now a sergeant, working swing shifts when casualties roll in around the clock. He's earned the respect of his commanding officers, who helped him with his studies to receive his regent degree through a partnership with the University of Northern Carolina State.

"Cory, need you to take the graveyard watch tonight. After finals, I need to you to monitor Private Dill's condition. IED did a number on his abdomen."

Rotating his eyes away from this screen, he replies quickly, "Yes, Captain I got it—night watch."

Once the sun sets, Cory takes his place going over charts during bed check to help the nurses.

"Thanks, Sergeant. You're a sweetheart. Wanna get a drink tomorrow or something?" the newest nurse to his unit asks.

The other nurses snicker, knowing she's about to get shot down.

"Maybe." That causes an uproar, as no one expected him to accept.

"About time," he hears the head nurse comment, reading over charts on the other side of Cory.

The young blond nurse has a bright blemish appear on her pale cheeks.

"Good. Can't wait. See you tomorrow, Sergeant."

Tapping her foot on the floor, the head nurse reminds Cory of regulations. "You know you can't have a relationship. You're still an enlisted man, and she's a lieutenant."

Cory cuts up. "I know, but it's just a drink, ma'am. I don't do relationships—you know that."

"I know, just reminding you in case you forgot."

They look at each other and laugh.

"Good one, Captain," he tells her, placing his last chart on the end of the bed before heading to the charge station for his shift.

Going over notes from his online lectures, Cory's night goes from peaceful to shattered when the MPs come rushing through the door.

"Sergeant Cory Dubois?" one of them questions, standing after he stops at the desk.

"Yes, I've done nothing wrong. What's this about?"

Taking their position in parade rest, they explain their actions. "We're here on behalf of the chaplain. Your father has passed away, and you are being shipped home for bereavement leave. Ten days at home, and then you report back to your unit."

"Forget it. I'm not going!" He tells them, taking his seat.

"Colonel's orders, Sergeant. You have no choice. His demands are for you to be sent home since you have skipped required R&R for the last two deployments."

Slamming his fist on the table, Cory awakens every patient in the bay. "I said I'm not going. Court-martial me if you must, because I am not going back to RiverCreek!"

A day later, Cory is proven wrong when he's flying back to Germany for a direct flight to New York and then jumping onto a connecting flight to St. Paul Regional Airport.

When he's on the ground in Minnesota, he's welcomed home with a loud squeal when his mother spots him walking from the gate.

"Cory, son!"

He cringes at the sound of his name.

"Hi, Mom," he says, opening his eyes to see his mother, who has aged more than he has expected, standing in front of him.

"You look so good," she says, wrapping her arms over her son for the first time since he left home.

All he can do is stand there with his arms to his side. "Sorry to hear about Dad. I just came in to be at the funeral, and I'm taking off again."

Squeezing even harder, his mother begs, "Please stay longer. You've gone for so long."

Even standing there, Cory already feels the agony creeping back into his mind.

"We'll see, Mom, but I'm not making any promises."

Once she's able to let him go, Mrs. Dubois keeps her hands on his shoulders. "Look at you, so handsome, and with short hair. Oh, son, please don't make it another six years before I see you again after you leave this time. I know Tara would love to see you."

"Don't bring that bitch's name up around me."

Shocked, Mrs. Dubois seems lost by his actions. "Why? She's been golden, helping out when she can. She even made sure that—"

Cory's pain takes control as he interrupts his mother's sentence. "I said to shut up about her, or I'm out right now." He acts as if he's about to turn around to leave.

"No, you got it. She's not coming out of my mouth again. I won't even tell her you're home."

His pissed-off demeanor written on his face, Cory follows his mother out to her Ford Explorer, where she makes the drive home.

They pass the welcoming sign, making their way home.

"We're here, back in RiverCreek. The little town where nothing has changed."

Pulling up, Cory feels that tingling shiver crawl through his spine.

"You all right, son?"

Staring at the house, he sits there in silence.

"Come on inside. It's been remodeled for the most part. Kind of had to after your dad went downhill after his stroke."

"I had no idea—"

He's cut off before he can begin to show sympathy.

"I love ya, son, but don't sit there and pretend like you missed us. You disappeared more than six years ago, and it broke your dad's heart. We never understood why, but it took its toll on all of us."

"Sorry, Mom. After what I got in the mail, I was done with this place. I couldn't bring myself to come back. Too many bad memories. I got my chance to go, and I took it."

They sit there for another moment, trying to bury the hatchet. They get out of the SUV. Cory stares at the simple vinyl-tiled ranch-style home.

"Well, let's get inside, son. You need to rest up before the viewing and the funeral."

Snapping back from his cold, dead stare off into space, Cory follows his mother inside, where his attention is taken by the place where the kitchen table used to sit.

"Is that where Dad stayed? What's with all the equipment?"

Over on the hospital bed, Mrs. Dubois runs her hand back and forth where she found him the morning he died.

"He gave up when he realized you wasn't ever coming home. He slowly allowed his organs to fail by stopping his visits to see his specialist."

Cory stands there in the middle of the living room with his eyes glazed over. "I don't know what to say."

Looking down at the hardwood floor, Mrs. Dubois breaks her promise to her son. "Listen to me—just listen. Tara spent so much time here with him. She pampered and nursed your father to show him that someone mattered in their life to him. Even after you abandoned us, she never did."

Throwing his bag on the couch, Cory unzips his bag, roughly taking the letter to show his mother. "Here, you want to know so damn bad, then read it."

Cory flippantly tosses Tara's letter into his mother's lap. Not wanting to wait around to see her response, Cory takes off, walking down the street.

At the end of block, Cory bumps into an old acquaintance. "Joe, Joe Winters, is that you, man?"

Joe pauses to turn around with his kids holding his hand. "Cory? Really, you're home? Oh, wow, long time, old man."

Cory smirks with a slight chuckle. "Look at you. You're going bald and getting kinda chunky, old friend. And who are these little people with you? Can't be your kids—they're too cute to have come from you."

With a sarcastic laugh, Joe introduces his children. "Cory, this is Shay, my oldest daughter, and this is Vicky, my youngest daughter."

The two little sandy-brown-haired girls giggle and hide behind their father.

"They're beautiful, Joe. You're a lucky man."

Patting Cory on the arm, Joe smiles and waves as he returns to his walk up the sidewalk with his little girls.

Cory resumes his walk to his destination of nowhere. He wanders around, eventually finding his way to his father's old garage. He hears the familiar racket of air ratchets buzzing in the air.

"Who's running this place?" he asks out loud, heading around the side of the building.

As he peeks around the corner, he catches a glimpse of a tall African American man barking out orders.

"C'mon, Russell. I need this brake job done yesterday. Get the lead out of your ass!"

Unable to pinpoint why the man's voice sounds familiar, Cory stands there ransacking his memories when something else catches his eye.

Drawn from the corner of the building, Cory steps out, where he's noticed staring with intensity at his old car.

"Hey, pal, you ... Cory, is that really you?" the tall man calls out.

"No way. Rick?" Cory freezes in his tracks, gawking at his former best friend.

"Yeah, homie, it's me. When did you get back to town?"

Still bewildered, Cory musters. "A little bit ago. What are you doing here?"

"Well, I got out on parole with a ton of support from your parents and Tara. Kay's family even kept up getting me to look good with the parole board. I'm still on it now and will be for another four months. Forget all that, though. Come here, man. It's been way too long."

Rick makes his way over to Cory, embracing him in a long-overdue hug. "I am so sorry about your dad. He cut me a deal on this place before he gave it up."

"Glad someone kept this place going. Anyway, what's with my car still sitting here? I figured it'd be scrap by now." Cory points to his car, with its badly faded paint job from sitting out in the weather over the years.

"Your dad didn't have the heart to get rid of it. Still runs like a top since we kept up the maintenance on her. Go ahead. Just flushed it and changed the oil."

Reaching into his overalls pocket, Rick pulls out the key, handing it over.

"Yeah, wanna take a ride?" Cory asks.

Rick smacks him dead square center on the back.

"Can't leave these jokers without a manager. Nothing would get done, but hey if you get hungry, check out the Italian place in Minneapolis. Little joint called Rocco's Slice of Italy."

Cory suspects something's up when Rick winks after giving him the name.

"Yeah, okay, sure, buddy boy."

Shoving Cory off so he can return to work, Rick motions for him to go get into his car and take a ride. "Get a move on. It's a long haul up there."

Stepping up to his Celica, Cory slips into the driver's seat, adjusting it for his comfort. He fires the engine up, giving it some fuel, shutting his eyes, and feeling the urge to give it hell right out of the gate.

Away from the garage, it doesn't take him long to get up to speed, heading back to the house. He arrives hoping to avoid a confrontation over the letter. Inside, he sees his mother sitting in her chair with the letter in her hand.

"So this is what kept you away all this time. This crock of shit? Really, you couldn't have called or written asking about this at all?"

"I did call—several times actually—and no one ever picked up the damn phone, Mom. There was nothing for me to come back to here, and there still isn't anything here. As soon as Dad's funeral is over, I'm gone again, and I'm not coming back until I have to bury you beside him."

Crumpling the letter and dropping it on the floor, Mrs. Dubois never takes her eyes off her son. "After the viewing, stay close. We're taking a trip, and no, you have no choice. You will go and keep your mouth shut."

It's a struggle to keep his mouth shut. Cory goes back to his old room, flopping on his bed until he must get ready to leave with his mother for the funeral home. When they arrive, they mingle with the guests who have come to pay their respect. When Cory notices his mother talking to Olivia, he walks away. He takes off outside, drawing attention, slamming the front doors wide open and nearly dragging them off the hinges.

Unable to understand his actions, Mrs. Dubois takes off after him. "Cory! Hey! Stop right there. Hot damn it, son, what in the blue blazes was up with making a scene like that?"

Breathing hard to contain his emotions, Cory snaps.

"The fuck is that bitch's mother doing here? We have no need for the Roses to be here, Mom. I came, I saw Dad, and now I'm good to go."

With her hand braced above her eyes, Mrs. Dubois can't contain her own anguish anymore.

"Give me another hour, and after the viewing ends, we will go get this settled once and for all. I don't ever remember you being such a heartless bastard. Where the hell is my loving, warm-hearted son? I can't stand the prick you are now. Your father would be so disappointed in you."

"Dad's the lucky one. He doesn't have to put up with this bullshit anymore. He got away from you and this town finally, and he'll never come back. I fought like hell to stay in Iraq doing what I do best. I didn't want to be here. I was forced to come home."

Removing her hand, his mother stands there, heartbroken. "If that's how you honestly feel, then go. I don't need you to take care of me. I can manage. Just go back and forget you even have a mother."

Behind them, waiting for the moment to come, is someone unable to wrap their mind around how much Cory has changed. Prepared to take on the battle head on, Tara steps up, ready to tackle the super volcano about to erupt.

"Now, that's enough, you dumbass. You will not ever talk to your mom like that again. She's one of the best people I know."

Breathing deeper than before, Cory recognizes her voice, causing his face to shake. Every ounce of rage goes beyond his breaking point. "You … why the fuck are you here?" he groans, nearly grinding his teeth as he talks.

Sensing things are about to get ugly, Tara goes over and whispers in Mrs. Dubois' ear.

"Go inside, Momma, and calm down. I can handle him. Go, take care of little man. He's looking for you."

Mrs. Dubois nods at her advice. She reluctantly walks away.

"You want a piece of me. Here I am, big boy. Come get me," she provokes him, trying to get him to turn around.

"Go fuck yourself, you bitch," he says, still facing away from her.

"I still have your ring on. You never officially ended it with me. So, my fiancé, wanna finish it? Then let's do this. I'm not some frightened teenage girl anymore. Turn around, you coward. My Cory wouldn't keep his back to me like a little scared bitch."

Out of anger, he twists his body around, getting right up in Tara's face. "You two-faced little slut. How could you write me like that huh? You wanna tell me that I'm not good enough for you and leave me in a goddamn 'Dear, Cory' letter and then talk to me like this?"

Still calm, wiping the spit from her cheek, Tara maintains her composure, even though she's scared out of her mind.

"I never said you wasn't good enough. I said I wasn't, and we never agreed it was over. I mean it, I still have the ring on, see."

She pulls her hand up, exposing the engagement ring on her finger. Using his speed and strength, Cory clamps her wrist with one hand, forcing the ring off with the other.

"Not anymore. This worthless piece of shit is history."

He chucks the family heirloom and watches as it grows smaller the farther it travels. His action forces Tara's hand in the matter.

"You bastard. I love that ring. I still love you, you big clueless idiot! I was trying to get your temper out of the way so we could talk. Do you hate me that much?"

Seeing her eyes go from sarcastic smartass to destroyed and crushed, he stands there, hanging onto his expression.

"Yes." He watches as he forgets to free her wrist, as he is beginning to get upset.

"I'm sorry. I was so afraid back then that I made the worst mistake of my life," Tara says, now upset over the matter.

On the inside, part of him wants to calm down and embrace her to escape the pain. The other part wants to keep up his current mood as protection in the case she's lying to get her way.

"I made the worst one the day I agreed to escort you around school. I was stupid to think I loved you," he continues, trying to keep his façade as his regret grows the longer he maintains eye contact with her.

"I know you don't mean it. I can still see it in your eyes. I never moved on, either. I couldn't. I've loved you all these years, and I don't know why. Cory, please, let me go. You're hurting me. Damn it, let me go!" She hauls off, hitting him with an open palm across the face.

Realizing his strength is out of control, Cory releases his grip and begins to walk away.

"Goodbye. Take care of my mother for me please," he murmurs, reacting to the urge to get away.

"Stop! Stay, please. I need to talk to you."

Blocking out the sound of her voice, Cory continues walking away at a slow, steady pace, his mind going numb to the world around him.

"Cory, come back. We need to settle this. We have to talk. You have to learn the truth!"

Unwilling to go after him and afraid that he'd lose control if she does, Tara heads inside, still clutching her wrist.

"Everything all right, sweetheart?" Olivia asks, standing at the door. She witnessed everything that happened.

"Yes, Mom. I think I made it worse. He won't listen. It's like he's not even himself anymore."

Checking on her daughter's wrist, Olivia and Tara are interrupted when a young man with almond brown hair and blue eyes walks up to them in his little tan khakis, accompanied with his white dress shirt.

"Mommy, did you get a ouchy?" he says in a lighthearted voice.

"Yeah, baby, Mommy got a little boo-boo. Wanna kiss it and make it all better, like I do for you?"

She bends over, allowing her little boy to kiss the back of her wrist. "All better?"

She smiles, picking him up. "Yes, CJ, you made Mommy feel all better." She gives him a kiss on the cheek, which he wipes away, wriggling to get away from her grip.

"Go stop him and tell him the truth. Tell him that his son is here waiting to meet him. He has a right to see him at least once," Olivia explains, knowing the situation that Tara lied about back then.

"Yes, Mom. Take CJ home with you. I'll pick him up later, I promise. I hope he can forgive me."

Turned around, she slips out of her heels, holding them in her hand as she exits the funeral home. Tara sprints like a scolded dog after Cory, praying as she runs that she can repair the damage inflected without a war erupting in the process. At the end of the block she stops, looking around in every direction, trying to find Cory.

"Shit, where are you?" she cries out as the guilt returns, hitting her instantly.

"How is it you can still make me cry. How?" she babbles on, giving up and returning to the funeral home.

Back near the steps, she's forced to stop when everyone begins to leave.

"I take it you didn't find him?" her mother states, carrying a sleepy CJ in her arms.

"Good guess, Mom."

In a disappointedly sigh, her mother says, "Come on. Let's go home. If his mom sees him, she'll call."

Putting CJ in his booster seat, Tara leaves to go to her mother's, staying the night since she doesn't feel like driving back to Minneapolis to return for the funeral service in the morning.

In the driveway, she doesn't get the chance to get out, as Cory flings his car into the driveway behind her. Cracking his car door open, he stands there, glaring at her.

"Get in the fucking car," he demands with a look to kill on his face.

"Hang on. I need to take my son inside and put him to bed. Can I even get back into regular clothes?"

"Your son?"

Tara confirms his confusion. "Yes, my son, *our son*, actually." She stands there feeling six years of regret and remorse cripple her soul.

"I wanna see him! I wanna see my boy," he says, feeling a wave of calm come over him in that instant.

"Sure, I know you wouldn't harm him. He's a spitting image of you, especially with his hair styled like yours when we met. He has my nose and your smile."

Curious to see him for the first time, Cory sluggishly goes behind Tara to get CJ from his booster seat.

"Already out cold, so be gentle taking him inside, please," Tara educates him as she quietly opens the car door, unlatching him from his restraint.

"He looks a lot like Dad, actually. There's no mistaking it—he's mine," Cory says as his eyes swell with tears.

Tara stands there speechless.

"We're not finished," he reminds her, picking him up, twisting him from side to side, cherishing the feel of his boy in his arms.

"Take him inside and put him in my old room, please. I'll get changed and meet you at the point—I promise."

Cory takes him upstairs, laying him down on the bed. "Sweet dreams, my boy. Daddy loves you."

Tara's still at a loss for words. "I found this when I was walking away. Keep it, for all I care."

He opens his palm to reveal the ring he threw.

Taking the ring from his hand, Cory slips away, returning to his car and driving away. Tara goes to the drawer where she keeps her spare clothes. Once she's changed, she heads downstairs, where her mother is waiting.

"Be careful. He's not the Cory we remember."

Stopping at the bottom step, Tara tells her mother, "He won't hurt me, not after seeing CJ."

Ready to rumble with Cory all over again, Tara realizes she's going to have to come up with a plan quickly. She goes over every possible scenario in her mind on her way to the point. As the sun drops from the sky, and prepared for the fight of her life, she still feels her heart pounding like it used to back in the day when she was around Cory.

When she arrives, she sees his car sitting there, but he's not in the Celica waiting. Memories flood back from years ago, nearly causing her to pull away.

"No, you can do this," Tara whispers to herself, climbing out the car.

She heads down the path to the dock, where she sees Cory standing there under the lights, waiting to get this confrontation settled once and for all.

CHAPTER 21

Regrettable Fear

Nervous about the faceoff, Tara scoots her feet inch by inch, trying to get a read on the situation since she played her trump card earlier than she wanted.

"Hurry up. I don't have all night," she hears, causing her to pause in her tracks.

"Can I say something first? Can you let me explain?" she begins, letting Cory hear the shakiness in her voice.

"Go ahead. This I got to hear."

Crossing his arms, Cory waits while Tara struggles to find the words to justify six years of actions. Everything she thinks of sounds weak in her head. The silence between them makes Cory stir with anticipation.

"I'm waiting, Tara. If you can't think of anything, then I'll begin."

She raises her hands to grab his attention as she blurts out the first thing that comes to mind.

"Your father loved him and thought the world of CJ. I know I screwed up royally, and I can never take that back. I was scared. I didn't wanna leave my mom and dad yet. We were kids, we were so young. I thought I could do it on my own, and I was wrong. If it wasn't for both our families, I'd have been flat on my ass from the start. Please, don't hate my son, our son. He didn't do anything wrong."

Cory begins to laugh, sending mixed signals. "I wouldn't ever hold it against him. You, though, you tore me apart with that letter. I've beaten myself over and over for six long years. You kept him from me, as much as I want to rip you apart in every way I can, and I won't. My heart still beats for you. You, standing there even now, the biggest part of me wants to hold you and tell you it'll be all right and pick up where we left off. The other part though says to leave you hanging right here and never return."

After hearing that, Tara drops to her knees, ready to break.

"We can. I don't need anyone else other than you and CJ in my life. I'll do anything to make this up to you. Let me make this right!" She plants her hands on the ground to balance herself, feeling the weight of the world crashing over her, unsure of what's about to happen.

"No, I have an entirely different life now. I'm even signed to re-up when I get back to Germany. I save lives every day and go into hot zones every so often. You couldn't handle it if I get killed, and I wouldn't hurt CJ like that. He's better off never knowing what I do."

"You're wrong, Cory. He needs his daddy. He is always asking about you. He cries, thinking that you don't love him. He's such a sweet boy. He is so much like you, and it's unforgiveable what I did. Can you forgive me?"

Standing there without flinching, only a single word is uttered—"No"—the one word that destroys Tara's heart.

There's a struggle to breathe. Tara's body feels as if she's trapped under water with chains strapped to her ankles.

"Cory … help … please … I can't … I can't …"

She grabs at her chest, wheezing loudly.

"Hang on." Cory jumps into action, rushing over rolling Tara into his arms so she can face the night's sky.

"I got you. Relax. It'll pass. Look at my eyes, Tara. Focus only on my voice." He maintains a calm, cool tone as he begins to slightly rock back and forth. "You're safe. I won't let you go until it passes."

They sit there for what feels like several minutes as it begins to pass.

"Thank you, Cory. Can I please hold you while I cry?"

Unwilling to comply with her request, Cory gives Tara assistance to her feet and goes back to where he was. Only now, he's sitting on the edge of the deck rail.

"Is there anything I can do? What will it take to earn your affection again?"

As he inhales deeply, his attention is guided to the sky. It isn't long before he reverts to being a rude smartass. "I got nothing because there is *nothing* that you can do, Tara."

His eyes locked to the sky, he's taken by surprise when Tara makes a move of desperation, yanking him from his makeshift seat, slamming him face first on the deck. Tara rolls Cory over with her weight on top of him, pinning his arms down with all her might.

The wind knocked out of his body, Cory is caught off guard when he feels Tara kissing him. Without thinking, he reacts, returning the favor, until he moans. The reunion kiss snaps him back to reality.

"Get the hell off me," he yells, bucking his hips, rolling her off his torso.

"I had to try, and you kissed me back. That's all I needed to know. Even if you don't believe me, I love you Cory, and I always have. I meant it earlier when I was in your face. I never took your ring off, waiting on you to come home. Naive as all get out, but I held on to a slimmer of hope."

"You're a fool to think I'd take you back instantly. I've been through hell, while you went and done God knows what with God knows who."

She pushes Cory, feeling insulted.

"You think I was out fucking guys left and right, don't you? Sorry to burst your bubble, but you're wrong."

Back to his old tone from high school, Cory sits up. "Could've fooled me. I'm done with this, and I'll get a JAG representative to setup something with CJ later."

Cory hobbles to his feet, trying to make his getaway.

"Wait, please. I won't let you go and leave this unsettled. Cory, stop, damn it, and listen to me. I'm not okay with this, and you aren't either. I know you. Come back, you spineless ass hat!"

She sits there screaming at the top of her lungs.

Heading for his car, Cory takes out the key and gets in. He fights the impulse telling him to turn around and take her in his arms all over again.

"She burnt your ass. Don't look back. Don't … look … back."

The key is in the ignition. He presses the clutch to the floor. Sprinting to stop him from leaving, Tara gives it her all, attempting to get in front of the Celica. Cory doesn't waste time utilizing the boost from the turbo, putting distance between himself and Tara. Frantic mode sets in when Tara tries to catch him, but soon, his taillights disappear.

She drives to his mother's, where she crawls by the house with headlights off, trying to see if he's there. When she doesn't see the car, she parks down the street, waiting for him to arrive. More than an hour and a half passes by, and no sign of Cory anywhere. Her eyes burn with exhaustion. Tara finally packs it in, returning to her mother's.

She's brought to back to reality when CJ turns on the morning cartoons. Tara whimpers, throwing her arm over her eyes.

"Didn't go as planned, I'm guessing," her mother comments, lifting her daughter's feet, taking a seat on the couch.

"I tried, and he walked away without looking back."

"Maybe then it is time to let him go and find someone else. You can't wait forever, and CJ needs a man in his life."

Insulted at the notion, Tara yanks her feet back to sit up. "No, I refuse to accept that fact. I'll chase him down anywhere in the world. Seeing him yesterday reminded me how much he will always mean to me. Now, if you will excuse me, I have a funeral to go to."

Up on her feet, Tara looks down, smiling at the ring that was returned to her. "Oh, by the way. You saw him throw my engagement ring. If there was nothing there, then why did I get it back?"

Examining her daughter's hand, Olivia is at a loss for words. Tara stomps the entire way up the steps, showers, and dresses for the funeral.

"I'll be back, and thank you for keeping CJ for me while I go. Love ya, Mom."

With a peck her mom on the cheek and forcing CJ to take a mommy kiss on his cheek, she smiles, running her fingers through his thick hair.

"Love ya too, my sweet girl, and don't worry about us. It's Mom-Mom–CJ day!" As she teases her grandson, he yells, "Yay," repeatedly jumping up and down.

"Have fun, y'all. I'll see you soon." Tara gets her purse, then darts out the door, already running late.

She rushes to the funeral home, nervous about what she'll do when she tries to get close to Cory. Pulling up into the parking lot, she's guided to a spot that isn't following the hearse to the cemetery.

Once inside, she's motioned up to take her seat beside Mrs. Dubois.

"Not to make a bad day worse, but Cory left last night. He found Rick and convinced him to take him to St. Paul for a red-eye flight back to Europe. He's gone, honey, and I'm sorry nothing got fixed with you two. I always wanted you for a daughter-in-law."

Unable to respond, Tara's cracked heart shatters at that very moment when it hits her that she is too late.

"I know, honey—it hurts—but you tried. At least he came home for a day and got to see CJ. Yeah, I know, he spilled everything to Rick, even how he wanted to give in to you, but he's still not over that letter. Speaking of which, we need to have a heart-to-heart over that one day soon."

Ashamed about how everything has come to an end, Tara nods, turning her attention to the pastor as he signals the ushers to close the doors for the memorial service to begin.

A couple of weeks later, after Cory has had a chance to catch up with his work at the field hospital, he slowly begins to come around to mending his relationship with his mother.

"Hey, Mom. How's it going?" he greets her via Yahoo Chat webcam.

"Oh, there ya are, son. Can you hear me okay?" she says loudly into the microphone, excited to see him in uniform.

"Perfectly. So how're CJ and Tara?"

Thrilled over this new way to keep in touch, Mrs. Dubois begins to rant.

"I finally had my heart-to-heart with her over that letter, and she feels so bad about it. She's gonna be here later. Would you like to talk to her and try to work things out?"

Cory gives the indication he's thinking it over with the expression written on his face. "Not really, Mom. You know I'm here for another couple of months. I have decided though that I'm not signing a new contract, and I will come back to the States for medical school."

Squealing with delight, Mrs. Dubois can't contain herself. "Oh, yes! I don't care where, either. I will come visit you every chance I can. That is such great news."

Cory smiles for the first time without sarcasm. "Yeah, I guess it's time to pick up where I left off in high school. I know it'll be great to not have to do PT every day anymore."

His mother laughs, nearly spilling her coffee.

"Just having you home and no longer worrying is good enough. I couldn't care less about you going to school. I only want you home where you're safe."

Cory begins to break down his plans, even with the sounds of a ruckus stirring outside.

"Well I have my goals, Mom and … Captain, what is it? What's going on? Hey, you can't …"

He moves away from the camera, causing his mom to stir in her chair.

"Cory … son … are you all right?" She listens as she hears screaming and yelling in the background.

"We're a hospital, not a prison. If you want your men, take them—"

Right before the connection goes dead, she catches the sounds of gunfire, accompanied with higher pitched screams of despair.

"No! Cory, no!" she screams, clutching the monitor in her hands, shaking it nearly off the desk.

Panic sets in when she can't reestablish the connection. Worried, she sits there waiting for nearly twelve hours.

"God, please, let me him be okay." She begins to slowly chew on her fingernails the longer she's forced to wait, until company arrives.

Unable to hear the knocking at her door, Mrs. Dubois is oblivious when Rick enters the house.

"Hello, is anyone home?"

Snapping back to reality, she hollers to expose her location. "Rick, back here, hurry!"

Able to detect the urgency in her voice, Rick flies through the house to the back room.

"What's wrong?" He stands behind her, resting his hands on her shoulders.

"There was a scuffle, and I, I, I think I heard gunshots, with people screaming. Then this just a dead, blank screen." She continues to stare at the screen with a terrified expression.

"Lord have mercy, Cory. I'm sure he's all right. Come on, miss lady. We have our dinner date. It's fish-taco Tuesday. You need to eat, so come on."

Reluctantly, Mrs. Dubois gets to her feet, fainting when she takes her first step.

Concerned over her well-being, Rick picks up Mrs. Dubois, carrying her to the hospital bed. He then crashes on the couch. He remains at the house for a few days to ensure her recovery. He maintains an eye on MSNBC's coverage. His heart drops when a special report about an attack flashes along the bottom news ticker.

"Army hospital back under control of US military. Casualties from both Iraqi and Taliban forces and among them some army personnel. More as the story develops," Rick reads to himself, feeling his heart sink to his stomach.

"I know you're alive. You've worked too hard since leaving here to fix things to have them end like this. Please, let there have been an angel there protecting him," Rick prays as time stands still.

Taking out his phone, Rick knows he must be the one to deliver the worst news. Praying to get to voicemail, his hopes are crushed when Tara answers.

"Hey, stranger, you and Momma never showed up. Did something come up?"

Heavy breathes into the phone. Tara can sense that everything isn't all right.

"Please tell me nothing's happened."

Unable to find the words, he begins to stutter.

"Mrs. Dubois is fine. She's been resting for a few days now. Sorry we couldn't make it. She's, uh, out of it right now."

Sensing his demeanor, Tara can't take the anticipation. "Rick, just spill it. What's wrong?"

Like the grim reaper about to take the essence of her soul, Rick spits it out to the best of his ability.

"Something happened over there, something bad. I've been watching the news, and I think Mrs. Dubois listened to Cory and his friends get killed at the hospital he was at in Iraq."

Suddenly, a thud is heard over the phone, along with voices of people around Tara.

"Boss, boss, are you okay? Someone, get a cold rag pronto. Tara fainted out of nowhere."

The phone away from his ear, Rick ends the call, dropping his phone on the coffee table. He stares at his phone for a little while with the news reporting in the background. Rick's attention is pulled to the front door when Olivia bursts through in a cold sweat.

"My God, is it true? Tara called me. What happened?"

Rick sits there, staring at her. "I read on the news thingy that there was an attack on a hospital and people were killed. Mrs. Dubois heard it begin on Cory's webcam, and that's all I know."

She joins Rick on the couch. They sit, watch, and wait for any updates, but they never materialize beyond the vague description on the ticker feed.

"All we can do is wait and pray," Olivia states, twisting her clammy hands together.

"Yeah, that's the hard part."

After a few more days of patiently watching the news, they decide it's time to move on. They accept the outcome that Cory must have been killed, with no word getting to them otherwise.

That time is hell on Tara. It's affected everything in her life. She's lost her spark that's kept her smile alive for so long. Every time she looks at her son, he provides a constant reminder that Cory might not ever come home.

Going through the motions of her daily life, somedays Tara can barely get herself out of bed. She picks herself up, reminding herself that CJ still needs her. Somehow, due to her strength from the love of her child, she keeps putting one foot in front of the other until she begins to feel numb enough to function normally.

As time continues to go by, with no word on Cory's condition, Tara can finally put on a convincing smile for the world to see. Knowing her daughter needs support, her mother begins to put a little bug in her ear.

"Sweetheart, you need to move on. You deserve to be happy, and CJ needs you to be happy again."

"I am happy, Mom. I am. I have a job that I love, and I have you, CJ, Mrs. Dubois, and Rick. Even Lloyd comes to visit when he's not busy playing mayor to RiverCreek. Why do I need a man?"

Her mother can hear her tone heighten from the core of her suffering.

"I don't need a man to boss me around. How can he tell me how to live my life? To possibly hurt my son, all I have left of his father? To love a woman whose heart doesn't beat all that much these days."

Hugging her only child, Olivia attempts to help Tara heal. "I know you miss him. We all do, but sometimes we have to accept the unbearable truth."

Tara's only card she can use is all that she has left from acceptance. "There's not been a phone call, a letter, a body bag, or a preacher show up for last rites. He's alive. He's just lost, Mom—that's all. He couldn't be killed. He's Cory. He's been my Superman. He's the father to my son. Cory's alive—I can feel it. I don't know how, but I just know!"

"He was just a man, honey pie, flesh and blood that could be killed as easily as you or me. It's time to move on. This ain't healthy for you or my grandbaby. If you need to, I can stay with you, or let me take CJ home with me. You need time to grieve properly."

Refusing the offer, Tara pushes her mother out of her house.

"Go. I won't accept it until I have proof."

Standing there with the same furious glare Cory gave her that night at the dock, Tara slams the door shut, then begins crying again, knowing her mother is right.

"I can't say goodbye, not yet," she whispers to herself, wiping away the familiar painful tears.

To give Tara time to cool down, Olivia decides that enough is enough and takes matters into her own hands to close the matter once and for all. She begins making phone calls to anyone who could help her obtain information.

"Yes, Senator, I understand but if you could—"

She's cut off as she listens to him rant again that he can't give her the information she needs. Hanging up and shuffling through her list from top to bottom again, Olivia doesn't give up at all. Her luck changes when she's connected to a doctor out at Walter Reed Medical Facility in Washington, D.C.

Not willing to give up, Olivia is persistent.

"Yes, sir. I hate to be a bother, but I need some answers."

Intrigued by her opening line, the doctor agrees to listen.

"You have my attention, ma'am. Please, tell me what you need."

"Yes, thank you. My name is Olivia Rose. I live in RiverCreek, Minnesota. I'm searching for any answers on the whereabouts of a young man named Cory Dubois. His hospital, I think, was attacked in Iraq. Anyway, my daughter and he have a little boy together, and she's torn apart because we can't find him. So, if you could please make a call or search for him, I'd be eternally grateful, sir."

She listens as there is some shuffling in the background.

"Okay, give me his name again, and I'll see what I can do. I normally don't do this, but I have a son that's serving too. I can understand your fear of the unknown."

Breathing a sigh of relief, Olivia feels a burden slightly lift from the abyss. "It's Cory Dubois, D-U-B-O-I-S, and my number is 612-555-0883. Thank you—anything would be great."

"My pleasure. It might take me some time, but I will return

your call. Have a good day, Mrs. Rose." He hangs up on his end, passing the information onto his assistant, who begins the search.

Two days go by before Olivia's phone rings with the number from Walter Reed appearing on the caller ID.

"Hello."

She waits as the connections is filled with static.

"Uh, yes, Mr. Olivia Rose, please," the doctor begins.

"This is she. Have you found anything on Cory?"

She listens as he explains the information that a friend of his stationed in Germany has confirmed Cory's whereabouts.

"Yes, and it's big news ..."

He explains everything, causing Olivia nearly to drop her phone.

"Oh, wow. Yeah, thank you, sir. Again, you'll never know how much I appreciate you getting this for me. Goodbye, and God bless."

She hangs up and drops her phone, immediately breaking down, covering her face with her hands.

Once she's calmed down, she comes up with a plan to bring the news to Tara. She calls Rick and Mrs. Dubois, formulating the plan that will finally bring closure.

"Yeah, Rick, you'll be the distraction at dinner. That way, I know she can't get away or shove us all away at once," Olivia explains as Rick accepts the idea.

Hoping she'll take the bait, Olivia calls her daughter to get the initial plan set into motion.

"Hey, Mom. It's not a good day to badger me."

In a strong tone, Olivia begins, "I wanted to apologize, but listen—I have an idea. Let me make this up to you and treat you to dinner. Drop CJ off at the babysitter on Saturday, and it'll be my treat to you."

Tapping her finger against the back of the phone, Tara takes her time deciding.

"As long as I can drink."

Seeing her opportunity, she jumps at the chance. "Yes, I'll drive so you can drink all you want."

"Fine. What time?"

Already prepared, she tells Tara, "Be ready by five o'clock sharp." Olivia is all smiles at this point.

"Fine. See you then. Love ya. Mean it. Bye."

Locking her phone after the conversation ends, she's satisfied to know this can finally be put to bed at last.

Saturday arrives in a flash, and Olivia begins to feel anxious. She heads to Minneapolis with a surprise guest for dinner. When they arrive at Tara's cozy little split-level brick home, they wait for her to come out after they honk the horn.

Out to the car, Tara is caught off guard when she sees their guest sitting in the front seat.

"Mrs. Dubois, I wasn't aware you were coming to dinner."

Turning around to look at how beautiful Tara looks, she explains, "Well, your mom didn't want me being alone since Rick has a date tonight and it's game night. Hope I don't ruin things."

Partially offended, Tara speaks her mind. "Uh, no, you won't ruin things. You know I love you, Momma. You are always welcome with me."

She sees Mrs. Dubois smile and rubs her hand when she feels Tara touch the edge of her shoulder.

Tara ignores her own mother the entire trip to the restaurant. By the time they get seated, the smile across Olivia's face becomes infectious.

"Okay, what's up?" Tara questions, looking at them.

"Well, wait. We have something for you."

Startled at the comment, Tara senses something is off. "I swear, if you set me up on a date, I'll disown you after I beat your ass, Mom. I'm not in the mood or drunk enough to care yet."

Stretching her smile even more, Olivia pulls out her phone, sending a text to get the all-clear.

Stall will be there in fifteen, she reads, trying to think of some way to keep Tara occupied.

"Well, tell you what. I have something to confess. After I left, I made some calls. What if I said I found someone who knew Cory?"

She listens to the structure of her mother's statement, Tara bites at the bait. "You said 'knew' as in past tense? Like I knew him in high school or how he looked naked?"

Mrs. Dubois is caught off guard. "Tara, I don't wanna think about you two naked together."

A sarcastic laughing Tara smarts off, "How else do you think you became a grandmother? He was so hot ..."

Thinking about what she says, she clamps her mouth shut.

"Uh, huh, you've accepted it. He's gone," her mother mentions with her fingers locked together.

"Yeah, it's been hard but after all this time. If he ain't home by now or called, he's gone."

Staring down at the table, Tara lets that feeling sink in a little more.

"Hey, it'll be okay—I promise. Order a drink and let's celebrate. Have one for Cory," Olivia suggest, waving down a server.

Olivia orders the first round of drinks. She tries to buy time to keep Tara distracted. By the time the second round is finished, Olivia's phone dings.

Here, getting into position now, the message states as butterflies flutter in her stomach.

"So don't get mad, but we have someone coming who wants to see you."

Mixing the alcohol with her suffering, Tara's eyes grow to the size of silver dollars.

"I said no way. I'm out of here!" she shrieks, shooting out of the booth.

"Leaving so soon?" a voice says after she bumps into his body.

"Rick, what are you doing here?"

With a smile, he plays his part perfectly. "I'm your date, hot stuff. Didn't you know?" he teases, moving each time she tries to get past him.

"Move, Rick. I'm out of here."

"What if I get in your way?" A frail, rickety voice calls out, standing about six feet behind her.

Unable to move, Mrs. Dubois simply puts her hands over her nose and mouth at the sight.

"Don't play games with me. Whoever you are, you can't be Cory. He's dead." She tries to hide her hands, which are trembling with hope.

She listens as he steps closer.

"Tara, turn around and face me," he orders, stopping inches from her body.

Unhurriedly, Tara turns her body around. She drops her head, clinching her eyes shut. She can't take being disappointed. Feeling a set of hands take hers, he leans in, giving her peck on the cheek.

"Open your eyes," he whispers softly in her ear.

Tara forces her eyes to obey. She lunges forward after they focus to see Cory is the one holding her hands.

"You're alive!" she screams, crashing their bodies together violently, sending them both to the floor.

"Yeah, sorry for the delay, but they wanted to get my discharge papers finalized before I was sent home. I'm here, though—barely—but I am home, for good."

She has no control over the grip around his neck.

"What happened?" she cries out, burying her face against the side of his.

"I got shot trying to protect patients and nearly bled out. Luckily, the few that weren't slaughtered managed to save all the ones who could be saved."

Rick leans over, breaking Tara's grip so Cory can get off the floor.

He continues telling his story.

"After they patched me up, I laid around until I was well enough to fly to Germany to receive proper treatment and therapy for my injuries. Your mom calling got things sped up. You owe her big time; the doctor she called had a friend pull some strings, and here I am," he finishes in a raspy voice.

Rick snatches an empty chair from the table across from the booth and waits for Cory and Tara to settle into their seat.

"I can't believe it. You're really here."

Taking her hand, Cory assures her it's real. "I am here, and if you wouldn't mind, I'd like to start over. Nearly getting killed puts things in perspective. I love you, and I don't want to go another day without you."

Tara can't control her strength when she tightly clings to his arm. Tara leans her head on his shoulder.

"You don't need to ask. I've always been yours and yours alone."

His head against hers, Cory relaxes, knowing it'll be a long and difficult road ahead, but together, they can face it.

When that night comes to an end they hatch new plans together. They patch things up over time. CJ meets his father for the first time officially, not long after Cory returns home. Once he's settled, he begins therapy and rehab at the VA Medical Center.

Tara doesn't waste time moving Cory in, and in time, they tie the knot. They're expecting another addition to the family, a little girl they plan on naming Makayla. Life is slowly repaying what it has taken from them.

Being able to pick each other up when life gets tough isn't always easy. When times get rough, they remember what it was like alone. Those memories guide them together for the rest of their lives.

After all, they both achieved their primary goal. They escaped RiverCreek, and now they can return to their dream together. Raising their family in a quaint little home, focusing on what made them inseparable in the first place, the couple is constantly reminded that their love will overcome all things.

The end